THE NINTH INNING

THE BOYS OF BASEBALL, #1

by
J. Sterling

Other Books by J. Sterling

About the Author

Jenn Sterling is a Southern California native who loves writing stories from the heart. Every story she tells has pieces of her truth as well as her life experience. She has her bachelor's degree in radio/TV/film and has worked in the entertainment industry the majority of her life.

Jenn loves hearing from her readers and can be found online at:

Blog & Website:
www.j-sterling.com

Twitter:
twitter.com/AuthorJSterling

Facebook:
facebook.com/AuthorJSterling

Instagram:
instagram.com/AuthorJSterling

Dedication

This story is for every girl struggling to figure out if he really likes her or not. For all those late nights spent overanalyzing his every move, word, and expression with your girlfriends. For those girlfriends who might get tired of hearing the same thing over and over again yet still remain steadfast by your side. Basically, this book is about the boys, but it's for the girls.

Baseball Parties

Cole

THE ONE RULE I had about parties at the house during baseball season was that they happened *after* we finished a weekend series. So, no parties on Friday or Saturday nights when we had games the next day, but Sunday nights were up for grabs. Which was why the baseball house at Fullton State was currently at capacity.

Why would anyone listen to me, you might be asking yourself? Because I was the damn captain of the team, and I lived in the house. What I said went. When the other guys lived here and I was gone, they could do whatever they wanted. They could burn down my rules and make new ones for all I cared. But as long as I was a senior and this was my last chance to get drafted and play professional baseball, they would do what I said. Or they could all get the hell out and find a new location to party at.

No one gave me shit though, to be honest. I'd been on the team since I was a freshman. I'd paid my dues. Nothing had been handed to me, unlike some of the other guys here. Listen, just because we were teammates, it didn't mean that we were friends. I wouldn't associate with a handful of these guys off the field if I wasn't forced to. And that wasn't me being a dick. I was just being real.

Baseball players were known for their egos. I understood that. I was one, and I wouldn't pretend I didn't have one, but there was a time and place to be cocky. Most of the guys tended to forget that, whipping their proverbial dicks out every chance they got to see who had the bigger one. We never lost sight of the fact that it was a competition out there. A competition to be seen, to get bites from scouts, to beat out your teammates if you had to for a place in the minor leagues. This might have been a team sport, but only one person at a time got selected in the draft.

"Cole!" someone yelled my name, but I had no idea who.

Looking around the crowded space, I noticed Chance Carter waving me over from the backyard. I wiggled my bedroom door handle, making sure that it was locked, before tucking the keys in my pocket and heading toward Chance and the keg he stood next to.

If I thought it would take me only a second to reach him, I was wrong. Girls stopped me, pawing at my chest, congratulating me on our win, all of them practically foaming at the mouth in anticipation. It was bizarre, and I should be used to it by now, but a part of me still wasn't. These girls acted like we had magic keys to a castle only we could see but they were dying to get into. They treated us like gods, something to be envied, vied for, and hopefully won over.

I'd admit that my dick had loved it at first. The girls had made it so easy for me—an eighteen-year-old freshman who'd had sex one time in high school. Once they found out I was on the baseball team, they swarmed me every chance they got, flirting, pretending like they were interested in me when they were only interested in having a story to tell. I was too naive to put that together at the time—the fact that some girls simply wanted to be able to say they'd fucked me. I'd always thought that girls were all feelings, all the time, but that definitely wasn't true. Welcome to college.

My ego had initially loved the newfound attention, craved it even. Until I noticed how distracted pussy made the other players on the team. They stopped focusing solely on the game. My first year, I watched how females caused problems on the field, started fights between teammates, and incited unnecessary drama. I didn't have the time or desire for any of that, so I'd started keeping most girls at arm's length. That wasn't to say that I stopped hooking up completely—because I didn't. It just wasn't that often, no matter what other people said.

If you believed the things said about me on campus, then I wouldn't even have time to be on the baseball field, what with my apparent nonstop hopping from one chick's bed to another's. It was a lie, an exaggeration at best, but what did I care? As long as my game was on fire and the scouts were seeing me play well, my fellow students could say whatever they wanted.

The truth was that I rarely slept around. I definitely had a few one-night stands under my belt. I was a single guy in college on the hottest baseball team in the country. I used it to my advantage whenever I felt the need. I hadn't meant to turn into such a stereotypical jock, but it'd happened anyway.

"Cole, find me later?" a busty fake blonde whispered in my ear as I pushed through the crowd toward the sliding glass door.

"Not likely," I shot back without sparing her another glance.

I knew she was pouting, her injected bottom lip sticking out way too far for her face.

Why did girls keep doing that shit? Did they really think we liked the way it looked or even cared?

Ladies, we guys loved that you had a mouth in general. We daydreamed about the things we'd like to do to it or put in it or having it wrapped around our dicks. But we never daydreamed about you making them bigger. If anything, we wished you'd stop. There was enough fake shit in this world; you didn't need to fill your face with it.

"What's up, Carter?" I said, calling Chance by his last name once I finally reached him. I clapped him on the back as he handed me a beer in a red plastic cup.

Chance was the son of a baseball legend here at Fullton State and our pitching coach, Jack Carter. He was only a sophomore, but he was one of the best catchers I'd ever seen behind the plate, and he was starting this year, after playing second string to a senior last season.

The best part about Chance was that he never acted like he was owed a damn thing. He worked hard, even as a freshman, and I'd taken to him right away, respecting his work ethic and the way he carried himself. It was rare that someone so young could be so focused and driven, but then again, he'd grown up with a legend, so maybe it was to be expected.

"Hanging out at the keg isn't a great way to avoid the ladies, Chance," I teased, knowing that he had a rule about not dating or hooking up with any girls. *Ever.* I used to make fun of him for it when he first joined the team, but once my senior year had started, I'd understood all too well what he'd been trying to do.

Chance shrugged. "Coming to the baseball house isn't a great way to avoid the ladies," he said in response, and I laughed.

You see, most guys had to chase girls in college, but if you were on the baseball team, they came to you. And if you were Chance Carter, you tripled that number.

"You did it right, man," I said, tipping back my beer and taking a small sip. I didn't drink often during the season, and I never got drunk.

His eyes narrowed. "What'd I do right exactly?"

"The girls. You said no right from the start. I'm just saying no now. It feels like too little, too late," I admitted, as if my sex life had led to the fact that I hadn't gotten drafted at the end of last season. It had nothing to do with it and everything to do with my shitty batting average. I was great in the outfield, fast, with an arm like a rocket, but it wasn't enough. I needed to have the stats at the plate to go along with it.

You see, getting drafted was a bit *easier* if you were a pitcher or a catcher. Teams always clamored for as much pitching as they could get, convinced that the more pitching they had, the better off they'd be. And catchers were a close second. But being a position player, trying to get drafted, was a little tougher. They looked for a strong, powerful bat among your other attributes. But if you sucked at hitting, you weren't getting picked up. And by the end of last year, I had fallen into a slump I couldn't get out of.

Basically, I sucked at hitting.

But this season would be different. I'd been working on my form, my stance, my hips, and my body alignment and weight distribution at the plate. Chance and I were always at the cages, taking hacks and hitting more than anyone else on the team. I felt like I had the most to lose.

This was my last year on the field. It was my last chance to impress the baseball scouts enough for them to want to take a chance on me. I had been eligible for the draft after last season ended, but there wasn't even a single scout sniffing around or talking me up. No one reached out, told me they liked what they saw on the field but to get that batting average up over the summer. Not a damn scout had said a damn thing. And not a single agent had unofficially talked to me, letting me know they wanted to represent me when the time came.

That was when the panic had officially started to set in. I was on a clock that would eventually stop ticking. My days to further my baseball career were numbered, and I was getting down to the wire. What the hell would I do with my life if I didn't play baseball? I really didn't want to follow in my old man's footsteps. I wondered how long it would take to get over feeling like a failure if that happened.

It was the one question every athlete asked themselves. Most of us had been playing for so long that the sport was tied up in our identity. It was a part of who we were. If I didn't have the game and wasn't a baseball player, who was I exactly? I'd been working toward this dream, this goal for so long that I'd abandoned any other dreams I might have had, not that I could think of any in the moment.

Baseball was all I saw. And I was not unique in that perspective. Baseball was all most ballplayers saw. We all shared the same dream—to get to the minor leagues and hopefully get into the bigs one day.

I knew that I could go work for my dad if this dream died, but the last thing that interested me was being an electrician for other people to snub their noses at. Not that it wasn't a fine profession, and my dad made plenty of money; it just wasn't for me. But then again, outside of baseball, I wasn't sure what was.

"You think your parents ever hung out here at the house?" I asked, knowing it was a fucked up question, but every player at Fullton knew the story of Jack and Cassie Carter. Or at least, part of the story.

Jack had been the best pitcher the college had ever seen at the time. He had gotten drafted but not before falling for a sassy and mouthy girl he had to work to get. There was more to the story, but the part that had been most drilled into us was the part about the girls who would stop at nothing to hitch a ride to a player heading out of town. We had been warned to be careful, to think with the head on our shoulders and not the one in our pants.

"Dude. Really?" Chance grimaced, and I laughed. "I don't want to think about my parents right now."

He shuddered, like he was washing away a bad memory, and I laughed more, tossing the rest of my beer into the grass. I wasn't in the mood to get drunk even though we had just won the series and should be celebrating. The season was in full swing, and I needed to be in my best shape.

Beer made you round. I'd seen it happen. The last fucking thing I wanted to be was round.

"Who on the team do you think is most like your dad was?" Another weird question, but I found myself lost a little in time, thinking back to when the great Jack Carter had gone to school here and how it must have felt to be him.

Chance narrowed his eyes at me, knowing exactly what I was asking. Who was the biggest player? Within a second, he gave a nod of his head toward the door and said, "Mac. Hands down."

I followed his gaze and watched as Mac attacked some girl's face with his own. He had a different girl as often as he wanted, even when we traveled to away games. How the hell he seemed to pull it off with little to no drama was beyond me, but that was Mac for you. A line out the door of girls always wanting more. None of us understood it.

My smile dropped instantly when I spotted the familiar girl wiggling her way around Mac and his latest conquest. Her face twisted as she shot him a look of disgust before her eyes searched the yard for the keg. Or maybe they were searching for me. No. Of course, she would be looking for the keg and not me. I was probably the last person she wanted to see, but then again, she was at a party for my team, at my house.

Still, had to be the keg. Christina only drank beer. I remembered her telling me once that hard alcohol made you do stupid things but beer made you lazy. She'd said she preferred being lazy to stupid. That it gave people less things to talk about. The last thing Christina wanted was to be the topic of gossip. I always knew there was more to that story, but she never told me, and I never pushed. I should have pushed.

The soft blue eyes that I knew by heart locked on to my own, and I sat there like an idiot, watching her. I hadn't seen her face in seven months, and every part of me realized it all at once. My breath caught in my throat, but I shoved it down, acting like I was unaffected by the way her long, tanned legs stepped carefully through our lopsided yard. Her bare stomach peeked out from underneath her tube top, showcasing her hourglass figure. One that my hands were all too familiar with touching.

Christina Travers. The one girl who had been my constant since I started going here. At least, she had been until I finally cut her loose one hot night last August after a disastrous summer ball performance. It was Cole Anders's self-preservation at its finest. I was sure someone somewhere would have been proud, although I had no idea who.

Seven months. Seven torturous months since I'd laid eyes on her. At least in person. Attempted online stalking definitely didn't count. After that night last summer, she'd unfriended me on all social media and made her profiles private. I'd asked Christina to disappear from my life, and she'd given me exactly what I'd asked for. And I fucking hated it.

I tried in vain to find pictures of her online whenever I missed her, which was more often than I was willing to admit, but she'd made it impossible. She'd even gone so far as to block all of my friends and teammates, so I couldn't get to her through them. She'd always been smart. Except when it came to me.

I watched as she made her way toward the keg, which Chance and I still stood next to like we were its bodyguards. Her light-brown hair spilled around her shoulders, and I stopped myself from reaching out and grabbing her like she belonged to me. She didn't. And I'd told her that more times than I cared to remember.

"Hey, Chance. Hey, Cole." She gave us both a small smile before reaching for a plastic cup and pulling the black nozzle toward it.

I didn't think I'd even responded. She seemed so composed, so … unaffected by my presence, and here I was, coming undone from the inside out.

"Here, I'll get that for you," Chance said before taking her cup and filling it up.

The only thing that stopped me from raging at him, even though I had no right to, was the fact that I knew he wasn't flirting with her or trying to get in her pants. Chance was just being nice.

"Thanks." She looked at me once more and hesitated, those blue eyes saying something I couldn't quite decipher, but her friends screamed her name from inside the house, and the spell broke.

Her eyes tore away from mine, and I stood there like some kind of love-struck fool as she walked away without another word. I watched her hips move from side to side with each step she took, silently berating myself for letting her go.

I convinced myself it was for the best. Baseball came first. It had to. End of story.

Of Course He's Here

Christina

I HAD KNOWN that coming to the party tonight was a mistake. But that was all I seemed to do when it came to Cole Anders—make mistake after mistake. He was my own personal dark-haired, five-eleven kryptonite. I couldn't resist him if I tried. And dammit, I'd tried.

I'd been trying since freshman year. I was a senior now, so clearly, it hadn't worked. Although I'd been really good the past seven months at avoiding him, making sure I wasn't in places where I knew he'd be. It was too hard to see him and not give in. Any pep talks to *stay strong* that I'd given myself flew right out the window if he was around. And he knew it. Cole had always known the effect he had over me. I used to pretend that I had the same effect over him as well, so we were at least even in our fuckedupness, but it was a lie. I lied to myself all the time when it came to him, apparently. But I was done with all that.

I had very little life experience to pull from when it came to guys like Cole Anders, so everything about college athletes' real relationships and the idea of love were brand-new to me. If this were a class I was getting graded on, I'd currently be getting a big, fat F.

It wasn't as if I hadn't ever dated in high school—because I did. But not that often, and I'd definitely never been in love before. Trying to compare the boys from my high school to the guys here at Fullton State was like trying to force a square peg into a round hole. There was no comparison. Life here was different … and exactly what I craved. Fullton State had been my chance at a fresh start. The opportunity to get away from my small city in the valley where everyone knew everyone else.

After witnessing a vicious lie being spread around school about my best friend, I'd steered clear of all parties, jocks, and most guys. I watched how quickly someone's world could go from inspiring to devastating. That was when I started getting interested in social media and its influence on society. And why I'd chosen to major in it and planned to work with people nationwide.

I wanted to make a difference, but I wanted to do it with integrity. Something the internet seemed to lack in gross amount these days, no matter how hard people tried to pretend otherwise.

#RealLife.

#NoFilter.

#Bullshit.

After that night in August, I'd decided that Cole Anders had broken me for the last time. If he could look me in the eyes and tell me he didn't want me and never would, then it was high time I actually believed him.

When a girl liked a guy, we simply wanted him to like us back. And we had a really hard time believing that he didn't or that we couldn't change his mind. Why did we girls not believe the things that guys said to us? We never took their words at face value, always searching for hidden meanings or trying our damnedest to figure out what he really meant when he had basically laid it out point-blank. My guess was that it was all the contradictory hook-ups, the late-night phone calls, the kisses, and the occasional sex. It made us think that the *words* were the lies and the *actions* were the truth. At least, that was what I'd been telling myself since the first night I met him freshman year.

I'd finally decided to believe Cole's words. Screw his conflicting behavior that had left me feeling more confused than anything else. Forget all the times he'd told me he needed me when the sky was dark, only to act like he didn't when the light finally came.

That hot summer night was when I'd realized that whatever we had been doing all these years, even though it had never once been defined, was done. Cole had never been my boyfriend. Sure, we had slept together a handful of times, but he'd never once asked me on a real date. And I was done feeling like a fool because of it. How had I allowed this much time to pass, only to find that we were still in the exact same place? It was embarrassing. And I was embarrassed.

There had been times over the last seven months that I truly thought I was over Cole. And then the urge to text him or see him would wash over me so strongly that I felt like I'd made no progress at all. In times like those, I'd pull up the note app on my phone and read what I'd typed there.

DON'T YOU DARE CALL HIM. DO NOT TEXT HIM. HE
DOESN'T WANT YOU. HE LOOKED YOU IN THE EYES AND
TOLD YOU HE DIDN'T WANT TO BE WITH YOU. HE TOLD
YOU TO DISAPPEAR FROM HIS LIFE, SO GIVE HIM WHAT HE
ASKED FOR. SILENCE SPEAKS VOLUMES. AND IT HURTS A
HELL OF A LOT MORE THAN ANY WORDS EVER COULD.
HURT HIM BACK THE SAME WAY HE HURT YOU—BY
PRETENDING HE DOESN'T EXIST. YOU'LL THANK ME
TOMORROW.

I was pathetic.

At least, I felt like it each time I had to read that stupid note.

Why was it so hard to get over someone who was never truly mine to begin with? I was tired of being that girl—the one who waited around for a guy who'd never asked her to wait in the first place. I'd been there for Cole the last three years, taking the scraps he had given me like a starved animal and begging for more. I'd allowed it all to happen. I recognized that, and I accepted responsibility and acknowledged my role.

Each time we had been together, I had hoped for a different outcome. And yes, early on, I realized that was the definition of insanity, but while I was living in it, it didn't feel so insane. It felt more like a part of life, growing up, figuring out who you were and who you wanted to be. My mom had always said that relationships were hard work, and I'd assumed this was a part of what she meant.

You see, I was the one Cole had texted whenever he was

sad or down. It was me he called when he had a bad day. It was me he reached out to when he needed a friend, an ear, or someone to talk to. I considered the fact that maybe I wasn't the only girl he reached out to in his time of need, but I wasn't convinced that was true. The talks we shared were not things you simply told anyone who was willing to listen. And Cole wasn't the type to spill his guts to random girls even if he was the type to screw them.

Cole's conversations with me were personal.

Private.

Intimate.

And ours.

He gave them to me. And I cherished them. Like a silly schoolgirl with a crush, thinking I was getting insight into a man that no one else had gotten to see. I'd thought it made me special. In the end, it'd only made me stupid.

I found myself replaying our moments together, my finger hovering over the Delete button on the single selfie I had of the two of us in my phone. It was the first night we'd met, when we sat on top of the parking structure until dawn. He said we should remember the moment as he fished out his phone and pulled me tight against him before asking for my phone number so he could send it to me. We looked so sweet, so innocent, and so … hopeful.

I remembered thinking that it was the beginning of something bigger. That we would look back at that night as the one that had started it all for us. I'd stupidly thought we had something more. And over the years, I'd tried to convince myself that I wasn't just a casual hook-up. But what followed after was always a stab to the heart. I knew he hooked up with other girls; I heard all about it whenever I walked across campus or sat down in class. It sucked, having Cole's sex life thrown in my face, but he wasn't the only one screwing other people.

I went out with other guys, but nothing lasted, nothing stuck. Not the way that Cole seemed to. I definitely hadn't been an angel during my college years so far, but I wasn't sleeping with a new guy every week either. And Cole was the only one who seemed to be a constant presence, blowing in and out of my life like the wind, always coming back, no matter how far away he had gone.

When my roommate and best friend, Lauren, had suggested we come to the baseball party in the first place, I'd wanted to ask her if she'd lost her damn mind. She was the one person who knew all of Cole's and my history and had been there to witness most of it. Just last month, she'd offered to cut off his nuts for me if it would make me happy again. I hadn't realized that I wasn't—happy, that was—but she had been right. That night in August had taken something from me.

Lauren and I'd met in the dorms our first year even though we had been assigned to other suitemates.

She was convinced that her roommate was going to get kidnapped because she "doesn't pay attention to anything! Ever! She's always on her phone, staring down at it instead of looking at her surroundings!"

I remembered laughing at what she'd said because most teenagers were like that, but Lauren had been deadly serious. I stopped laughing and started nodding furiously, promising that I'd pay more attention whenever I walked alone. She seemed satisfied with my answer and declared us friends. We'd been inseparable ever since.

So, here she had been tonight, pushing for me to go see Cole in person, when I'd been doing so well at avoiding him for months.

I grimaced and shook my head, proclaiming that it was a really bad idea, but she still insisted we go. She told me it was a test.

"I hate tests," I whined.

"But this one's important." She jutted out her hip and placed her hand there.

"Please tell me why I'd willingly put myself in this position? I've been doing so well," I asked, waiting to hear her logic.

If I wanted to see Cole in real life, I'd go to a baseball game. And I hadn't done that so far this season even though I knew it was his last one.

Like I'd said, I was done making a fool of myself for him.

"To prove to yourself that you're over him. Once and for all. Cole Anders cannot have this effect on your life forever. And I've got twenty bucks that says you'll see him and feel nothing, but we won't know until we try." She pulled out a twenty and waved it around in the air like a maniac. "It's been seven months. We need to see."

She sounded so convincing in her argument that she actually had me believing I needed to know how it felt to look at him in real life, too, instead of just on the baseball website.

Which I didn't look at ... often.

And that was how I'd found myself here, at the baseball house, where Cole lived, dreading the moment I'd finally see him. A part of me reveling in whatever his reaction would be to seeing me in person, too, considering the fact that I'd dressed the part. If I was going to prove that I was over him, I was going to do it looking as hot as possible.

Please don't be with a girl. Please don't be with a girl, I repeated the mantra, irritated that I even cared in the first place, as I walked through the house in search of beer.

Someone pointed out the keg in the backyard, and I made a beeline for it. If I was going to run into Cole tonight, I needed a little liquid courage running through my veins.

I stepped into the yard, and my skin suddenly prickled with awareness. He was close by; I just knew it. My eyes searched and quickly spotted him. He looked different, bigger, more muscular. *Was he taller? Did guys still grow after twenty-one?* It felt like I was seeing him for the first time. One look at Cole's brown hair peeking through his backward hat, and I knew that I had failed Lauren's test.

He affected me. Looking at him affected me.

No matter how much time had passed, whatever it was between us still existed. At least, it did for me. And that was why I should have turned around and walked right out the same way I'd come in instead of heading straight toward the keg where he stood with another unattainable ballplayer.

Seven months of work down the drain with just one look. I was a fool for coming to this party, and now, I officially knew it.

Girls Versus Baseball

Cole

"CHRISTINA SEEMS LIKE a cool girl," Chance said as we both watched her walk away.

She looked fucking gorgeous, and I was kicking myself for being such an idiot.

I shot him a look. "Yeah, she's great. You interested or something?" My tone came out bitter, jealous, and possessive. All things I definitely was whenever it came to her even though I had no right.

Chance threw his hands in the air and made a sour face. "Not even remotely, bro. But you clearly are."

I palmed the side of my head, moving my hat up and down, thankful that no one else was hanging around the keg where we were; otherwise, I would have kept my mouth shut.

"I don't know what it is about that girl," I groaned before bending over at the waist like I was struggling to catch my breath. All I wanted to do was follow her inside the house and make up for the last seven months, but I stopped myself. I had to.

"Why haven't you guys ever gotten together?" he asked.

"We have," I argued, sounding like an angry lunatic.

Seven months without seeing her face had been seven months too long. I'd always known that I missed her, but I never realized *just how much* until I saw her. It was like a damn sledgehammer to the chest. Seeing her had knocked the wind out of me.

"I just meant"—Chance shook his head before laughing—"why isn't she your girlfriend? It's obvious you like her. She clearly likes you. What's the deal there?"

Is it really obvious that I like her? And vice versa, I wondered but didn't dare ask out loud.

I glanced up at the mini white lights in the yard before shaking my head. "It's not that simple."

"Look, man, I get it. When it comes to baseball and girls, it's hard to maintain balance and focus. They both require a lot of attention, but only one of them talks back and gives us shit over it."

Nodding my head, I looked directly at Chance. "I won't do girlfriends until I'm drafted. And I've always tried to keep her at arm's length, but we keep sharing these moments," I admitted, knowing that I sounded like a total pussy, but I wasn't sure how else to word it.

"Sharing moments? What kind of moments?" Chance questioned, knowing better than to make fun of me, as he kept his tone serious and inquisitive.

"You know, the kind of moments where you stay up, talking, and before you know it, it's six o'clock in the morning and you're watching the sun rise together and you don't realize how tired you are because talking to this girl is way better than sleeping could ever be."

I hadn't meant to say all that, but it'd spilled out.

Christina had gotten to me like no other girl ever had. She'd been doing it since freshman year. We circled around each other, always gravitating back, and I never understood why. Or more honestly, I never tried to figure out why. It was a puzzle I had carefully avoided putting together, hoping some of the pieces would simply get lost along the way so I'd never have to. I drowned myself in other girls, in baseball, working out, and anything else to convince myself that I didn't need her.

"Can't relate," Chance offered with a shrug. "But it sounds nice."

I laughed. "Yeah, in theory, it does sound nice. But it's my last chance at the draft. Who knows if I'll get signed or not? If I don't and she's my girlfriend, I'll blame her for it, you know? Make her the reason why it didn't work out for me. Maybe we'd fought too much. Or spent too much time together. Or maybe she'd wanted to spend time with me when I should have been working on my hitting. That kind of shit."

He stared at me for a beat before nodding. "You know, I get it. Of all people, I get it. But what if she's the right girl and you let her go? You know how hard it is to find a chick who understands this lifestyle?"

It wasn't like I hadn't considered it before. The thought had entered my head on more than one occasion, but I usually filed it away for later. Much later. Baseball and the draft now. Christina and relationships later.

"I can't think about that right now. I have to focus one hundred percent on the game. If she's the one girl in the world I'm supposed to be with, then we'll end up together, right?" It was some hokey, fate-like bullshit, but it was what I had to tell myself to move on and let go.

You always thought you had more chances with the sport you loved, more time to get better or to have a great season to prove them all wrong, but you didn't. Time ran out for each one of us, and my time was currently sprinting toward the finish line.

"I want to argue with you, but look at me"—he waved an arm around us in a circle—"no girls in sight."

That was why I had chosen to talk to Chance about this topic—because he not only understood it, but he also lived it. By choice.

"You plan on avoiding girls your whole life?"

He gave me a one-armed shrug. "You try growing up with Jack and Cassie Carter and tell me how excited you would be to meet girls after hearing all their horror stories."

"Your mom's hot as fuck," I said before thinking twice, and his face twisted.

"Don't say that shit." He bristled.

"I wasn't finished," I teased, but he interrupted what I was about to say next and stopped me cold.

"Speaking of moms," he started, and I felt my entire body tighten, "you never talk about yours."

" 'Cause she's not around. Nothing to say."

Chance's expression shifted. "Is she dead?" he asked point-blank, and a guttural laugh escaped from somewhere deep within me.

"No, man. She's not dead. My parents split up when I was ten. She met some rich guy online and moved across the country to be with him. She told me that a boy needs his father and took off. I used to see her a couple of times a year, but now, I don't see her at all."

It had hurt so bad at first, when my mom bailed. I remembered crying myself to sleep at night for weeks, wanting her to come back home. After a while, I'd learned to live without her, but it was to my own detriment. I knew that I was dysfunctional when it came to relationships since I'd never had a healthy one to learn and grow from. I had no idea how to do it right.

When I looked back, it wasn't that my mom was even all that maternal in the first place, but she was still the only mom I'd ever known. A boy might need their dad, but we needed our moms too.

"And your dad never remarried or anything?"

I shook my head once. "Nah. I think she hurt him real bad when she left, but he never talked to me about it. I mean, I was a ten-year-old kid; of course, he wasn't going to spill his guts to me. But soon after she was gone, he started burying himself in work. I couldn't even be pissed because he started making a lot of money, and I never wanted for anything again."

The second I said those words, I realized how familiar the concept was. I tended to do the same thing when I wanted to avoid overthinking about shit—buried myself in baseball and girls I had no feelings for.

"And the most ironic part was that my mom had apparently wanted more from my dad. Like, she wanted him to be more driven, more ambitious. Basically, she wanted him to have more money. And the second she left, that's exactly what he did."

"Karma?" Chance asked.

"Or something like it," I said with a shrug.

"Did you guys stay in the same house?"

"Yeah. Can you believe that?" I asked, my tone a little incredulous. "Once I was older and realized what had happened between them, I tried to get my dad to sell. I told him we needed to move out of the memories and into someplace new, but he always said no and shut me down. End of discussion," I said, swiping my hand through the air.

Chance stayed silent, and I had no idea what he was thinking. My mind spun as I started thinking about why my dad would want to stay in a place that caused him pain. We never talked about it.

"Your dad's an electrician, right? I think I heard you say that once to Mac or someone."

"Yeah," I answered before subconsciously bracing myself for what might come next even though I should have known better. Chance wasn't the kind of guy who would make fun of someone's occupation.

Even though everyone else always seemed to talk shit or look down on blue-collar workers, I never truly understood why. Those were the jobs that were always needed, that people needed other people to handle for them. Not to mention the fact that my dad had brought in well over six figures every year since he started his own company, and we had a good life.

"How does he feel about baseball as a career? I mean, does he want you to go pro, or does he want you to take over the business?"

Chance and I were talking more about our family dynamics than we ever had before. Maybe it was the fact that Christina had come in and ripped open a part of my heart I'd thought was closed, or maybe it was a full moon or high tide or some shit. Who the hell knew?

"My dad," I started to say before pausing.

My dad, as loyal and supportive as he was, always told me to make sure I had a backup plan. A plan B. The one thing he had done was pound me with stats about the number of baseball players in the country versus the percentage of them who actually got drafted into the minor leagues.

He acted as if I hadn't already known this information. Every ballplayer knew that the reality of going pro was slim, but that never stopped us. We didn't care if there was a one in a million chance of getting to play professional baseball; we still would go for it. That was the thing about dreams— you refused to give up on them, even when other people told you they couldn't come true.

"Um, he loves watching me play, but he thinks it's a pipe dream. He never says those actual words, but I can tell by the other things he says."

"That sucks." Chance grimaced.

"Yeah. Well, we all can't have Jack Carter for a father," I said, and Chance stood there, looking at me, clearly unsure of what to say.

"Having him for a dad hasn't sucked," he said quietly.

"Now, back to what I was saying about your mom before you interrupted me like a dickhead." A cautious grin appeared on his face, and I continued, "Your parents met here. At this school." I pointed down at the grass at our feet. "And here we are, on a girl strike."

"What the hell is your point?"

I looked around the yard again before searching the house for her. Christina stood inside there with her friends.

"I don't know. We can't all be Mac, I guess," I said as we both saw him still attached to some random chick's face.

Chance exhaled a dramatic and loud breath. "Go talk to her already. You guys clearly have unfinished business. So, go figure out exactly what it is."

He didn't have to tell me twice. It was like I had been waiting for his permission or some shit … someone to tell me it was okay to want her.

I tossed my cup to the ground and stormed inside, determination written all over my face even though my insides were a nervous wreck.

I'm Not Yours

Christina

I WALKED INTO the house and toward my girlfriends, a cold beer in my hand as I stopped and glanced around.

Lauren leaned close, whispering in my ear, "Pass or fail?" and I knew she was talking about her stupid Cole Anders test.

"Hard fail," I said before taking a large gulp of the cheap beer.

She pressed her lips together in a straight line before declaring, "Dammit. I really thought you'd pass."

Pulling the crisp twenty from her pocket, she shoved it down my shirt and into my bra. I left it there.

"You and me both," I said but knew it was a lie. "Can we go now?"

Lauren laughed like I had said the funniest thing in the world. "No. We'll get you over Cole by hooking you up with one of his friends."

"I don't think it works like that." I took a stuttering step backward, suddenly uncomfortable. The last thing I wanted was to betray Cole by getting together with one of his friends.

"Come on, Chris." Lauren leaned toward me. "It will make him seethe with jealousy. He won't be able to handle it."

She sounded like she knew what she was talking about, but that was impossible. Cole had said he didn't want me, so he wouldn't be jealous.

"He doesn't want me, remember? In order to make him jealous, he'd have to care in the first place."

I watched her look around before her expression changed into surprise. "Oh, he cares all right. And he's about to show you just how much."

What? I grew nervous as the sound of heavy footsteps echoed behind me, and Lauren grinned wickedly before moving away.

"Why are you here?" His voice was a masculine whisper in my ear. It wasn't kind, and I hated the way my body reacted to his nearness.

He wasn't even being nice, and here I was, chilled to the bone with his presence and the smell of him.

Sucking in a deep breath, I turned around to face him, his blue eyes mesmerizing me like always. "What?" I asked with as much confidence as I could muster.

"Why are you here, Christina? Did you come to see me?"
God, he is arrogant.

"Get over yourself." I tried to sound tough but wondered if the lie was written all over my face.

"You did. You came to see me," he said, confident and cocky.

Taking a sip of my beer, I decided to tell him the truth. "Fine. I did. I came to see how it would feel to see you in person."

"And? How does it feel?"

Like I want to hop in your arms and wrap my legs around your waist. Like I want to be yours forever and never let go.

"It feels like nothing," I lied before emphasizing, "*I* feel nothing."

"Liar," he said before grabbing the back of my neck and crushing his lips against mine.

I caved in that moment, all rational thoughts gone and out the window as his tongue found mine. The heat between our bodies pulsed, and all other sounds ceased as I completely lost myself in him, loving the way it felt to be his.

Then, it all instantly clicked into place. *I'm not his. He doesn't want me.*

I shoved Cole away with all my strength before slapping him across the face, hard and loud. I knew whoever was near us was most likely watching, but I couldn't have cared less in that moment.

"You don't get to do that. We are not a thing."

He rubbed at his cheek, his expression shocked but not angry, as his eyes never left mine. He almost looked amused. "We'll always be a thing. Look at us. We can't stay away from each other. We always come back."

"Not anymore. I'm done with this." I turned to walk away, and he grabbed my arm, stopping me mid-step. Before he could say a word or try to kiss me senseless again, I threw his own words from the summer back in his face. "You don't want me, remember? You. Don't. Want. Me."

"You're mine," he ground out, and his grip on my arm tightened.

I shook him off as anger radiated through me. "I'm not anyone's. Least of all yours. Leave me alone, Cole. I don't belong to you. I never did. You've made that perfectly clear."

If there were awards given out for resisting the one guy who held your heart in his hands, I would take home the gold. Every word that had come out of my mouth was a struggle, something I had to force out of me. My heart screamed at me, calling me a liar, but my head knew it was the right thing to do. I refused to let Cole dominate my senior year of college the way he had the last three before it. I was tired of being his doormat, the girl always there for him whenever he needed me. What about what I needed? What about my feelings? This one-sided whatever we were was over. I'd make sure of it.

My eyes searched the room and found Lauren, who was watching us with rapt attention. I took two steps toward her before he stopped me. Again. I had no idea if he was drunk or not. Cole didn't normally drink during the season, and his breath hadn't tasted like alcohol when he kissed me, but then again, my taste buds were full of beer, so I couldn't be positive.

"What if I've changed my mind?" he asked, and my heart pressed against the cage that held it.

"You wouldn't. And I've never asked you to."

It was the truth. I had never asked Cole to change his mind when it came to us and being in a relationship. He had always told me that he didn't want a girlfriend until he was drafted, and I understood his passion and drive, respected it even. Cole knew what he wanted, and he was going after it. I liked that about him.

But the honest-to-God truth was that it hurt. Him choosing baseball over me year after year sucked. Especially when other guys on the team found a way to have both. I heard myself making excuses for him, to either make myself feel better or to justify the fact that I continued to let him come around. I knew that if he'd really wanted me, he would have broken his self-imposed rules for me. And if he'd really liked me, he would have figured out a way to have us both. But he never did.

"I hate the idea of letting you go," he said, his voice low as if he wanted no one else to hear.

Even while we were in the crowded room, surrounded by people, he made me feel like some dirty little secret.

The words hit me with the force of a blow. *He hates the idea of letting me go.* I rolled the sentence around in my head, repeating it three times, each time making me angrier than the last. It wasn't that Cole wanted to be with me, but he didn't want anyone else to.

Cole loved that I'd always been there for him. Everything had always been on his terms. He called; I answered. He texted; I responded. I had been at his beck and call for years. The only one who could break this vicious cycle and get off the merry-go-round once and for all was me.

"You can't let go of something you never had in the first place." I glared at him before stalking toward Lauren and telling her I wanted to go home.

She pressed some buttons on her phone before reaching for the hem of my shirt and pulling me out the front door and into the darkness.

DURING THE RIDE back to our apartment, I oscillated between being so mad that it scared me and so hurt that I thought I might shatter to pieces in some stranger's car. My bones were crushing me from the inside out, leaving nothing but a pile of dust and skin.

"He's such an asshole," Lauren said from the passenger seat.

She always insisted on sitting up front when we drove in a ride-share car. She claimed she got car sick if she sat in the back, but I knew that was a lie. It was some weird safety precaution she had made up in her mind or seen on TV one time and adopted it as her own belief. If Lauren was up front, she considered us safer, less likely to be taken advantage of or caught off guard.

She hadn't only been paranoid about her roommate getting kidnapped freshman year. No, I learned soon after that Lauren was paranoid about *us* being kidnapped.

"Or sold into sex slavery or disappearing without a trace, never to be found again," she'd confessed to me one night.

She said it happened all the time. That college girls all

over the United States went missing, but no one ever seemed to talk about it.

She claimed it was an epidemic. I thought it stemmed from the fact that she was obsessed with the Investigation Discovery channel and watched every show there was to watch about missing persons, murders, and lies told online. Lauren said it made her more knowledgeable and aware. I thought it made her more paranoid.

"I can't believe he said those things to you," she added.

"I can." I wanted to argue but couldn't.

This was what Cole mastered in—absolute confusion. His words and actions never seemed to add up or match. It was why I was always so damn confused whenever the topic of us came up. I could never truly figure him out.

"I mean, I can't believe he said them out loud. For everyone to hear," she said.

I winced with the realization that we had had an audience back at the party. I'd been so caught up in what was happening between us that I had forgotten other people were around.

"Yeah. That was a bit out of character. Even for him."

Cole never created a scene. At least, not when it came to women. It wasn't his style.

"I can't believe you slapped him. That was some seriously awesome shit!" She laughed before telling our driver all about what had happened.

He pretended to laugh in all the right places, but I could tell he was annoyed. Or bored. Probably both. I convinced myself that he hated driving drunk college kids around late at night. Even though we weren't technically drunk.

My mind raced back to *the slap*.

I couldn't believe I'd done it either. I'd never hit a person in my life, and there I had been, slapping Cole Anders, the baseball player, at his very own baseball party.

"He deserved it," I said, but the words came out far less angry than I'd wanted them to.

The car rolled to a slow stop, and Lauren told the driver we'd get out here, in front of the security gates of our apartment complex. He nodded his head and unlocked the doors before pulling away. We typed in the code and walked through the gates. The night air was tolerable since there was no wind, and I was grateful. I knew I wouldn't have been able to handle it being as cold outside as I currently felt inside. I needed the contrast to keep me grounded.

Lauren looped an arm through mine as we walked to our building in silence, but I knew her wheels were spinning the same way that mine were. She pulled out her key fob and waited for the main door to unlatch. Once you stepped inside, our apartment complex looked very much like a hotel with long hallways and multiple doors with faux porch lights attached. It always reminded me of an Embassy Suites of sorts, but at least it was safe. And when Lauren and I had moved out of the dorms and into a place of our own, safety was her top concern. Obviously.

Like I'd said, kidnapping and disappearing without a trace. The girl was obsessed.

Once she unlocked our front door and we stepped inside, she locked the door again and made her way into the kitchen.

"I didn't even drink anything tonight," she said, pulling out two cold beers from the fridge, and I remembered that I hadn't even come close to finishing off the one beer I had gotten. It wasn't like we had been at the party for very long.

Taking one of the cold cans from her hand, I hopped up onto the counter and opened it with a loud fizz and pop before taking a gulp. She hopped up on the adjacent counter, opening her own and taking a long drink. It seemed funny, two girls drinking beer when all the other girls seemed to drink straight alcohol or mixed drinks.

Cole had always said he liked that I drank beer. It made me different, not typical or basic. I'd considered it a compliment at the time. Now, I didn't give a shit what he'd meant by it.

"So," Lauren started as she wrapped her blonde hair up in a twisted knot on top of her head. It stayed there, nothing holding it, except other hair, and it had always fascinated me that she could pull that off.

Whenever I tried to tie my long hair in a knot, it would undo itself right away, the dark pieces unraveling and falling slowly until it hung straight across my back once more.

Stupid hair.

"Stop cursing my hair." She shot me a look, and I laughed, hating the fact that she could read my mind so well sometimes.

I'd told her on more than one occasion how unfair it was that her hair followed directions when mine always laughed in my face. It was so fine, the strands so ridiculously soft, that I found myself filling it with dry shampoo daily just to give it some volume and texture.

"I wasn't," I lied with a smirk, and she shook her head, waving me off.

"Whatever. How are you feeling? What are you thinking?"

I offered a one-shouldered shrug because, really, what more could be said at this point? Hadn't I talked myself to death over the topic that was Cole Anders for the past three years? What could I possibly say that I hadn't already said a hundred times before?

"I don't know what to say. I'm pissed. I'm hurt. But mostly, I'm just sick of it. I promised myself I'd never give him the time of day after what happened in August. I shouldn't have gone tonight. I knew it was a mistake."

"I shouldn't have pushed you." She sounded truly apologetic. "I really did think that you'd see him and not feel anything. Or at least, I hoped. But honestly, I should have known better. You two are ..." She stopped, clearly searching for a word before not finding it and giving up. "Anyway, it wasn't my place or my call to make you do that."

I had been pissed at Lauren for all of two seconds before placing blame where it was due.

"You don't control me. I have free will. I could have said no. You suggested it, and obviously, a part of me wanted to go. And I know it's because I wanted you to be right. I wanted to feel nothing when I looked at him," I admitted before taking another sip. "But mostly, I wanted him to feel something when he looked at me."

"He did," she said with determination as her eyes locked on to mine. "I saw the way he was looking at you tonight. He wants you."

"He's wanted me since freshman year," I said.

Cole physically wanting me wasn't the issue. The issue was all the rest of it—the relationship parts he refused to give, all the things I wanted beyond us constantly making out and sometimes having sex. I needed to stop giving my body to a guy who refused to give me anything more than his. And I definitely needed to stop giving my heart to a guy who didn't deserve it.

"He doesn't want me in public though. He doesn't want me after the games or in the stands, where everyone can see us. He doesn't want me at the fundraisers or the awards dinners. He sure as shit doesn't want to take me on a date since he's never once asked. And to be kept in the shadows, it's not enough for me. Not anymore."

"You know he brings his dad to all those stupid baseball dinners," she said.

It was true. Cole had brought his dad to every baseball banquet and fundraiser since he started on the team, but I expected that. His dad would, and should, be there with him.

"All the players bring their parents. But they bring their girlfriends too."

Silence.

I knew exactly what Lauren was thinking but didn't want to say out loud, so I said it for the both of us, "See? I'm not his girlfriend. If you like someone, you want to be with them. In public." I added for emphasis, "Around other people."

"He likes you. I don't care what he says, Chris. Cole likes you. It's obvious. And not only to me," Lauren tried to reinforce her opinion, but it was too late.

Cole had inadvertently confessed his truth tonight, whether he had meant to or not, whether he even realized it or not. And I'd heard him loud and clear.

"He doesn't like me, Laur. He just doesn't want anyone else to have me. And that's not the same thing."

I was one hundred percent done with him. For good this time.

Play Hard, Practice Harder

Cole

I GOT TO practice early, like I always did. Chance was already here, which was no surprise. So was Mac Davies, our first baseman. For as big of a Jack Carter-in-training as Mac was off the field, he was serious about the game, our team, and his performance on it. It was why I liked him. He worked hard. And if things weren't going well, he worked even harder. Which was exactly why the three of us, give or take a pitcher or two, were in the locker room and on the field before anyone else on the team.

"You can't let go of something you never had in the first place." Christina's words had been tormenting me since the moment she delivered them, playing in a loop in my head.

I'd watched her inhale a single breath before walking away, and I wondered if that would be the last breath I'd ever watch her take. I would deserve it. I considered the fact that maybe, this time, I'd actually pushed her too far. Everyone had a breaking point, and I was pretty sure I'd found Christina's.

In August, I'd been especially cruel. I wasn't proud of the

things I'd said to her, but it was all done out of necessity. Hell, I hadn't even meant any of it, but if I didn't make her go away, I was afraid that I'd prioritize her over baseball, and that scared the hell out of me. How could I have both? It didn't seem like a possibility, so she had to go. Baseball wasn't expendable, but the girl was. How fucked up was that? And even after all this time, making her go away hadn't made me stop thinking about her. I still wanted her. I still missed her. And I hated myself for it.

I'd thought I'd put her away … shoved her in some box in my mind where I compartmentalized the other parts of my life, but seeing her last night had ripped it all wide open. She had been locked away tight, and now, she was out, ruining my nights and distracting my days. The very thing I'd been so desperately trying to avoid, and it was all happening anyway.

Some would call that ironic.

Lacing up my cleats, I pushed to a stand as Mac laughed from around the corner, suddenly appearing in my line of sight.

"How's your face feel?" he asked, his surfer-looking blond hair flopping in front of his eyes before he moved it back and put on his hat.

I narrowed my eyes at him. "My face?" I asked before remembering that Christina had slapped me in front of everyone at the party last night. "Oh, it's fine. Barely even stung," I lied, rubbing a hand down my cheek where she'd struck me.

"Surprised you even noticed, considering the fact that

you were glued to"—I paused, searching for the name of the girl I'd never seen before in my life—"some chick's face."

Chance laughed at that. "Mac sees everything," he added.

"It's true." Mac nodded. "I do. Even if I'm making out with Bambi." He stopped and shot us each a look. "Real name. Swear. I still see everything that's going on around us. And I hear everything too."

Mac was hinting at something, but I wasn't sure what.

"You have something to say?" I figured I'd get straight to the point instead of beating around the bush. We weren't a bunch of chicks here, leaving hints for one another to decipher.

"I'm not sure," Mac started, taking a single step closer to me and lowering his voice in case anyone else came in. "I just overheard Logan talking about the girl who hit you. Christina, right? And I heard your name." He paused. "More than once. Just sounded like he was up to something, is all," he warned, and my skin prickled.

Logan LeDeoux. Grade A douche bag and bad-attitude extraordinaire.

We were both seniors this year, beginning together on the team as freshmen. But when I had gotten to start in the outfield over him, our friendship had quickly disintegrated. He hated me and made sure I knew it every chance he got, reminding me that he should be the one playing center field and not me. He celebrated my failures with a golf clap and a wicked grin and pouted over my successes. It was one of the worst feelings to know that a teammate, someone who was supposed to have your back, was secretly—or not so secretly—hoping for your demise.

"Who was he talking to?" Chance asked, and I knew that he hated Logan just as much as I did.

Chance had zero tolerance for guys who tore teams apart. We both considered him a cancer, but Coach Jackson obviously didn't see it the same way; otherwise, he would cut him from the team.

Mac grabbed his glove and motioned for us to head out toward the field. "I'm not sure. I don't think it was anyone on our team. Maybe some frat guy? I really don't know."

The air around me buzzed, my anger simmering just below the surface. I hated that Logan had been talking about Christina, even breathing her name. I couldn't have cared less about whatever he was saying about me, but him talking about her made me uneasy.

"What are you thinking?" Chance asked as we stepped upstairs and into the daylight.

"I don't want him anywhere near her," I growled. "But there's no time for that now. We need to focus."

Chance and Mac both nodded as we picked up our bats and made our way toward the outdoor batting cages. Chance's dad and our pitching coach was already there, setting up the machines.

"Rough night last night?" he asked, and the three of us shot each other looks like we were somehow about to be in trouble.

"I didn't say anything," Chance said before we could blame him.

"Oh, please. Like we didn't do the exact same shit when I

was here. Sunday nights after a home series? Yeah, we partied. Don't act like that's changed." Coach Carter gave me a pat on the back. "Just don't"—he stopped short and looked directly at Mac—"get anyone pregnant."

Mac practically choked.

"Jesus, Dad," Chance said.

Coach Carter threw his hands in the air. "Just a little friendly advice, is all. You still on a girl strike?" he asked, directing his question at me.

I wondered how he knew so many personal details about us. I realized that he must listen in whenever we traveled on the bus and whenever he sat in the dugout. Or who knew what the pitching staff confessed to him back in the bullpen during practices and games? Jack obviously knew way more than any of us realized.

"I am. At least, I'm trying," I said, deciding to be honest.

His brows shot up, and a sly grin appeared. "Ah. You met a girl then," he said.

"I've always known her," I started to explain before feeling frustrated. "It doesn't matter, sir—Coach. I can't focus on that right now. I need to fix my swing." My tone came out almost pleading.

Every at bat felt like it might be my last. If I couldn't pull myself out of the hitting slump I had been in, there was a good chance that Coach Jackson would start putting Logan in instead of me. I knew Logan was waiting for it, chomping at the bit to take my position.

And I couldn't let that happen regardless of how I personally felt about Logan. It wasn't only that I hated him, but I was also terrified that if he, or anyone, got to start over me, what would happen if they went on a hitting streak? There was no way that Coach Jackson would pull a player whose bat was on fire and replace him with someone whose stick was lukewarm. I could very well spend the rest of the season warming the bench, never to see the outfield grass again.

That meant I wouldn't get drafted.

And there weren't any more chances after this one. It was my last.

So, like I'd said, I couldn't let anyone get a chance at playing over me. I had to fix my broken swing. You see, it wasn't enough that I was the best center fielder in the league. I had to be able to hit at the plate. The only people with an allowance to fuck up their at bats were pitchers and the occasional infielder who was too valuable to replace. But even that was rare. When you were up to bat, you had to perform. It was part of your job. And I was currently failing at mine.

Coach Carter turned serious. "Then, get in the cages," he directed before grabbing a bucket of balls and arranging a small L-shaped screen for him to sit behind as he threw me some live pitches.

Even though Jack was technically the pitching coach, he was so knowledgeable about baseball in general that if he offered extra help, you would be a fool to not take him up on it. He had hit the shit out of the ball when he was here at Fullton State. As far as we'd all heard, Jack struggled with nothing on the field and excelled at everything. We all wanted to be just like him in that regard.

I took a bunch of hacks with him in the cages, and Coach Carter shook his head as he stood up.

"Stop," he said, walking over to me, and I suddenly got anxious.

"How bad is it?" I asked, hoping he could tell me exactly where I was going wrong in my mechanics so that we could fix it. A swing was made up of a million different facets, and any one of them could throw the whole thing off.

"There's nothing wrong with your swing, Cole," he said, throwing the ball into his glove with a pop over and over again.

Say what? "Coach?"

"There's nothing wrong. Your swing looks good. You're balanced. You're centered. All your mechanics are tight."

Dammit. "So, why can't I hit the ball then?" I asked as my hand holding the bat dropped to my side. I tapped the end of it into the dirt, gripping it tight, knowing what he was going to say next.

If there was nothing wrong with my mechanics and everything technically looked good, then there was only one other explanation. My approach at the plate. Also known as a hitter's mentality when walking up to bat.

Mechanics could be adjusted and fixed with a few swings on the tee and live pitching, but your mental state? That was another issue altogether. There was no cure for being in your own dome. And the more you thought about it, the worse you made it.

I waited for him to say what I already knew but didn't

want to be true.

"It's your approach."

Annnnnd ... there it is.

I exhaled a loud, frustrated breath, my head shaking, as Coach Carter added, "You're in your own head. You're overthinking."

Tossing the bat onto the ground, I walked over to the three-foot concrete wall and hopped up on it, the heels of my cleats kicking against it like I was a five-year-old kid. Coach Carter hopped up next to me.

"Is there anything going on? I mean, I know it's your senior year, so that alone is enough to make a batter choke at the plate sometimes."

He said the words, and I winced. Visibly fucking winced. I wasn't choking at the plate. I just couldn't hit anything other than easily fielded ground balls to second base. *Shit. Maybe I am choking at the plate.*

"Cole?" he said, pulling my attention to him.

"Sorry, Coach. I appreciate you working with me and helping. It's just the worst-case scenario, you know?"

He nodded because he did know. Jack fucking Carter knew how important a baseball player's mentality was and how it affected everything. There was no other sport that was as superstitious as baseball.

"I know this sucks. And I should probably yell at you and tell you to stop being a fucking pussy and fix your shit, but I know that's not really helpful."

"Do you think it's because I'm worried about getting drafted?" I asked and watched him take off his hat and fuck with his hair.

"Do *you* think it's because you're worried about getting drafted?" He tossed my words back at me.

I shrugged with both shoulders, holding them up for a breath or two before dropping them. "I'm not, *not* worried about it."

"I know it's hard. And it sucks being one of the few seniors still here on the team after a draft year. I wish I could fix this for you, but I can't. You have to get out of your own head and stop trying so hard. You know it doesn't work like that. Keep swinging for the fences, and you're going to keep striking out or hitting fly balls. Whatever it is that's going on in there"—he tapped a finger against the side of my head—"figure it out and shut it up."

Jack pushed off the wall and hopped down right as Coach Jackson yelled, "Hey, Anders. Plan on joining us on the field today, or do you want to run till you puke?"

Jumping down, I extended my hand toward Coach Carter and gave it a firm shake. "Thanks again, Coach."

"Anytime. You got this," he said, and I wanted so badly to believe him, but I'd been struggling since fall ball. "Coach Jackson might still call you a pussy though," he added with a laugh, and I took off running toward the field and the rest of my teammates.

"Get out there." Coach Jackson pointed toward center field where Logan stood with a shit-eating grin on his face.

We rotated players during practice, each person taking grounders and fly balls respectively at their shared position, but I went first since I was the starting center fielder.

"How nice of you to join us," he said when I got onto the grass. Even something as simple as Logan going first in practice felt like I was losing my grip on the position, but I pretended to not give a shit until he added, "You can stand behind me. You should probably get used to it."

My anger simmered, threatening to explode. Logan was a cocky asshole who barely deserved to cast a shadow on the grass we stepped on.

"Don't get too comfortable," I said as the ball sailed my way, and I easily caught it before throwing it hard to second base for the cutoff.

"You and I both know I should be starting over you. You've had a shitty time at the plate, and I don't see that ending anytime soon." He was poking the proverbial bear, and he knew it. Logan knew if he was going to talk shit, to do it where it counted. "Coach will get sick of it and yank you. Watch. I give it two more games. Three, tops."

My heart spun in my fucking chest. It was my worst fear, being pulled from the lineup and forced to watch the games from the bench, but I couldn't let Logan know that. I had to make him think I wasn't worried. "It's not my fault you're not good enough to play here. Should have gone to a different school. Maybe a D2 university, so you would have had a better shot at starting."

Telling someone they weren't good enough to be playing at the top D1 level was a low blow. It felt like a win even if it was short-lived.

"Fuck you, Anders," Logan fired from behind me, and I grinned to myself, knowing I'd struck a chord.

"Nah, I'm good," I said without turning around.

I fielded a ground ball this time and threw it at home plate to Chance. It reached on one bounce, low and perfect at the plate for a potential tagged out. I heard a few of my teammates whistle in response.

"Heard Christina's done with you. That was fun to watch. I'm thinking about asking her out. She seems feisty," Logan said as we switched positions, and he stepped in front of me, waiting to take his turn.

The idea of Logan touching Christina made my blood go straight from simmering to a strong boil. I bit the inside of my cheek to stay focused and to stop myself from tackling him to the fucking ground and beating him senseless. No matter what instigating and vile things came of Logan's mouth, I would be the one who got in trouble if I did that.

Coach Jackson had no tolerance for fighting between teammates, especially over girls. It wasn't something he warned in vain to keep us all in line, but something he followed through on as well. I'd seen him do it my freshman year. When two of the guys on the team had fought over some chick, Coach had benched them both. During playoffs. We lost that year.

He'd followed up his decision with a speech that started with, "No pussy coming between my players," which of course forced us to all fight back laughter, and ended with, "You have all the time in the world to let females ruin your life. You don't have that with baseball. Get your head in the game or get off my field."

Teammates didn't poach on their teammates' exes. It

went without saying that if one of us had dated a girl, she was off-limits to the rest of us. But then again, Christina and I had never officially been together, so those rules didn't necessarily apply. An ex-girlfriend was one thing, but hooking up wasn't. And if they weren't even remotely on the same level, then why did I feel so betrayed?

"If you want my sloppy seconds, be my guest." It was rude as shit, and I didn't mean a single word of it, but Logan was trying to rattle me, and I couldn't let him know just how badly he had.

"I think I will," he said before Coach Jackson waved us in. We started jogging toward the dugout, and he turned to offer one last dig. "I won't ask for permission when I steal your position next."

This motherfucker thinks he's going to steal my girl and *my position? Over my dead body.*

Guys in Bands

Christina

THE PARTY HAD left me rattled emotionally. Seeing Cole had broken the proverbial cage I'd kept him in the past seven months wide open and obliterated it to pieces. It had been made of cheap plastic anyway, so it really was to be expected. But now, he was out in the open again, free to torment my days. I'd tossed and turned in the three nights since I last saw him, sleep eluding me as I replayed our interaction, angry that I was back in this fucked up, emotional place again.

I was pissed at myself. For going to the party, for letting Lauren suggest the idea, and for me agreeing that it was a good one. I had known that seeing Cole could potentially wreck me. Okay, I hadn't known, but I'd damn well suspected that could be the case. Sucking in a breath, I resisted my own thoughts. I was not wrecked. Cole did not wreck me. He'd stopped having that ability months ago, and I was not some weak girl who couldn't get over a guy.

Although, to be fair, him grabbing my face and kissing me like he actually missed me could have been so much hotter if it had actually meant something. But it hadn't. It was just more of his games. More of his bullshit. More things to add to my list of What Not to Look for in a Guy. I mean, if I'd had a list like that in the first place.

A quick knock on my bedroom door had me looking up.

"Are you almost ready to go?" Lauren asked, her purse and notebook in her hand.

Glancing down at my feet to make sure I had shoes on, I nodded. "Yep. One sec," I said as I pushed off the bed and made my way into my bathroom for a quick swish of mouthwash. I avoided overanalyzing the fact that my eyes looked tired and that I wasn't skilled enough in makeup techniques to cover the light bags that had started to appear underneath them.

"You didn't sleep again, did you?" Lauren asked as soon as I exited my room and met her in the hallway.

"I did," I lied, and she gave me an eye roll. "Just not very much."

"This is all my fault," she groaned as she walked toward the front door and held it open for me to go through before locking it behind us.

"It isn't. And I swear, I'm not trying to not sleep. I want to sleep. I want it so bad. I think it's avoiding me because I keep chasing it so hard," I said with a sick laugh, realizing the irony and apparent theme of my life.

"Well, if it makes you feel better," she said as we walked into the brisk morning air, "there's a live band playing at The Bar tonight. I think we should go."

The Bar was literally the name of the bar across the street

from campus where everyone who was old enough to drink hung out. If you were underage, you could definitely get away with using a good fake ID in there, but if you didn't have one, you weren't allowed on the premises.

"It's Wednesday," I argued as her car chirped to life as we neared it. "Who goes out on a Wednesday?"

"We're in college. We can go out any day." She smiled. "And I might know one of the guys in the band." Her cheeks crimsoned as she dropped into the driver's seat and out of view.

"Wait." I opened the door and sat quickly, fastening my seat belt. "You *might* know one of the guys in the band? Either you do or you don't."

She waved me off as she started the engine, her lips pressed together tight.

"Oh my gosh. You have a crush on some dude in a band!" I practically shouted because it was so unlike her.

"Why are you yelling? I'm right here. And I don't have a crush on him. I barely know him," she tried to argue, and I laughed.

"You don't have to know someone to think they're hot," I teased as she navigated the short drive to campus. "Wait," I said before remembering a conversation we'd had. "Doesn't a guy in a band go against all your safety rules?" I started to ask as it all came rushing back to me. "Yeah," I said, holding up one finger. "They never stay in one place for long, so if they commit a crime, they have the potential for getting away with it." Holding up a second finger, I added, "Two, they have access to drugs that other people might not and are willing to use them to their benefit." I said, adding a third finger in the air, "And three, no one stops a girl from going off with a guy in a band because they all assume she's a willing participant. So, basically, anything bad could happen, and no one would believe her."

"I'm impressed. Not only do you pay attention to what I say, but you retain it as well," she said, sounding like the future psychology teacher she wanted to be.

"Guess I'm more than just a pretty face," I said with a smile as we drove toward one of the farther student parking structures.

Lauren knew better than to park in the one where Cole and I had shared multiple nights on the top level, looking up at the stars, talking about life, and watching the sun rise. I avoided it too. Even if it was the closest one to my classes and not parking there added ten minutes to my walk, I never cared. I refused to park in there on principle alone.

"Barely." She pulled the car into a spot and cut the engine before turning to face me. "Fine. I sort of, maybe think the drummer is good-looking, okay? And I know, boys in bands break all my rules, but this is more for you than it is for me anyway."

I pulled back slightly before asking, "More for me how?"

I grew nervous and worried, hoping she hadn't set me up on another blind date before talking to me about it first. She had done that once before during freshman year, and it hadn't ended well.

Thinking back, I remembered us sitting in the library, studying, when two guys walked in, dressed in full Harry

Potter cosplay, wands and all.

I laughed and whispered how it wasn't even October, so what were they doing, all dressed up? Lauren only smiled as the guys headed straight for us.

"Wh-wh-whyy are they coming over here?" I stuttered as their pace quickened. "Lauren?" More steps. "Lauren!" I whisper-shouted as they stopped in front of our work table and sat down, the entire library focused in our direction.

"Hi, I'm Ron." The redhead stuck out his hand.

I stared at it, wondering three things:

1. Is his name Ron, or is he just in character?
2. Is his hair really red, or again, is he in character?
3. And the most important, WHY THE HELL IS HE INTRODUCING HIMSELF TO ME?!

I stared at his hand like I'd never seen one before, and he finally pulled it back, tucking it inside his cape sleeve, where it disappeared. Yeah, I'd said, cape sleeve.

"Sorry. This is Christina. She's just really shy." Lauren broke the awkwardness, and I punched her leg under the table. "Ow!" she said before trying to play it off.

I was not shy. I just had no idea what the hell was going on.

"We should get going, or we're going to be late," the other Potter person said.

I looked between the three of them as Lauren slowly gathered up her things and started shoving them in her messenger bag. She was clearly leaving with them.

"*Be late for what? I'm not going anywhere,*" I argued. "*I have a test tomorrow.*"

Fake Ron—or Real Ron, I still had no idea—pulled a chocolate frog from a pocket in his cape and handed it to me. A chocolate frog! Like from the movie! I stared at it like it might come to life and start hopping around, leaving little chocolate frog prints all over the books and the shelves and the walls. How pissed off would the janitorial staff be if they had to find all those little things and clean them off? I imagined that a frog hopped around a lot before you actually caught it.

What the hell is wrong with me? *I shook my head.*

"*Are you coming?*" *Lauren asked, and I realized that no one had told me where they were going yet.*

"*Where?*"

"*To the party,*" *the other Potter said like I was an idiot who should know exactly what party he spoke of.*

"*Is it a costume party?*" *I asked, still completely confused.*

"*What? No. Why would you say that?*" *Fake/Real Ron asked seriously, and I wondered if I'd fallen and hit my head.*

Was I sleeping? *I pinched my arm and flinched.* No. Definitely not asleep.

"*You guys go ahead,*" *I said slowly, wondering briefly if I was being filmed for a prank show. Glancing down at my books, I pointed to them with my finger—because, unlike the Potter people, I didn't have a wand to point with.* "*I have to study.*"

"*I thought you said she'd agreed to come?*" *Fake/Real*

Ron pointed his wand at Lauren, and she backed up a step before apologizing. "I don't want to be a third wheel. You promised, Lauren." He was getting riled up, his wand waving all over the place, and I thought he might stab her in the eye with it if he wasn't careful. "You said she liked Harry Potter and this wouldn't be weird."

Lauren looked back at me with a pleading look in her still-intact eyes, and I shook my head. I loved that girl, but I wasn't going anywhere with them.

I'd assumed we'd both learned our lesson when it came to coordinating blind dates without asking, but now, I wasn't so sure.

"Stop looking at me like that. I did not set you up with anyone," she reprimanded me as she read my thoughts. "I promised I'd never do that again." She reached for her door handle and pushed it open, stepping out.

I did the same, getting out of the car and looking across the top of it at her. "Tell me how this is more for me then."

"Fine." She huffed out a quick breath like whatever admittance came next was going to physically pain her. "I stalked him. Then stalked the band. And their social media pages are crap. Not updated at all. How can you expect to grow if you don't even do the simplest thing, like tell people you have a show coming up? It's like they're not even trying."

Realization dawned on me as we weaved through cars in the parking lot and walked toward the tree-lined campus. "And that's where I come in."

"That's where you come in." She felt satisfied with her idea, I could tell. And she wasn't wrong to feel that way.

Social media management was what I planned to do with my life, and she knew that I was always looking for a good addition to include in my online portfolio. So far, I handled a few accounts for professors who had creative side gigs regularly as well as a handful of people who wanted me to focus on highlighting particular activities or events. Those were short-term gigs but still resulted in huge awareness and success on all fronts.

When I'd mentioned what I was doing to Cole one time, he'd told me that when he got drafted, I'd be his second hire—after his agent, of course. He said he wanted me to handle all of his online accounts. That there wasn't anyone else he could think of trusting more than me. I remembered blushing and feeling so incredibly flattered. I went home that night and researched other baseball players, taking notes on what their sites were like, when and how often they posted. I'd read all their comments, noting if they ever responded or not. I had a social media file with Cole's name on it that I should have tossed in the trash after last August, but I could never bring myself to do it.

"I mean, if their social media is that bad, I'd be doing them a favor by helping." I grinned, and she pretended not to be overly excited at my agreement.

The one thing I knew for sure was that I wanted to start my own social media management company. I assumed that I would have to work for someone else after graduation to get more real-life experience, but being my own boss and getting hired as an independent contractor was my end goal. I wanted to work with multiple clients and offer a sliding scale of services—from the basic, light finessing to total hands-on management every day. Whatever a person needed on their social networks, I planned on being their one-stop shop.

I had originally debated between specializing in high-profile companies or individuals. I carefully weighed out the professional pros and cons versus what I thought would interest me the most in the long run. I didn't want to get into something that I'd burn out on quickly, so making the initial decision wasn't as easy as it might have seemed.

Working for high-profile companies would come with a huge paycheck and stability, but I worried that I might get bored at some point or be bound too tightly by their company policies and politics or that I'd feel stuck with what I could and couldn't do creatively. I absolutely wanted the safety and financial security that a large company could provide but not at the cost of my heart.

I didn't want to play it safe when it came to my passions, and that was when I had known ... that working for individual people was the right choice for me. I remembered feeling instantly lighter after the realization, and it only reinforced the decision I'd made. I knew that I'd still be bound by beliefs and what my clients wanted to show to their followers, but I'd be more involved in how they presented it. My job would have a more intimate approach rather than me feeling like a replaceable cog on a corporate wheel.

We walked toward our respective buildings, *our* parking structure closing in on me as it neared in the distance.

"Don't look at it." Lauren nudged my shoulder with her own, knowing all that it represented, and I shot her a look.

"I wasn't planning on it. I wish they'd demolish it."

The stupid building hovered, calling to me like a bright beacon of neon, highlighting all the memories I had shared there with Cole. It taunted me. Haunted me.

Lauren laughed. "It's not the parking structure's fault. They just can't demolish something because you're mad at it."

"Stop being logical. If I want logic, I'll ask for it." I frowned, wanting to change the subject. The topic of conversation needed to stop revolving around Cole Anders.

I was about to ask Lauren the name of the band, so I could do some online research before the show tonight, but some not-so-quiet pieces of conversation caught my ear.

"Yeah, that's her."

"Slapped him."

"He hates her for it."

"I hooked up with him that night anyway. It's not like he's into her."

My steps faltered only the tiniest bit, but Lauren locked her movements in time with mine and smiled big for any girls looking our way to see. "Don't listen to them."

The girls on campus had always said things under their breath about me or Cole whenever I was around. It was petty and immature, and you would think I'd be used to it by now, but I hated the way being the topic of conversation felt. Especially when it wasn't ever anything nice or complimentary. A girl could only take hearing, "She's not even that cute," so many times before she wanted to beat someone senseless.

And it was all Cole's fault. It'd felt like everyone on campus knew about the two of us hooking up the minute after it happened, and apparently, it was everyone's business. Other females made sure I knew that I wasn't the only one spending time with Cole. Heaven forbid a girl felt special for two seconds. Oh no, not when it came to a highly desired baseball player at Fullton State. Cole Anders was a hot commodity, and I would not be the one to take him off the market. Or so I'd been told by a drunk sorority girl at a party one night.

The craziest part to me was the fact that I'd never even been Cole's official girlfriend in the first place, but for some reason, other girls loved throwing his sex life in my face. Over the years, I'd been told more times than I could count about Cole hooking up with someone who wasn't me. They whispered when I walked into the commissary, said things as they sat next to me in class, made sure I overheard them at frat parties. It was always the same; first would be his name to get my attention, and then things like, "She's not the only one. She knows that, doesn't she? I was with him last night. He sure knows how to use his hands," would immediately follow.

I never understood why they cared so much to try to hurt me when it was obvious that Cole and I weren't a couple. What did they have to gain by bringing me down? Why did we women enjoy seeing each other suffer or hurt? We were competitive. No matter how much girl power we preached, it was kind of bullshit. I thought it was ingrained in our DNA to be competitive with one another or something. Fight for the most virile man.

I used to care a lot more in the beginning. I'd stayed silent and let them talk while I sat there and took it. I stopped taking it about a year ago and started speaking up. Once I'd started talking, they'd stopped. For the most part.

The two girls had already passed us by, but I turned around and shouted, "Hey!" to get their attention.

They stopped and turned to face me, nervous looks on their faces.

Yeah, not so tough when I call you out, are you? I thought to myself. "Just for the record and just so we're clear, I don't give a shit what or who Cole does. You make sure and let him know, 'kay?"

The girls who'd had so much to say when they were strutting past me were suddenly at a loss for words. I was not surprised. What did surprise me was seeing Cole. He was taking the steps two at a time up the side staircase of *our* parking structure.

I watched where he was going until he reached the top level and disappeared out of view.

Of course.

The one place that I avoided like the plague because it held way too many memories, he continued to use it like it meant nothing. Like our lives hadn't become intertwined up there on that top floor. Me and that stupid structure were the same to him … just a place to hang out until he had somewhere else to be.

Social Media Guru

Christina

I SPENT MY afternoon after classes researching the band, The Long Ones', social media sites and taking a ton of notes. There were four members, all local surfers, born and raised in Southern California. Their Facebook page had been set up but never posted on. It was a literal ghost town. They had a YouTube account, but it only had one video on it. And their Instagram had sporadic posts at best. The only thing that was up-to-date was their website, which, in the grand scheme of things, was a good sign. They weren't completely dysfunctional.

None of this had truly surprised me, however. Most of the time, the people who I considered "the talent" didn't have the extra hours, knowledge, or the desire to handle the social media side of things. It truly was a full-time job in and of itself and overwhelmed even the most organized professionals. The fact that they even had an account set up at each one of the appropriate channels showed me that they at least wanted to maintain them, but for whatever reason, they hadn't been able to.

And that was where I would step in tonight and offer my services. I definitely was at the point where I could charge a fee for my knowledge, expertise, and time, but since these guys were all students, I knew they wouldn't be able to pay me. I would build their accounts, upload content, and maintain them until I graduated. Then, my days of doing things for free would have to be over. Not because I didn't believe in helping people when I could, but because I deserved to be paid for my work, and I would have bills that my parents no longer covered.

Graduating meant it was time to grow up, be an adult, and pay for your own way. As terrifying as the concept was, I also felt ready to tackle it. I knew a big part of that was because I knew what I wanted to do with my life and was taking the steps to get there. The majority of students who put off graduating for as long as possible did it because they had no idea what they wanted to be when they grew up. I totally understood that but was thankful I couldn't relate.

Closing my notebook, I glanced at the clock. Hours had flown by, as they usually did whenever I was excited about the prospect of a potential client. Lauren used to tease me about how I wouldn't even notice that the sun had risen and fallen while I was immersed in work. And it was true. I was too busy paying attention to all the details online to notice the ones off of it. She'd come home an hour or so ago, and she knew better than to distract me, so when I stretched my arms over my head and looked around, I was surprised to see her sitting on the living room couch, reading.

"Have you been there the whole time?" I asked, and she

laughed, her head nodding as her feet tucked up underneath her.

"Pretty much. But I've been quiet, so you haven't noticed me," she said like she was a proud child waiting for a reward from a parent.

"We'd better start getting ready." I stood up from the chair and stretched some more. My body was tight from staying in one position for so long.

Lauren slammed her book shut and breathed out, "Finally! But I'm hungry. And I was afraid to bang around in the kitchen while you were in it. You know how grumpy you get."

I frowned. "I don't get grumpy. I just hate getting distracted. It takes me out of my mindset and throws me all out of whack, and then I have to start over."

"Yeah, yeah. Grumpy. Anyway, I need to eat something before we go because I am not eating at The Bar."

"Why not? Their food's decent?"

The Bar's food was definitely edible but greasy. Maybe she wasn't in the mood for anything fried.

"I don't want to eat in front of the drummer," she admitted, and I gave her a half-smile.

"Understandable," I said because drinking in front of a crush was one thing but trying to eat greasy bar food in front of them was something else altogether.

Walking into the kitchen, I pulled open the fridge and frowned. We were pretty bad at keeping food stocked. Like most students, we ate out way more than we could afford to.

"There isn't much here," I said as she appeared behind

me, looking over my shoulder.

"Please don't make me eat another salad," she whined, noting how much lettuce was in our vegetable drawer.

"I don't make you eat anything," I said with a laugh. "And you love salads."

The girl ate more salads than anyone I'd ever met in my life.

"I know; I know." She waved me off. "Don't get me wrong. I just feel like they steal joy from my life every time I eat one for a meal. I know I'm supposed to eat it, and it's good for me, but it's not fun. I get tired of eating them all the time."

I laughed, not only because she was an absolute crazy pants, but because I also totally agreed with her. I loved a good salad myself, but she was right; they weren't necessarily fun to eat. They felt like something you were forced to put in your mouth, not something you wanted to. And it was such a female thing because how many guys did you see walking around, eating salads for meals? None. Unless they were vegetarians, but they didn't count for the sake of this argument.

"Joy-stealers. That's our new name for salads from here on out," I said with a laugh.

Lauren cracked up. "Yes! I love it! Now, make me one of your famous grilled cheeses, please!" She reached for the bread on the counter and slid it toward me.

I grabbed the freshly sliced deli American white cheese and salted butter. "All right. But don't blame me when you feel all bloated and full and gross."

"I'll feel delicious because your grilled cheese is the best. And I won't even be sorry because it will bring me joy and make me so happy to eat it!" she singsonged as she spun around in circles.

"If you say so." I went to work on the sandwiches, making them exactly the way my grandmother had taught me when I was young. It wasn't like you could *really* go wrong when making a grilled cheese, but you could improve it and make a good thing even better. And that was what I did. I made a really great grilled cheese, thanks to Grandma Travers.

After the sandwiches were made and eaten and the dishes placed in the sink for later, we headed into our separate bathrooms to shower and start getting ready. It took me no time at all since I wasn't looking for anything other than some new clients. Heading into Lauren's room, I looked around at the mayhem. There were a ton of clothes all over her floor, and her room was usually impeccable. It was only then that I realized how nervous she must be.

"Do you want some help?" I asked as she clearly struggled over what to wear.

"Yes! And fair warning: I have no idea what kind of music they play. They might totally suck. I have no clue." She offered me a short shrug before pulling on her third skirt since I'd walked in. Tight. Black. With a slit in the thigh.

"That's hot as hell. Do not change. Wear that," I said, knowing that she would fight me on it a little.

"It's pretty attention-grabbing," she mulled, looking in the mirror from all angles.

"Look, you're allowed to dress sexy because you like a guy in a band and not worry about getting kidnapped and sold into sex slavery, okay? Girls go out, looking hot, every night! I won't let anyone steal you," I said, telling her exactly what she needed to hear.

"Okay, but if I get taken, it's on you." She pointed a finger in my direction.

"Deal."

"And you'll have to tell Jason what happened," she added, and I squinted at her.

"Jason who?"

"The drummer!"

"Okay. I'll claim responsibility, and I'll tell Drummer Boy it was all my fault. Happy now?"

"Yes." She smiled before offering to call a ride, but I jingled my car keys and promised that I wouldn't drink more than one beer all night.

This wasn't a social call for me. I was in work mode and didn't want to forget anything, so drinking too much was not on the agenda. After I grabbed my notebook and pen, we headed out the door and into the night.

I pulled into The Bar's parking lot, and the first thing I noticed was how crowded it was. There were some parking spots available, but it definitely wasn't as dead as I'd assumed it would be on a Wednesday night. When we stepped out of the car, we could hear the music pouring out. They'd already started, and I hated the fact that we were late. It screamed unprofessional.

When we showed the bouncer our IDs, he said we had a

table reserved, and both Lauren and I shot each other surprised yet thankful looks. He directed us to the lone empty table in the entire place with a handwritten Reserved sign on top. The Bar was packed and not just with college-aged kids. It was a younger crowd, but some people had clearly come here straight from work, dressed in business attire and loosened ties. I watched as they rocked out, their heads nodding along with the beat.

We sat at our high-top table, both of us enjoying the music and the way in which the band commanded the stage. The lead singer reminded me of a male Gwen Stefani from back in the day, if such a thing existed. They were really good. A mix of old school punk and ska with catchy melodies and lyrics. It was easy to see why the place was so packed.

While Lauren was laser-locked on to Drummer Boy, my eyes wandered, and I mentally took notes on the amount of people here on a Wednesday night. I questioned if they had come to see the band or if they just liked to drink during the middle of the week. The majority of people who not only knew the lyrics, but were also actually singing along gave me my answer.

They were fans.

And they had come here to watch the band.

I felt proud and excited, and I hadn't even met the guys yet. The realization that they already had a fan base made me smile. And it could be so much bigger if they kept their online presence up-to-date and informed people where they were playing and when, among other things.

But my first order of business was to find out if they even wanted that growth in the first place. It seemed like a question that went without saying, but it wasn't. Not every band was trying to make it big. I needed to know what their ultimate end goal was. Was it a record deal, radio airplay, sold-out concerts, or were they content with being a big fish in a little local bar scene? In order to serve them the best way that I could, I needed to learn exactly what they wanted.

All things I would ask them once I got the chance to sit down and talk to them. Hopefully, they'd all be on the same page. That was the first challenge when it came to working with multiple people—aligning their goals, especially if it was something they had never discussed before. Putting your dreams and desires into words made them real. Almost like once you'd said them out loud, you weren't allowed to take them back. That was a very scary concept for some people, especially artists I'd learned.

"I'm going to go get us some drinks," I yelled toward Lauren, who nodded her head but didn't make eye contact with me.

I'd already lost her. She was encapsulated in the wonder of live music. And to be fair, there was something about seeing a band perform live that was a step above anything you could ever hear through your speakers. Well, most of the time anyway.

I made my way toward the bartender, wiggling and sucking in my stomach as I pushed through the crowd. When the bartender finally noticed me—or should I say, when he noticed the top of my head—I shouted my order and pushed all the way in, my chest firmly pressed against the dark wood that currently smelled like spilled beer.

"This is a nice surprise," a guy to my left said.

I racked my brain, wondering how and if I knew him. He looked familiar.

"I'm not sure we've ever formally met. I'm Logan LeDeoux." He wiped his hand on his shorts before holding it out toward me.

Logan LeDeoux ... Logan LeDeoux ...

Recognition dawned on me. Baseball player. I should have known or at least put it together, but then again, why would I have? There was more to my life than just the Fullton State baseball team.

"Christina," I said with an unsure smile, not knowing what he wanted or what was about to come out of his mouth. Anything having to do with Cole always made me a little uneasy.

"Nice to meet you." He gripped my hand and gave it a firm shake right as the band announced they were taking a twenty-minute break.

"You too. I actually have to go." I broke our contact and thumbed toward the band, who were putting down their instruments.

"Come back. I'll buy you another beer," he said as I made my way toward Lauren without answering him.

Lauren was smiling at Drummer Boy as he walked toward our table. It was cute, seeing her so enamored. And he seemed to feel the same way. At least if I was reading his expression right anyway.

The four band members surrounded our table as I handed Lauren her drink, and a waitress appeared, giving the guys each a beer and water. *Where was she when we needed drinks?*

"You guys are really good."

"Thank you," Jason, the drummer, said.

"This is my roommate, Christina. The one I told you about." Lauren started the introductions, and I paid attention even though I already knew their names and what they played from my research earlier, "And this is Jason, the drummer. Aaron, the bassist. Frazier, on guitar, and Charley, the lead singer."

Drummer Boy wiped the sweat off his head with a towel before dropping it to the ground. "It's nice to meet the social media guru."

A loud laugh came out of me without warning. "I'm not sure I'd go that far," I started to say, "but okay."

The group laughed along while they all stared at me, so I decided to get right into it. We only had twenty minutes anyway, and it wasn't enough time.

"So, I took a look at all your sites today, and you guys have a lot that needs to be done," I started my pitch.

Charley interrupted, "We can't pay you."

"I mean, we barely get paid to play," Frazier added.

"I know," I said, hoping to calm them down.

I felt their fear, their apprehension. They were struggling artists who knew that nothing was free or cheap in this industry. It was one thing to hope for a break, a helping hand, or someone to throw them a bone, but that rarely happened.

And the majority of people who offered it usually had a hidden agenda.

"I didn't come here, hoping to get the big bucks."

"That's good. 'Cause we got no bucks," Aaron said.

"What did you come here hoping for then?" the lead singer asked with a wink.

Is he flirting?

He leaned his body closer to mine.

Yeah, he was definitely flirting, but I shook him off and focused on the business at hand.

"I came here, hoping you guys would hire me. And I'll work for free for the next three months until I graduate. I'll take pictures and video tonight to add to your pages, I'll update all your sites, and I'll build you guys a solid foundation that you can use, going forward. We also need to have one big meeting where we sit down and talk about each individual social media channel and your goals. I have a lot of things I want to ask you, but I need way more than twenty minutes."

I could tell that I was starting to lose them, overwhelm them. Social media was like a giant Oak tree that had a few large branches but what felt like a million smaller ones sprouting off in all directions. It was easy to get lost on a tiny branch and never get back to anything else.

"Okay, let's start small," I started, and I swear they all breathed out in relief in unison. "Which one of you has your login for Instagram? I want to log in to your account and go live when you guys start playing again."

Frazier raised his hand and then scooted next to me,

giving me the password and login information, and I entered it into my phone. The Long Ones was added to my list of Instagram handles and logins. I planned on updating their site with some clips from tonight, and then I'd schedule a meeting with them ASAP to discuss the rest.

"Are you guys all good with this?" I asked before I started taking over because I knew that I could move a million miles a minute.

They all said, "Yes," and, "Thank you," as they downed their water before finishing off their beers as well.

"All right! I'll start tonight. We'll schedule that meeting for as soon as you guys can do it."

I was overloaded with excitement and possibility as the guys made their way to say hello to other people that they knew. Jason walked off but not before giving Lauren a sweat-covered hug, which she pretended to not like but secretly loved, I could tell.

"This is going to be so much fun." I beamed at her, surprised to see that her vodka and cranberry drink was already empty.

"You're really good at this, you know." She smiled.

"Thank you." I felt like I was glowing from the inside out.

Nothing had ever made me feel more personally fulfilled or confident. I never questioned if I was good enough to do this job or if someone might be better at it than I was. That never mattered to me. There was more than enough business to go around, and I planned on being one of the best.

"Who was the guy at the bar?" Lauren asked.

I'd already forgotten all about him.

"Oh. Some guy named Logan," I said without looking at him.

"Baseball player, right?"

"How'd you know that?"

Lauren remembered everyone. His face was probably stored in a file in her mind labeled Potential Kidnapper. I stopped myself from laughing.

"I recognize him. He was at the baseball party the other night."

"He seemed nice. Offered to buy me a beer," I said and waited for her reaction.

"Don't let him hand you one that's already opened!" she started, and I shook my head.

"I know the rules, Mom," I teased because, apparently, roofies helped you get kidnapped easier. Made you compliant, pliable, and forgetful.

"Do you think he knows who you are?" She rattled the ice in her glass around before sliding it away.

"I'm not sure," I said because I wasn't. "He did say we hadn't formally met before, but I don't know what he meant by that. So, maybe he's seen me around?"

A waitress arrived, carrying two drinks—another beer for me even though mine was still full and another vodka and cranberry for Lauren. "From the guy in the hat," she said, pointing toward Logan, and he tipped his glass in the air in our direction.

"Thanks," I said to the waitress.

Lauren waved Logan over before I could argue. "Might

as well see what he wants," she said.

I figured we might as well. *What's the worst thing that could happen?*

Gave His Blessing

Christina

"**Y**OU TWO KNOW the guys in the band?" Logan was at our table before I could blink twice. He moved his body in between Lauren and me, placing his drink on our table as he introduced himself to her, shouting over the music.

"They're her clients," Lauren offered a little too quickly.

She was clearly trying to shove Logan off onto me, but I didn't want him. At least, I didn't think that I did.

My brain couldn't have cared less about any of that because all it focused on were Lauren's words.

My. Clients.

"They are my clients," I agreed a little too loudly. Something about saying those words out loud to other people made me feel so satisfied. "Thanks for the drink, by the way."

"Yeah, thank you," Lauren added as she sipped hers through the tiny straw it came with.

I always thought those were for stirring and mixing, not actually trying to drink through, but what did I know? I rarely drank hard alcohol.

"Not a problem. So, the band is your client?" Logan's brow furrowed as he turned toward me. "Fill me in. I'm lost."

"I handle all their social media," I said before quickly wondering if he had ever looked at their stuff online before. It wouldn't look like I had done a very good job if he had. "Or at least, I will after tonight."

"I wasn't going to say anything"—he laughed—"but their accounts are pretty bad."

I sat up straighter in my chair, my back rigid. "They just need a little help," I said, feeling defensive of the guys already.

He leaned a little closer to me, as if he wasn't already close enough. "I'm sure you'll be just what they need."

I couldn't tell if he was being genuine or sort of smarmy since he came off a little of both.

"You were at the party last week, right?" Lauren asked, and he reached for whatever he was drinking and finished it off. "At the baseball house?" she clarified.

"I was."

"I thought so. Hey, I'm going to go to the restroom. I'll be right back." She gave me a grin like she was somehow helping me out by leaving us alone, and I wanted to roll my eyes at her but didn't.

"I saw what happened between you and Cole." His dark eyes were focused right on mine.

I tried so hard to read him but failed. It wasn't like I trusted my judgment when it came to guys at this point anyway.

"Oh," I picked at the label wrapped around my bottle. "Yeah, sorry about that." I found myself apologizing even though I had nothing to be sorry for.

Logan laughed. "Knowing Cole, I'm sure he deserved it."

I knew that was supposed to make me feel better, but it didn't. All it did was make me was wonder what else he knew about Cole that I didn't. Why would Cole have deserved it? The Cole I'd thought I knew never did things to cause a scene. And even though girls constantly threw themselves at him, they usually didn't walk around, slapping his pretty face.

"He did," I said, pushing my lukewarm beer away. I'd lost my taste for it. "Deserve it, I mean." I noticed another guy who looked sort of familiar, staring at us from across the bar. "Do you know him?" I asked, nudging my head in his direction. "He's been watching us this whole time."

Logan turned and craned his neck to see, a scowl appearing on his face before he dropped it. "Mac. He's one of my teammates."

"You don't like him?" I asked as I watched the guy switch between looking at his cell phone and us.

"Why would you say that?"

"The look on your face," I said, not wanting to dig up trouble, but I wasn't going to pretend like I hadn't noticed the scowl. "And the fact that you two aren't hanging out together."

"He's one of Cole's cronies," he said the words with disgust.

I figured out one thing pretty quickly that I knew I was

right about—Logan was not a fan of Cole's.

"Cronies?" I questioned. "Guess that's why he's staring," I said, annoyed with how it didn't seem possible for me to go a single day without Cole being brought into my life.

"He's also not old enough to be in here." Logan took a step away from the table, and I placed a hand on his shoulder to stop him.

"So what? Don't get him kicked out. That will cause problems for you on the field. Who cares if he's in here?"

Logan faced me, his hard features softening. "You're right; you're right."

"I'm back!" Lauren announced. She looked between the two of us, picking up on the fact that something had happened in the minutes she was gone. "What'd I miss?"

"Nothing much. Just some teammate drama." I tried to lighten the mood, but it had already soured somehow. There was a dynamic going on that I knew nothing about and wasn't my business.

Thankfully, the band started up again and I excused myself from the table as I went live on social media and started videoing their performance. The number of viewers steadily increased and I caught a few of the excited comments scrolling across my screen as I moved around the stage, filming the guys and their instruments.

After the song ended and they started into another, I ended the live stream, but continued to take short video clips and tons of pictures. I wanted to make sure I had enough material to last a month, if necessary.

Once I was done, I walked back toward the table,

surprised to find Logan still there with Lauren. "They're so good." I shouted through my excitement.

"I know!" Lauren yelled back.

I reached for her arm and tugged her closer. "I'm ready to go. I have a lot of work to do for the band, and I really want to get started. I'm too excited to wait. You coming or staying?"

I knew Lauren wasn't quite ready, and I honestly felt bad for asking her to go, but all I wanted to do was leave this place and get to work with the footage I'd taken.

"I can leave. He'll call me later," she said, motioning toward Jason on the stage as he rocked out, his eyes on us.

We both gave him a good-bye wave, and he smiled, letting us know he saw us without ever missing a beat.

"Can I walk you out?" Logan asked and I nodded.

Heading outside, the three of us walked through the small parking lot as I pulled the key from the front pocket of my jeans and pressed the button. The headlights turned on at the same time the doors unlocked with a loud beep that echoed.

"Is it too forward if I ask for your number?" Logan said as he stopped in front of the driver's door with me.

"What are your intentions?" Lauren asked from the other side of the car.

"Uh"—he let out an uncomfortable laugh—"I plan on asking her out on a date."

I shifted my weight and kicked at nothing.

"Eventually," he added carefully.

"A ... a date?" I squeaked out.

"Don't sound so excited."

"No, it's not that." I laughed awkwardly, knowing how bad that must have come off.

"I'll let you two talk this out," Lauren said before slipping into the car and shutting us out.

A date. And not just with a guy from class, but with someone who was also on Cole's team. *Wasn't this against bro code or something?*

I wondered how it would make me look—to date more than one person on the same sports team at the same school. Would people call me names or label me a baseball groupie? Cole had told me all about those kinds of girls before, and I had never once considered myself one of them. But was I? Would I become one if I said yes to a date with Logan?

"If you're worried about Cole, I already asked him," he said.

My heart stopped beating and fell to the ground at my feet. A second ago, I had been more worried about my reputation, but now, all I was thinking about was Cole's reaction and just when the hell Logan had had the time and forethought to ask him.

"You did?" I questioned. "You asked him about me? When?"

"After the party. It was during practice one day. I asked him if he would care if I got to know you better." Logan sounded sincere and nonchalant as my entire world was once again tilting around like an amusement park ride.

"What did he say?"

"He gave me his blessing. Told me to go for it. Said he didn't care what either one of us did, to be honest."

I had been right earlier in my assessment; Logan and Cole hated each other.

Whatever emotion I had been feeling instantly turned to anger.

He didn't care?

"So, what do you say, Christina?" Logan asked. "Can I get your number?"

"Say yes, Christina," Lauren shouted from inside the car where she could clearly still hear us even though I'd thought she couldn't, and it made me laugh.

"Fine. Yes," I said before taking his phone and putting my phone number in it.

Screw Cole Anders.

Screw him right to hell.

Where Is She?

Cole

M Y PHONE PINGED four times in a row, and I almost shut it off instead of looking at it. That shit annoyed me—the bombarding of messages like rapid fire. Why couldn't people just say it all in one text?

MAC: YOUR GIRL IS HERE.

MAC: WITH LOGAN.

MAC: THEY LOOK CHUMMY.

MAC: GET THE FUCK OVER HERE.

Jesus. Christina was where? And with Logan? I fired off a text response to Mac, asking for all the details, and waited twenty seconds too long for his response. I almost tore my room to pieces in those twenty seconds. I hated the idea of her being with him. Logan had warned me, but a part of me hadn't thought he'd be that stupid. He must be getting desperate if he actually crossed the line into my territory.

I told Mac I was on my way. Tossing on a tight Under Armour shirt over my low-slung black sweats, I hopped into my old, beat-up 4Runner and drove toward The Bar. The last thing I cared about was what I looked like or what I was wearing. All I wanted to do was get there and get there quick.

I had no fucking idea what the hell I was going to do or say once I did. But it didn't matter. Logic didn't matter. I was running on fumes and desperation. You could probably smell them both on my skin. Slamming the car door after I parked, I practically sprinted inside, the security guard not even asking to see my ID—he knew who I was. Looking around like crazy, I didn't see Christina. Or Logan. But Mac came up to me, as if appearing out of thin air.

"You just missed them."

"They left? Together?" I ground out, my jaw flexing, my hands balling into fists.

"They did. He went outside with her and he didn't come back."

"Do you think he left with her?"

"I don't know." Mac gave me a slow shrug.

"How'd you get in?" I asked as I remembered that Mac wasn't twenty-one.

"I have a fake. And I wanted to see the band that was playing. They're so good."

I looked around at the guys gathering up their equipment from the small stage. I knew who they all were, and Mac was right; they were awesome.

"Did they come together? Her and him? Were they on a date?" My mind started racing, my anger soaring, my jealousy fucking raging like a wild beast. I had no right to be jealous. I had no right to be or do anything, yet here I was, in my fucking sweatpants, running here in the middle of the night because I would do anything to stop her from being with him.

I tried to convince myself that I'd be okay if it was with anyone but him, but that was a lie. I'd never be okay, seeing Christina with anyone who wasn't me. So, why couldn't I man the fuck up and tell her that? Why did I refuse to cross that line and risk losing her forever?

"Cole." Jason, the drummer of the band, walked up to me, his hand extended.

"Hey, man. How was it?"

"It was packed. Great show. Sorry you missed it, but to be honest, I don't even know how half these people knew we'd be here tonight," he said with a lopsided grin as he pulled his sweat-filled hair back and slapped on a ball cap.

"What do you mean? You guys are incredible."

"Nah, it's just that we haven't updated our social media in months. But that all changed tonight, man!" he started to say, and I knew instantly what was coming next. "We got a social media manager. It's going to change our lives. She's fucking smart as hell."

"That's great. Is it Christina?"

"You know her?" He tossed his head back. "Shit. Of course you know her. But yeah."

"Hey," Mac said, hitting my shoulder, and I focused on the front door where Logan had walked back through with a shit-eating grin on his face.

"Hey, Jason. Was she with that guy tonight?" I asked, and he warily looked at me, almost too scared to give me the answer. "Tell me," I pushed.

"They were definitely hanging out." He backed away. "I gotta go pack up."

"All right. Thanks, man. Good to see you. I'll come to your next show," I said as Jason headed back toward the stage, his eyes looking somewhere over my shoulder.

"Unless we have a game. Then, we'll both miss it." Logan's voice hit my ears, and I saw red.

I turned slowly to face him, trying my best to keep my temper in check.

"What do you want?" I bit out, and he grinned.

"Surprised it took you this long to show up, Anders," he taunted before shooting a glare at Mac. He obviously knew that he was the one who had ratted out his location. "Were you hoping to catch Christina?" he asked, his tone like a barb straight to my fucking guts, but I tried my best to pull myself together and appear unaffected. I couldn't let him know he had me. "You just missed her. But don't worry. She's in good hands."

"Yeah, her own since she's not here," Mac said.

I let out a hollow laugh, hoping my detached act would have its desired effect and Logan would back off, thinking I couldn't care less that he was pursuing her.

But I cared too much, and Logan fucking sensed it. He was about to contradict what Mac had said, and I couldn't stomach the idea of hearing it. I bailed before he could say another word about her or him or them. I heard Mac shouting my name from behind me, but I was too far gone to care.

I practically sprinted outside and exhaled, watching my

breath fan out like smoke before it floated away. The night air was freezing, but I had my anger to keep me warm as I reached for my phone and fired off a single text message to Christina that read:

PLEASE DON'T GO OUT WITH HIM.

Screw Cole

Christina

I STARED AT the unexpected text message, my heart lodged in my throat and my fingers hovering over the keypad on my phone. After seven months, this was the first text Cole had sent. No text had come after the slap at the party. No text after that awful evening in August when he'd destroyed whatever we had. Not a word until tonight.

I heard Lauren on the phone, her high-pitched responses reverberating through the thin walls of our apartment. I knew she was talking to Jason, the drummer, and I didn't want to interrupt, so I couldn't ask her for advice. Although I was pretty sure what she'd tell me to text Cole back. And it wouldn't be pretty. Not that Cole deserved pretty.

He'd given Logan his blessing. His blessing! And now, he wanted to take it back? He wanted to tell me not to go out with him after he told Logan he didn't care?

I wanted to respond to him in a hundred different ways. I wanted to tell him to fuck off, to ask him why he cared, tell him it was none of his business what I did, or say if it bothered him so much, then why weren't we together? I wanted to remind him he couldn't have his cake and eat it, too, although that was exactly what I'd been giving him the last three years. But mostly, I wanted him to leave me alone. Since we were not going to be together, I needed him to go away.

More thoughts raced. Like how had he even found out so fast? Mac, the other baseball player's face, came to my mind. I remembered seeing him oscillate between watching me and Logan and typing on his phone. It didn't take a genius to figure out that Mac had texted Cole. But it did take one to figure out why Cole cared.

He had no right to ask me not to go. He had no say in my personal life after he decided that he didn't want to be a part of it. I promised myself that when the time came and Logan decided to ask me out on a real date, I would definitely say yes. I deserved to move on.

Lauren's bedroom door opened, and she walked out with an empty glass, surprised to see me still working at the kitchen table. "Oh. I'm glad you're still up. I got some interesting news," she said through a yawn.

"I got an annoying text"—I held up my phone—"but you first."

"Apparently, Cole showed up at the bar. And he was looking for you," she said as she filled her glass up with water.

"He was there? How do you know?"

"Jason told me. They're friends, I guess. Cole was asking him about you. Jason said he looked scary."

"Looked scary?" I said with a laugh because it sounded

ridiculous. Then again, there were apparently sides to Cole that I hadn't seen and didn't know existed, so it wasn't beyond the realm of possibility.

"He was asking about you. He was asking about Logan. He was pissed. He and Logan had words. That's all I know," she said, sounding completely annoyed, before taking a drink. "Now, show me that text."

I held up my phone, and she grabbed it before groaning. "This guy has some nerve."

"Right? That's exactly what I thought."

"He's such an asshole. The biggest game player and mindfuck I've ever met. And that's saying a lot because, hello, we're in college, and I'm majoring in psychology." She sounded more wounded than I felt. "Are you going to respond?"

"No," I said with finality.

"Good. Silence hurts more than any words ever could." She gave me a quick hug. "You okay?"

"Yep."

"You're sure?" She jutted out her hip and waited.

"Promise."

"Okay then. Night."

"Night," I said as she started walking toward her bedroom. "Wait." She stopped and turned to face me. "How's Jason?" I asked.

A huge smile covered her face, and she tried to hide behind her hand. "He's so nice. And normal. I thought that since he was in a band, he might be more of a jerk than he originally let on, but he's not at all."

"I really liked him too. All the guys were super chill," I said, giving her my approval that she hadn't asked for and didn't need.

"Agreed. Get back to work. And don't forget"—she leveled me with an overly dramatic expression—"silence."

I laughed. "You don't have to worry. I'm not responding. I have nothing to say," I reassured her, but I meant it. There wasn't anything left to say to Cole that hadn't been said a hundred times in a hundred different ways.

And I didn't even feel bad about it. I felt sort of good, empowered even. For once, I was in control. Something I had rarely, if ever, felt when it came to me and Cole.

Get My Head in the Game

Cole

CHRISTINA NEVER RESPONDED to my text. The one where I'd asked her not to go out with Logan. I basically begged her, my heart aching as I willed myself not to puke up my guts in the parking lot where I'd apparently just missed her. I was more vulnerably honest in that single text message than I'd ever allowed myself to be. I wondered if she realized that. Maybe if she knew just how twisted up I was inside, she wouldn't have ignored it.

Maybe she wouldn't have ignored me.

It had been three days. I knew she'd read the message right after I sent it, but she never said a thing. I'd waited over an hour before I finally let myself fall asleep that night, assuming that when I woke up the next morning, there would be a text waiting.

But there wasn't.

And it fucking killed me. I could text her again. Hell, I'd thought about it a hundred times, but my pride would shut it down every time I got close. If she wanted to talk to me, she would have responded. Or called. Or done any-damn-thing.

But she didn't, and so I couldn't either.

It was like she'd opened the door just a little by showing up at the baseball party, and now, I couldn't stop thinking about her or get her out of my head. Wherever I had her compartmentalized had been blown to hell and back. I was going crazy, trying to stay away from her and not talk to her. Or at least, I felt like I was. And once you tossed my nemesis into the mix, I could barely focus on anything else when all I should be focused on was my game.

After taking infield, I hustled into the locker room to take a piss and lace up my cleats one more time before the game started. Baseball players were superstitious, and apparently, I had some shit with my shoes. There was absolutely no rhyme or reason for it, but every game, you could find me pulling out my laces and tying them back in, nice and tight. Sometimes, I only did it once. Sometimes, I would do it as many as three times. But I always did it.

As I laced them up, I did my best to keep an eye out for Logan LeDouche. If he knew what was good for him, he would stay outside in the dugout while I was going through my pregame ritual in the locker room. I was afraid that I might snap his scrawny little head off his neck if he showed it around me before game time. And even though it annoyed me to no end, it was probably a damn good thing that Mac knew what was going on. I wasn't really in the state of mind where I should be left unsupervised even though I refused to admit that fact to anyone other than myself.

I pushed to a stand, my laces done. "You don't have to follow me around," I growled, and Mac shot me a bored look.

"I'm not," was all he said in response.

He hadn't even tried to come up with a bullshit lie or excuse. Chance suddenly appeared, and they both fell in step behind me like my own personal shadows.

"Are you two on double duty?" I spat at them both even though they didn't deserve my anger.

"Don't be an asshole," Chance chided me, and I bristled, wanting to put the sophomore in his place. "Mac filled me in. We can see what Logan's trying to do to you. And it's clearly working."

"It's not working. Both of you, shut up." I swatted my gloved hand through the air in their direction, hoping I'd hit one or both of them as we walked through the underground tunnel toward the dugout, but I missed.

Chance reached for my shoulder, his grip tight, as he forced me to stop. Leaning close, he spoke quiet enough that no one could overhear but loud enough that I could, "It's working. It's written all over your face. He's in your head. It's what he wants, Cole. He wants you rattled."

I shook Chance's arm off and snarled at them both. "He won't beat me. Not on or off the field. I'm not a rookie. I know what's at stake. Stop trying to babysit me."

The metal spikes of my cleats echoed in the tunnel as I left them behind and waited to hear the two of them start walking again. I appreciated them looking out for me, but I also meant it; Logan wouldn't win, and I didn't need a fucking babysitter.

The sound of the crowd grew louder as I neared the

entrance to the dugout, the music blaring, and I wondered for a split second if Christina was here. She hadn't attended any games yet this season. And trust me, I knew. Closing my eyes for a breath, I chastised myself and pushed thoughts of her away. My teammates were walking around the dugout, grabbing cups of water and hitting their fists into their gloves, making loud popping sounds. I walked up to the edge and leaned against the railing, watching the other team wrap up their infield practice.

Spitting onto the dirt, I glanced to my right and caught Logan eying me. He stared at me with a wicked grin on his face like he was moments away from taking away everything I had ever loved. I flipped him off and kept eye contact. His expression morphed into something I couldn't quite read, and I pretended that I couldn't care less about it. *This team was mine. This game was mine. Center field was mine. Christina was mine.*

Dammit.

"Let's go," Coach yelled, and we ran out onto the field before huddling up in a tight circle.

The announcer started speaking animatedly into the microphone, but we listened to coach giving us a quick pregame speech.

As a team, we shouted, "Win!" before sprinting to our positions to await the national anthem.

I stood in center field, next to the other two outfielders, my hat in my hand and my head bowed as the anthem played. And no matter how hard I tried to sing along in my head or focus on the upcoming game, Christina's face kept reappearing in my mind. Chance had been right; I was rattled, and I needed to fix it before I fucked it all up.

The first half of the inning went by quick. Our pitcher was on fire, and he struck out all three batters. Three up, three down. Glancing once more at the lineup, I saw my name in the fifth position. I was half-surprised that Coach hadn't dropped me down to eighth or ninth in the batting order. I grabbed a helmet and my bat and sat at the end of the bench, mentally giving myself a pep talk.

After a minute, I stood up and watched the pitcher. I kept track of his pitches and the way he moved depending on the pitch he was about to throw as he warmed up. Reading body language was one of a hitter's best weapons. That, and learning how a pitcher reacted to a batter and his ability. Nine times out of ten, you knew exactly which pitch was coming for you, but that didn't mean you would be able to hit it.

We took an early lead, thanks to a leadoff home run by Chance Carter. That kid was a fucking amazing ballplayer. I high-fived him when he came into the dugout with the rest of the team before focusing my attention back on the opposing team's pitcher, wondering if he was the type to lose control or pull it together after giving up a home run so early on. Pitchers were notoriously the most mental cases on any baseball team.

Chance had apparently pissed him off. And the kid threw better when he was angry, not worse.

Good to know, I thought to myself.

We had one out and one guy on base as I made my way to the on-deck circle. The crowd was loud, cheering and screaming, and I found myself wanting to do something I never did.

I wanted to look in the stands.

It was an unspoken rule among baseball players. You kept your head in the game, and you never looked in the crowd. I'd never even been tempted to do it before this moment. And I had no idea why the pull was so strong, but I gave in to it.

I looked.

Christina was here. My eyes went directly to her, and don't ask me how the hell I knew where she was sitting because I hadn't even been sure she'd be here at all. Our stadium was huge, sold out for every game, but there she was, behind home plate about twenty rows up with a baseball hat covering her dark hair.

Why did I know exactly where to find her? Why is she here? Did Logan given her a ticket? My eyes locked on to hers. Even through the shading of my helmet and her hat, I could still see her eyes. She was looking right at me. And she refused to look away.

Jesus, Cole, get your head out of the stands.

"Strike three!" the umpire yelled, and I refocused.

Looking at Coach at third base, I watched him go through the signs, waiting for what he would ask me to do. Hit away. Stepping into the batter's box, I sucked in a quick breath and readied myself to watch the pitcher's hand and grip on the ball. My stance felt good, but my head wasn't in it. I was out of sorts, and I felt it in every part of me. He threw the first pitch, and I watched it pass me by. A perfect fucking fast ball that I should have hit out of this park, and I hadn't even swung.

Tossing a hand in the air toward the umpire, I waited for him to shout, "Time!" before I stepped out of the box.

Coach Jackson stared me down from the third base line, a frown marring his features. I knew he was wondering what the fuck my problem was or what the hell I was doing. I squeezed my eyes shut for a second to clear my damn head. Her blue eyes appeared. Grimacing, I slapped the side of my helmet. *Talk about being a mental case.*

What if, all this time, I'd thought the draft and it being my last year were blocking me at the plate, but it was losing her that had messed me up? What if, in making sure I cut her out of my life so I could focus on baseball, I'd ruined my focus instead?

"Batter?" The umpire walked up next to me. "You okay?"

"Fine. I'm fine," I said with attitude before making my way back toward home plate. Each step gave me more clarity until I saw it all so clearly. The realization was like a thousand arrows raining down from the sky, aiming to strike me all at once. Everything suddenly made sense, and the tension that had been present moments ago eased from my body. I felt strong, assured, confident.

I moved my legs into position in the batter's box and waited as elation filled my veins. The pitcher knew I had been in a hitting slump, and I'd just watched a perfect fast ball go by without so much as flinching. He was going to give it to me again. And I counted on it.

He did. Another fast ball right down the middle, and I swung perfectly, the bat connecting with the ball with a *TING* so loud and so smooth that I knew instantly that it was a no-doubter. Dropping the bat to the ground, I started running to first as I watched to make sure the ball cleared the fences in left field. Once it did, I slowed my pace and jogged around the bases toward my waiting teammates, the cheering stands filling my ears.

When my foot slapped down on home plate, I took my helmet off and pointed it in Christina's direction, holding it in the air. I saw her jaw drop slightly, and I grinned before high-fiving and tapping helmets with my teammates, a newfound motivation growing inside me.

I'd told her that I needed her gone in order to focus, but I couldn't focus for shit after she left.

I'd thought I'd be fine without her, but I hadn't been fine since the day I forced her to go.

I'd believed that I was doing the right thing, but being without her was wrong.

I'd been such an idiot. How had I never put it together before now?

Christina had always been there, by my side, since day one, and I had never struggled at the plate. She wasn't bad for me or distracting me from my goals. She was the exact opposite. And as soon as the game was over, I was going to find her and tell her.

Am I in the Twilight Zone?

Christina

"Uh," Lauren stuttered, her shock as apparent as mine, "did he just point his hat thing at you?"

"It's a helmet. How many times do I have to tell you, it's a helmet?" I asked, knowing that no matter how often I tried to explain baseball to Lauren, she would never truly get it. I honestly didn't care. I was just happy she'd agreed to come with me.

I'd had no intentions of coming to this game until Logan texted that he had left me two tickets. It felt rude to not show, but if Lauren hadn't said she'd come with me, I would have stayed home, manners be damned.

"Okay, fine. His helmet," she enunciated dramatically. "He pointed it at you. I mean"—she looked around us—"who else would he have pointed it at?"

I shrugged my shoulders because the last thing I wanted to do was assume that Cole had meant that little gesture for me. It could have been for anyone. Maybe his dad was here? Or some other family member? Or some girl he'd screwed last night? I had no idea. But I did know that there was no mistaking the look he had given me when he was on deck earlier.

Maybe the helmet gesture was meant for me. But if it was, then why? We weren't even on speaking terms.

"He was definitely pointing it at you," a girl chimed in from behind us, her tone not at all happy or pleasant.

I angled my head to look at her.

"Although none of us can figure out why." She flipped her long blonde hair over her shoulder.

"Oh, Jesus, really? Let us know when you wrap your tiny brain around the answer, okay?" Lauren said, and I couldn't help but laugh.

Hair-Flipper leaned between us and whispered, "You don't have to be such a bitch."

"You're one to talk," I said, defending whichever one of us she was trying to offend.

"Cole can't commit to you, but he can't let you go either. Ever wonder why that is, Christina?" she said my name like it disgusted her.

"No," I lied with conviction, "but you sure seem to." I stopped paying attention to the game as I concentrated on the girls behind me. I had no idea who they were, but they all knew me. I wished that I could say I was surprised, but I wasn't.

"We do have a theory." Hair-Flipper leaned back in her stadium seat, and I turned my body to face her and her group of clones.

They literally all looked exactly the same with blonde hair extensions, fake eyelashes, and filled lips. I felt like I was staring at a group of social media *influencers* who should be posing up against the pink wall in LA for likes and mentions, not sitting in the stands of a baseball game. And even though I was passionate about social media, this was one facet of it that I didn't enjoy or want to be a part of. I would never understand the fascination with looking as plastic as possible at such a young age. And honestly, what were all those people influencing anyway? Nothing. I hated the fakeness of it all and the way it perpetuated girls to feel like they weren't enough if they didn't look exactly like these three girls did.

"You have a theory about me and Cole? Two people who have nothing to do with you?" I tried to make her feel as stupid as she sounded, but it obviously wasn't working.

"Yes." She sounded pleased with herself, and I wondered for a second if this was all some sort of joke that I was about to be the butt of. Hair-Flipper sat there, grinning at us, her too-white teeth practically blinding me.

"Care to share the theory with the rest of the class?" Lauren interjected, and I shot her a questionable glance, unsure of what was about to be said.

"Oh, right." Hair-Flipper clasped her hands together before looking at her cohorts for permission. She cleared her throat like she was about to give a presentation she'd practiced for months. "We think that Cole won't commit to you because you're not marriage material," she started, and I practically choked on my laughter.

"What?" I shook my head like she was insane as the stadium erupted in cheers around us.

I glanced toward the field to see the guys jogging back toward the dugout. I hadn't even noticed them take the field in the first place because I'd been so distracted.

"You see, there's no point in settling down with you if you're not the one." She sounded so convinced in her assumption and so impressed with herself that she continued without prompting, "Cole's going places, and he obviously doesn't see you there with him. If he thought you were cut out to be a baseball player's wife, you'd be a baseball player's girlfriend first. But you're not. And you never have been. So, it's clear he sees no future with you, and that's why he won't commit."

She wrapped up the first part of her argument with a wide smile while her doppelgängers all nodded their collective heads in response. I was actually a little stunned, a part of me wondering how much truth existed in her analysis. I'd never even gotten to marriage in my own head when it came to me and Cole, so it seemed a little far-fetched that he would be thinking that far ahead. But what if she was right? What if Cole couldn't see a future with me, and that was why he never let me get too close?

Hair-Flipper cleared her throat to get my attention. I'd zoned out for too long, lost in my own thoughts, and I hated that I'd probably given her some sort of satisfaction about it.

"And—" she started up again.

"There's more of this?" Lauren interrupted, and I knew she was only trying to help me. There was no way that she had missed the way I'd gone all internal and quiet.

"Well, there were two points, and I only addressed the

first one," she said, looking almost wounded.

"Oh. Well then, by all means"—Lauren waved a hand in their direction—"please continue."

Hair-Flipper clearly wasn't fluent in the language of sarcasm because she grew giddy. "We also think that Cole can't let you go because he met you first. If he had met any other girl before he met you, he would be doing this with her. But he didn't. It could have been someone else, but it just happened to be you. And now, he's stuck on you by default."

That exact idea was something I had considered multiple times before, but hearing it from a complete stranger stung more than when it had been born from my own thoughts. It was one thing to think it for myself on the nights I stayed up way too late, overanalyzing everything ever said between us. But it was embarrassing to learn that other people had come to the same conclusion.

It made me feel stupid.

"Anything else?" I asked, trying my best to sound bored, but I was coming unglued inside. I needed to get the hell out of this stadium and away from these Barbie lookalikes who had clearly struck a nerve. I refused to let them see how much they had gotten under my skin. Girls like them had been saying things to me for years, but this felt different somehow.

"Nope. That's it. So, what do you think? How close are we? Pretty accurate, right?"

"Are you seriously asking her what she thinks about your half-cocked, stupid-ass theories? It's actually embarrassing that you have nothing better to do with your time than focus on two people you don't even know," Lauren ranted, her tone bitchy. "You really should focus more on those shitty extensions you put in your head. They'll probably get you kidnapped."

"What?" She reached for a fistful of hair and ran her fingers through it. "They aren't shitty. It's real hair. I paid good money for these."

Hair-Flipper looked at her friends, and they all reassured her that her luscious locks were "beautiful" and "looked real" and we were "just mean girls who are jealous."

Right.

We are the jealous and mean ones.

"I have to go to the restroom," I said before pushing to a stand, thankful that I was sitting at the end of the row and didn't have to create a scene to get out.

"Don't leave me here with the bad-hair triplets," Lauren said loud enough for the girls behind us to hear, and I couldn't help but laugh. They deserved it.

Hustling up the cement steps with Lauren on my heels, I made my way out of the crowded seats and into the open walkway.

"I can't stay here," I said as soon as we got to the top.

"I know," Lauren said before she wrapped an arm around my shoulders. "Baseball's so boring anyway."

"It is not," I argued as we headed away from the field and toward the parking lot.

I loved watching Cole play. Even though we were never officially together and even when I was mad at him, I still wanted him to succeed. There wasn't ever a part of me that rooted for him to fail. Not even when he deserved it. And there were plenty of times when he had deserved it.

Letting out a long breath, I clicked the key fob on my car and opened the driver's door. My mind was replaying the two theories, her words repeating on a loop.

"So"—Lauren buckled herself in—"what are we going to do about this Cole situation?"

"Do you think the helmet was for me? Be honest," I insisted as my car revved to life. I didn't care what her answer was. I just wanted to hear her opinion.

"I do."

I nodded because my gut told me it was for me too. "Do you think what those girls said was true?"

"Hell no!" she argued. "Cole isn't thinking about marriage. That was the stupidest thing I'd ever heard. He likes you. He's always liked you. He's just too stupid to do anything about it. And once he realizes it, it's going to be too late."

I didn't say anything in response. I drove back to our apartment before realizing that I'd left the game because of Cole, but I'd gone to it because of Logan. "Think Logan will be upset that I left?"

"I'm sure you can make it up to him if he is." She waggled her eyebrows.

A small laugh escaped. "I'm sure you're right."

"Promise me you'll at least give Logan a chance."

"I promise," I said, and I meant it.

"One hat wave from Cole doesn't change the past three years," she added, and my stomach instantly dropped.

"I know," I reluctantly agreed because she was right.

The gesture changed nothing. And I refused to be the last one to realize it.

She's with Him

Cole

CHRISTINA HAD LEFT sometime during the game. I thought she might have gone to the restroom, but she never came back. I checked her seat without getting caught by Coach whenever I ran on and off the field. I wanted to tell her to wait for me when the game ended, so I could talk to her right away. Once I realized that I wanted her, I didn't want to wait a minute longer than necessary to tell her. But her leaving had put a pin in my plans.

"Looks like you're back, kid," Coach Carter said as he clapped my shoulder.

I grinned, feeling on top of the world. "I am."

"You looked great at the plate today."

I'd had five at bats during the game and got hits in four of them.

"Thanks. I felt great."

"Keep it up."

"I will," I said with confidence because I would. Everything had finally clicked into place.

Logan, on the other hand, looked like someone had

kicked his dog. He was most likely pissed off that my hitting was back on track. There was no fucking way he was taking my position now, and he knew it. Baseball was over for him.

I watched as he headed my direction. "Come to congratulate me?" It was a dick thing to say, but Logan didn't deserve my respect or kindness.

"On what? Finally hitting the fucking ball?" he said a little too snarky for my liking, and before I knew it, Mac was at my side making sure I didn't lose my cool.

"For starters, yeah," I bit back, putting a cap on my anger. Logan wasn't worth it.

"Wow, Cole. One game. Doesn't mean shit. Try keeping it up," he said before throwing one last barb in my direction, "Heard you saw Christina."

I bristled. I fucking hated the way he said her name. It made me want to hurt him. "I think it was the other way around."

That classic LeDouche shit-eating grin was back on his face. "She was here for me today. Not you. You might be keeping your position for now, but you've lost the girl."

I laughed, hoping it would rattle his confidence when it came to her. "We'll see about that."

Logan didn't have history with her the way I did. They couldn't have the same kind of connection that she and I shared. There was no way. I refused to believe it. No matter how many signs told me otherwise.

I SHOOK OFF my Mac's and Chance's shadows after reassuring them both that I was fine and that I'd see them later at the party. Even though it was a Saturday, today had been the last game of the series, and we'd swept the opposing team, winning all three games. Coach had actually smiled during our team talk and then proceeded to give us the day off tomorrow. He rarely did either.

I headed toward my truck with a half-baked plan in mind. Since Christina had ignored my text from a few days ago, I knew that any more of that type of communication was off the table. If I waited for her to respond to something new, I'd most likely be waiting forever. Texting wasn't effective. I had to be more aggressive. Showing up at her apartment, uninvited, seemed to fit the bill. Her roommate wouldn't like it, but as long as I promised not to sell her off to the highest bidder, she might be willing to let me in. Then again...

I considered stopping for flowers, but I wanted to get over there as quickly as possible. Anything, even romantic gestures at this point, would take too long. I'd been an idiot for long enough. And now that I'd realized it, I didn't want to waste another minute being apart from her.

When I hit the gated entrance to her complex, I cursed under my breath, forgetting all about the barrier that had helped them decide on this place to begin with. Rolling down my window, I punched four numbers into the keypad and waited, hoping it was still the same code that she'd given me from when they first moved in. It had always worked before, but I hadn't tried it in months. There was a slight possibility that it could have changed. Just when I was about to give up hope, the gate unlatched and swung open, allowing me inside.

I navigated the small road toward her building, searching for her car as I drove. This plan would be shot to hell if she wasn't home. I hadn't even considered that she might not be here, and I reminded myself that I could be really fucking stupid sometimes. Spotting her car, I felt myself grin as I eased my truck into the spot next to hers and shut down the engine.

Instantly, I regretted not getting the flowers. Walking up to her place empty-handed seemed like a bad idea now that I was here. I hesitated, my hand resting on the door handle before I convinced myself that I was doing the right thing.

I'll drown her with flowers after she's mine, I promised myself.

Huffing out a quick, calming breath, I pushed the door open and hopped out. I was at my next obstacle within seconds. Christina's building had its own secured entrance. If you didn't have a key fob to enter, you had to be buzzed in by a resident. Pacing back and forth, I wondered what my other options were. I hated the idea of using the coded phone system. It would be too easy to either ignore my call or decline my entrance. And I refused to be denied right now.

No sooner had the thought entered my mind when the door swung open, and a twenty-something-year-old female walked out. She shot me an appreciative glance, and I gave her my most charming smile as I reached for the door, holding it open for her before I let myself inside.

I walked the hallway like I belonged there, like I could remember how to get to her place blindfolded or in my sleep. And to be fair, I could. I made a right, followed by a sharp left, before I stood, staring at her front door, my hand held in the air, ready to knock. *What the hell am I going to say to her?*

Maybe coming here with absolutely zero plans in mind isn't the best idea I've ever had.

Rapping my knuckles against the wood, I leaned back on my heels and waited, my heart lodged in my throat. The peephole in the door grew dark before it lightened again, and I knew that it was too late to turn back now—not that I wanted to.

The door creaked open.

"How did you get in here?" Lauren asked from a mere two-inch space. She refused to open the door any wider, letting me know that I was not only *not* wanted, but also not welcome.

"Good Samaritan?" I said, trying to be cute, but Lauren didn't even crack a smile.

She wasn't happy to see me, which could only mean one thing—Christina wouldn't be happy to see me either.

"How'd you even get on the premises?" she asked, her tone even sharper than before, and I stuffed my hands in my front pockets.

"I have the code." I admitted with a shrug, knowing that I

probably should have lied, but I didn't want to.

"I'll have to make sure they change it," she said, and it made me laugh because I'd expected that reaction from her. "Why are you here, Hat Boy?"

Hat Boy? I thought to myself before realizing that she was talking about my helmet pointing into the stands from earlier.

"I'm here for Christina. Is she home?" I pulled my hands out of my pockets and fidgeted.

She let out a clicking sound before saying, "Sorry, you just missed her."

"Where is she? I really need to talk to her." I leaned against the doorframe, hoping that she would sense my sincerity.

"She's on a date," Lauren said before adding with a finger point, "and you should let her enjoy it."

I swallowed hard as I choked down my fear. "Who is she with, Lauren?" I asked, knowing damn well what the answer would be. My fingers gripped the doorframe so tight that I thought it might splinter.

"Who do you think?" Lauren was taunting me, and she enjoyed it.

"Logan?" I asked, my tone wary, desperate to be wrong.

"He isn't just a great baseball player, ladies and gentlemen; he's smart too." She pretended to address a crowd in the empty hallway.

"Do you know where they went?" I all but ground out through clenched teeth, my fists clenched. I needed to get to Christina before things with her and Logan went too far.

"No. And even if I did, I wouldn't tell you. Look at you, acting all caveman right now, like she owes you anything. You'd go there and cause a scene. She doesn't deserve that, Cole. She deserves better. And you've never been the one to give it to her."

Her words were like weapons, blunted, sharp, and aimed to kill. I took a step back like she had struck me before pulling it together—barely.

"Lauren. Please. Listen," I started, but she interrupted, finally pulling the door wide enough so that she could step through it.

"No. You listen," she said, jabbing a bony finger into my chest. "You've done nothing but hurt and confuse her. You don't get to do it anymore. She has a chance to be happy, and if you give a shit about her at all, you'll let her be."

"But Logan isn't a good guy," I said, my head shaking, wishing that Lauren could see the real Logan and not whatever fictitious one he was pretending to be.

"Says the guy who is worse than all of them," she said, glaring.

I wanted to tell her that she was wrong about me. That I'd changed and seen the error of my ways and that I needed Christina at a level that scared the hell out of me, but there was no use. Lauren would never believe it, and those words weren't meant for her anyway.

"I'm not sure why you did that thing during the game today, Cole. And I have no idea why you're here right now, but I do know that it's not fair." She shook her head as she made her way back into her apartment, her hand holding on to the door. "And you know it. You've played her like a yo-yo for years. Cut the damn string already and go find a new toy to play with."

The door closed without another word, and the sound of the dead bolt clicking into place reverberated throughout the hallway. I stood there like a kid who had just been scolded by his parents, staring at my shoes, wondering what the hell to do next.

Crossed the Line

Cole

TUCKED MY tail between my legs and drove back to the baseball house. But not before driving past five local restaurants and three bars, all looking for Logan's car. It wouldn't be my fault if we all happened to end up in the same place at the same time. I wasn't sure which of us I deemed the lucky one when I finally gave up.

When I walked through the front door, I saw some of the guys who didn't live in the house were already hanging out, drinking and getting ready for the party. They called my name and waved for me to come into the kitchen. Ignoring them, I headed straight for my bedroom instead and locked the door behind me. Usually, one or two of my teammates would end up in my room to shoot the shit, and I wasn't in the mood. I needed to shower and think in peace.

As Lauren's words played through my mind, I shook them away, refusing to get pissed off. I knew that she was only sticking up for her friend and wanted the best for her. What Lauren didn't realize was that the best thing for Christina, was me. It damn sure wasn't Logan. But the only

119

person I needed to prove that to was Christina, and I still planned on doing exactly that. I'd let her have this date today with Logan even if it ripped me apart inside, but tomorrow, all bets were off.

I'D WRONGFULLY ASSUMED that she wouldn't show up here tonight. Especially not on Logan's arm, with his hand wrapped around her waist as they navigated their way through the crowd of people blocking the doorway. My senses heightened the moment they arrived, calling my attention over my shoulder to where she stood ... *with him.* This scene was growing far too familiar—her in my house. But the rest of it, who she was here with, was all wrong.

I shouldn't have been so surprised to see her here, but I was. I'd looked in the stands for her today, called out my home run, and gone to her apartment with my heart in my fucking hands. If the girl was trying to show me that she didn't need me in her life, I was starting to believe her. Because a private date was one thing, but showing up here, to my house for a party, was a fucking statement. A slap in the face. A knife in the goddamn back.

Logan's arm was still holding her, and I wanted to tear him limb from limb for even thinking that he could even though I had no right. My eyes moved from where his hand touched her exposed skin, to her baby blues, and back again.

I couldn't stop. She watched me, her expression unreadable. The heat that raged to life inside of me started radiating out of my pores, and it was a damn wonder that I didn't light things on fire with my presence. I wondered if everyone else in the room could feel my rage as they grew closer to me in the kitchen.

Like clockwork, my two shadows appeared at my side, flanking me.

"Jesus, fuck," I growled, and they only moved in closer. "Shouldn't you be making out with some poor girl already?" I asked Mac.

"There's plenty of time for that," he said with a laugh before growing more serious. "He's only doing it to get to you," he reaffirmed what I had already known, but it changed nothing.

I didn't give a shit about Logan or his reasons for doing anything. I only cared about Christina. And she had come here tonight with him, knowing that I'd be here and that I'd see them together.

"He knows you have your head on straight. We can all see it. That your balance is back. He wants you off-balance again," Chance informed me, and I shot them both annoyed glares. "Using her is his last-ditch effort."

"It's all he has left in his arsenal," Mac added. "He knows if this doesn't work, nothing will."

I wanted to call Logan out on it. Make him admit that he was only using her to get to me, but I knew that it would embarrass Christina. And no matter how desperate I was to show her the truth, I'd never willingly put her through that.

"Hey, Cole," Logan said as the two of them walked straight up to me, Mac, and Chance. "You know my date, Christina, don't you?"

I looked straight at her. "Hi," I said, only to her, but she didn't respond.

She looked uncomfortable as she wiggled her body to move out of Logan's grip, but he refused to let her go.

Instinctively, I reached out and removed his hand from her. "She wants you to let go."

He cocked his head and sweetly looked at her. "I'm sorry, babe. Was I holding on too tight?"

"No, I just"—she stumbled on her words before recovering—"want to go out back and get a beer."

"I'll go with you," Logan started to say, but I put a hand up to stop him.

"I'll go with her," I offered with a grin. "Unless you have an issue with that?"

It was a challenge. One I knew that Logan wouldn't accept. He cared too much about what people thought of him to act ruffled over me walking his date to the keg.

"No issue," he said just like I had known he would, and I waved a hand toward the backyard and waited for Christina to start walking.

She kept her pace ahead of mine and didn't look back at me. "You don't have to come with me."

"I know I don't have to. I want to," I said as I reached for her arm, forcing her to stop moving.

"Why are you doing this?" She sounded exhausted. But only like she was exhausted with me ... like I exhausted her.

I wanted to tell her everything that I had realized during the game today ... everything that I had been dying to tell her since the second I figured it all out. But I couldn't. Not here. Not right now. The timing was off, and I knew she wouldn't believe me anyway. Christina would convince herself that I'd only said those things because she'd come here with someone else.

"I didn't want you to walk out here by yourself. And I really want a beer. We have the day off tomorrow," I said with a smile as I reached for the keg and started filling her cup.

"I know. I heard," she said, the words grating on my nerves, knowing exactly where she'd already gotten the information from.

Logan suddenly appeared and ruined the moment. "You were taking too long. I missed you," he said, and I shot Christina a look, wondering how much of Logan's shit she actually believed.

She offered him an awkward smile, and I handed her a half-filled cup. "Only half?"

"It gets warm otherwise, and you hate warm beer," I said, remembering when she had told me that once before.

"It's so gross when it's warm," she said, and I agreed.

"It's chilly out here. Let's go back in, yeah?" Logan asked, and she nodded before walking away and leaving me behind.

I sulked for only a moment before I followed them back inside, heading straight for wherever they were. It was going to destroy me to watch her with him, but I figured that I deserved the torture for everything I'd put her through.

Watching him with her was like throwing gasoline on my guts. I was afraid to breathe too hard, worried it might come out in flames.

Watch me burn it all down, motherfuckers.

"You good?" Chance sidled up next to me.

"Not in the slightest," I answered honestly as I took a swig of beer.

"Why don't we go sit over there?" He nodded toward the empty couch in the living room. "You can still see them from there. This is awkward as hell. You're making shit weird."

As much as I wanted to throw some sort of childish tantrum and stalk off, pouting, I didn't. If I left Christina and Logan alone, it would give them privacy, and I refused to grant them a single ounce of it. I was going to stand wherever they were and make it uncomfortable as fuck. If they even thought about leaving the room, I'd follow. If LeDouche wanted to touch my girl, he'd have to do it in front of me and pray to God—or whoever he believed in—that I didn't rip his fucking arm off and feed it to him.

"Then, it's working," I growled.

"What is?"

"My plan."

Chance laughed. "What plan? The one where you stand here, staring at the two of them like some sort of psycho? 'Cause that's what you look like. Not to mention, bitter, jealous, and rageful. All things that are making Logan so happy that he looks like he might shit a rainbow."

I choked on my beer, the liquid going down the wrong

pipe as I looked at Chance. "So, you're saying we should move over there then?"

"I think it might be a good idea," he said matter-of-factly.

"Fine," I grunted like the caveman Lauren had called me earlier. "Where's Mac?" I was getting used to his bodyguard tendencies.

Chance pointed, and I saw him making out with some redhead.

"Seriously, how does he do it?"

"I have no idea," he said as he walked with me into the living room.

I sat down on the couch, noticing that it still gave me a perfect view of where Christina was, just like Chance had said it would.

"Want to tell me what's going on?"

"Not particularly."

"I'm going to guess then. And you can tell me if I'm right or wrong."

Chance wasn't going to quit anytime soon, and he was clearly trying to distract me from the shitshow I couldn't stop watching.

"Fine. Guess away." I waved my hand toward him but kept my eyes focused on her.

"You realized she's worth it," he said in a serious tone.

I waited for whatever else he planned on adding to the end of that statement, but nothing came. That was it. Five words.

I turned my head to look at him and almost let myself feel defeated before I swallowed it down. "I'm not even going to try to argue."

"Good," Chance said with a laugh. " 'Cause you're a piss-poor liar."

In that moment, I watched as Logan tried to talk Christina into taking a shot of something, shoving the small glass in front of her. She shook her head, but he asked again, a giant smile covering his face so he appeared harmless.

He had to know she didn't drink that shit. Christina only drank beer. That was what she had always said to me. I was certain she would have told Logan the same thing. It was one of her hard rules. At least, I'd always thought it was.

I watched curiously, wondering what she would do, as her eyes shot over to mine. She liked that I was watching her every move, got off on it maybe. It made her feel like she was in control, and I realized that for so long, I'd probably made her feel powerless. I mentally added that to the list of things I had fucked up and needed to make right when it came to her.

Christina cocked an eyebrow in my direction, and I wondered what the hell she was thinking behind those mischievous blue eyes.

Don't do it, baby, I silently pleaded, hoping she wouldn't drink it.

Her lips formed a wicked half-grin as she reached for the shot glass and downed the contents in one swig, her eyes on me the entire time. Immediately, I pushed off the couch, the sound of Chance calling my name from behind me as I stalked into the kitchen.

Grabbing her by the arm, I pulled her a few feet away

from the crowd of shot takers. "What are you doing?"

"What does it look like I'm doing? Get off me," she said, shaking my hand from her arm.

I released her, but she didn't move away from me.

"I thought you didn't drink hard liquor," I whispered, trying not to create any more of a scene.

"What I do or don't drink is none of your business." Her words were meant as a warning, but they were laughable at best. Everything she did was my damn business, and we both knew it.

"You plan on accosting my date all night, or can I have her back?" Logan asked, and I turned my head so fast to look at him that I gave myself whiplash.

I grabbed Christina by the shoulders and deposited her in front of Logan but not without a final warning to him. "Stop giving her shots. Only feed her beer."

"I think I'll give her whatever she wants," Logan sneered.

I stormed away before I did something I'd regret. Like break his damn face and get thrown off the team for it.

I thought I was strong enough to watch her with him all night, but this proved to be too much. When she acted out of character, it hurt me even more. I hated feeling like Logan knew a side of her that I didn't or that she was willing to do things with him that she never did with me. Although I'd never asked her to drink anything other than beer because I respected what she had always told me. *Was I an idiot this whole time?*

Striding into the backyard, I started pacing before tossing

out my warm beer into the grass and filling up my cup.

"What was that all about?" Mac asked, suddenly appearing, sans redhead.

"Where's your lady of the night?" I asked.

He shrugged his shoulders before pointing lazily toward the house. "In there. Out here. Who knows?"

Chance was clearing out the few people who were lingering around us, telling them all to give us some space and go inside. They all listened. He was lucky that he garnered that much respect as a sophomore. If he were anyone else, they would have told him to fuck off and stayed put until he physically forced them to leave.

"I saw the whole thing. The way she was looking at you when she took that shot," Chance said once the three of us were alone. "Then, you flipped out."

"She told me she didn't drink hard alcohol. Only beer. It was one of her rules," I said, trying to explain why I'd gone so crazy.

"Okay." Mac shot Chance a look, and I knew they both must think I was losing my mind. "Then, don't look inside right now," Mac added, and of course, I did the exact opposite.

I watched as she downed a shot, quickly followed by another. " 'Alcohol makes you stupid,' " I said, repeating the words that she had once told me.

"What?"

"That's what she always said. 'Alcohol makes you stupid. And gives people something to talk about.' Why is she doing this?" I asked to no one in particular.

But Chance answered, "That's obvious."

"Spell it out for me then."

"She's trying to get your attention. She's mad at you. She's hurt. This is her way of lashing out," he said, sounding so sure of himself.

"Mac, do you agree with that?" I asked, looking for either a consensus or an opposing viewpoint.

"Sounds about right to me," he said.

I continued to watch Christina. When she stumbled on her feet and Logan's arms wrapped around her, I'd had enough.

"Oh shit," Chance and Mac said from somewhere behind me as I threw my cup to the ground and started moving indoors.

I didn't have to look behind me to know they were following. It was a good thing. I might need them.

"Oh, goodie, you're back," Logan sneered, still holding Christina, and I zoomed in on his fingers splayed across her lower waist.

"Stop giving her shots. I already asked you nicely," I ground out, my tone dead. Fucking. Serious.

He let her go and took a menacing step toward me, his hands balled into fists at his sides, and I almost prayed that he'd hit me first, so I could finally end this shit between us. But his maneuver was too quick, and Christina swayed, clearly unbalanced on her own two feet. I rushed to her side before she could topple over and held her upright, all thoughts of Logan wiped away.

"Let's get you home, huh?" I said protectively.

She looked up at me and batted those long, dark lashes. "I didn't come here with you," she said, her words slower than usual.

"That's okay. You can still leave with me." I tried to be cute, but she wasn't having any of it.

She swatted me away, forcing me to let her go as she braced herself against the counter. "No. I'm not going anywhere with you. I'm not your property or your problem, Cole. Stop acting like I'm either."

"I want you to be both," I admitted quietly, but I didn't think she'd heard me.

"Logan?" she said out loud, and he was suddenly at her side, pushing me away.

His hand splayed across her ass, and my eyes burned as I stared at his fingers, wishing they'd fall off one by one.

"Right here, babe," he said the words so sickly sweet that they soured my mouth.

"I'm ready to go now."

"Christina." My voice came out pleading, and I swallowed hard to clear my throat as I prepared to say the one thing I had just promised myself I wouldn't say in front of an audience. "He doesn't want you. He just really fucking hates me." I leveled my gaze to Logan, who was smiling now, his expression taunting me as my anger toward him multiplied.

Christina's face twisted, like she couldn't believe I'd just said that out loud. "Oh, right. 'Cause no one could ever want me since you don't," she bit out before grabbing his hand and interlocking their fingers together.

"It's the truth," I said, feeling like an asshole, but I couldn't let him do this to her. I knew it was hypocritical since I'd been the one to hurt her so many times before. It seemed like I was saying no one else was allowed too mess with her, except for me, but it wasn't like that. It fucking killed me to know that he was tricking her intentionally, maliciously. "Just ask him."

"I don't have to ask him. I wish I'd never met you," she said, and the proverbial knife in my stomach gutted me clean and hollowed me out. "Can we go?"

"Of course." Logan leaned down to plant a kiss on her cheek but kept his eyes open and on me the entire time like a fucking creep.

That single action confirmed every one of my suspicions; Logan was only using her to get under my skin. To distract me. To make me angry, push all my buttons, and get me to fall apart at the seams like a battered baseball.

Chance and Mac both stood in front of me the second I took a step toward Logan.

"Don't," they each said before turning to face him in unison like they'd practiced it.

"Just get out of here," Mac yelled at Logan. "Before we let him go."

Logan laughed like he wasn't the least bit intimidated as he walked out of the house with my fucking girl on his arm.

What the Hell?

Christina

THE MINUTE THE front doors slammed behind us, I dropped Logan's hand and turned on him, feeling a little more sobered up than I had five minutes earlier. "What the hell was that all about? I've never seen Cole so mad before. He looked like he was going to rip you to pieces."

Logan kicked at the ground before walking to his car in the driveway. He opened the passenger door and practically shoved me inside, but I braced an arm against the cold paneling and refused to cooperate.

"Tell me. Is it true? What Cole said?"

"Which part?" Logan asked with a sickening laugh.

"The part where you're only with me because you hate him."

"No." He repeated the word, "No, Christina. I'd never do that. What kind of guy do you think I am?"

He asked the question, and I couldn't answer it because I didn't know. I barely knew Logan at all, but he'd come on to me like a freight train out of nowhere and not stopped since the night at The Bar. Doing it out of vengeance didn't seem like such an impossible notion.

I might be pissed off at Cole, but I could tell he believed what he said. The look on his face when he had seen me tonight almost brought me to my knees. I'd never seen that kind of pain in his eyes before or the way it grew tenfold when he saw exactly who I had come to the party with. It was more than just a knee-jerk, jealous reaction, more than him not wanting someone else to have me.

I had been stupid to ever agree to come here tonight with Logan, but even Lauren had pushed me to do it. She said it served Cole right to see me moving on and with someone else. I knew it was a bad idea from the start, but a part of me liked the thought of making Cole hurt the way he'd hurt me so many times before. I thought it would make me happy to see him in pain.

But when I had seen the agony on his face, it'd made me anything but happy. Hurting Cole hurt me as well even though it shouldn't have. I didn't feel vindicated or justified. His pain was my pain. We were connected, and we both sensed it. I was so tired of denying it or pretending like it didn't exist.

"Christina, babe," Logan said, and I scoffed at him.

"Stop calling me that. I hate it. Take me home, please," I said as I folded my arms across my chest.

Logan knew that everything had changed. "Why are you listening to him? Why would you believe Cole over me?"

The aftertaste of vodka still burned in my throat, and I wished I'd never taken the shots. But Logan had pushed them in front of me, and I'd still wanted to punish Cole.

"Because I know him better than I know you." The words slipped out of my intoxicated mouth. "And I don't trust you."

"Find your own way home then," he said before slamming the car door and walking off into the dark.

I pulled out my phone and called Lauren.

Going Out of My Mind

Cole

I STOOD IN the front entry of the baseball house and waited for Logan to come back. I knew he would. Staying away when he could poke the bear more would prove to be too tempting for him. He had to come back to see what his handiwork had accomplished. To see how far he'd pushed me. To see just how far I'd cracked.

I couldn't stop pacing. I paced from the front door to my bedroom door. Twelve steps. My door to the kitchen— nineteen steps. Then, I'd turn around and do it all over again. When my teammate Brandon asked me what the hell I was doing, I shot him a glare that made whatever smart-ass remark he was about to say next die in his throat.

Mac and Chance had deemed me less of a threat apparently since Mac was attached to the redhead's face again, and Chance was nowhere to be found. I pulled out my phone, tempted to text Christina and make sure she was okay and home safe. Somewhere in there, I planned on apologizing as well, but all I could see right now was Logan's hand on her ass and the look he had given *me* when he put it there.

And while I was ninety-nine percent convinced that Logan was doing this for sport, that one percent ate away at me. *What if I'm wrong? What if Logan really does like her and my ego is playing tricks on me? Haven't I been the one to let her go over and over again? How could be so stupid for so long?*

The more time that passed, the more pissed at myself I became.

Pissed that I'd ever let her go.

Pissed that I had convinced myself all this time that I never felt anything real for her.

Pissed that I'd pushed her into someone else's arms.

Pissed that I had no one to blame but myself for it.

Pissed that I'd wrongfully assumed she'd keep waiting for me.

Every single year, the two of us would circle back to one another, hanging out off and on before I pulled my usual bullshit and pushed her away. I think a fucked up part of me thought I'd never be able to push her far enough that she wouldn't come back.

I could see everything I'd done to her so clearly now, and it stung. I'd given her scraps of my attention, little bits on a fishing line that kept her hooked. If I thought she had moved too far away, I'd give the line a little tug, and she'd be right back in my arms like she'd never left. Looking back, I wasn't proud of how I'd treated her, but I had been too arrogant to see what I was truly doing. And too stupid to put all the pieces together at the time. I'd never had a solid relationship to look up to or build from, so I didn't know how to do one right. It was no excuse, but it still felt relevant. *Maybe she'll understand?*

My thoughts were interrupted as Logan walked through the door, his chest puffed out, and I stormed to him, ready for a fight. "Where is she?"

He tossed me a *go fuck yourself* look. "Home. Apparently, she had too much to drink. Who knew?"

It hit me then—Christina's beer-only policy. Logan had known about it.

"You asshole," I said before charging him and slamming him up against the front door.

The sound of his body hitting the wood echoed in the house, and before I knew it, our teammates were between us, splitting us up and yelling for us to stop.

"Hit me. I dare you to fucking hit me!" Logan yelled, baiting me.

"Coach has a no-fighting policy. He'll bench you," Chance was screaming in my face. "He will bench you, and you know it, Cole. He doesn't make exceptions," he ground out, his arms gripping my shoulders as he worked to hold me back.

I pushed Chance to the side as I screamed around him, "You knew!" I pointed a finger at Logan, who was being held back by Mac and Brandon.

"Knew what?" he asked, his tone equally as pissed as my own as he fidgeted against them.

"You knew that she didn't drink hard alcohol. You knew, and you gave her shots anyway."

The possessive way I felt for Christina was almost animalistic. He had intentionally tried to hurt her even more than I'd originally suspected, and I wanted to fucking destroy him for it.

"Yeah, I knew," he admitted. "Is that what you want to hear? I knew she hated shots, but I got her to drink them anyway. I wanted her to loosen up. She's always so tense. Was she like that with you? Wound up tight like a teenage virgin? Is that why you didn't keep her around?"

I shoved Chance aside with one last hard push and charged for Logan, my vision blurred red with my anger. "You'd better not have touched her," I roared. "I'll fucking kill you if you put your hands on her after getting her drunk."

Mac blocked Logan's body with his own, knowing that I would never hit him. Reaching around Mac, I tried to get at Logan, but Mac wouldn't allow it. He used his shoulders to completely block me, making me flail around like a fucking idiot.

"Get out of my way," I said through a clenched jaw.

"No," Mac ground out, using his force to keep me at bay.

"Tell me you didn't touch her." I continued making a scene as a crowd gathered around us, but I didn't care anymore. At this point, Christina's safety was the only thing on my mind, not a bunch of baseball groupies.

"I'm not telling you shit," he spat over Mac's shoulder, toward me.

"Get the fuck out of here, Logan." Chance's voice was loud, boisterous, and demanding.

"Why am I the bad guy here?" Logan actually had the

nerve to ask. "Cole's the one all wound up over some chick who isn't even his. You can't be mad at me for wanting her."

"You don't want her. You just want to fuck with him," Chance said, sounded exasperated. "And we all know it. Stop playing games."

"Tell me you didn't touch her," I yelled again, demanding he answer me, but he refused and stayed silent, giving me nothing but a wink he knew I'd interpret badly.

Mac turned Logan around and shoved him toward the front door where someone opened it. "It's time you leave," Mac growled, but Logan shrugged him off.

"Or what?"

"Or I'll let Cole go," Chance said above the noise, and I made a show of struggling.

"You won't. And we both know it," he said matter-of-factly, but I knew his confidence was because of Coach's rule.

Logan moved toward the door. "Way to pick sides, assholes. We're supposed to be a team," he shouted before looking right at me. "This isn't over." He slammed the door so hard that it rattled on its frame, and I watched as Mac rushed out after him, most likely to make sure he actually left.

Chance still gripped my shoulders, making sure I stayed put.

"You heard him, right? You heard him say that he knew she didn't drink liquor," I asked, my words coming out in a mixture of anger and disbelief as the truth settled in.

"I heard him. We all did."

I stood there, shaking my head back and forth. "It's not right. You don't do things like that," I said to no one in particular as Mac walked back into the house and announced that Logan was gone.

Cheers filled the air, and everyone dispersed back to wherever they had been before all the chaos broke out. Chance finally released me, and I thanked him for having my back as Mac walked over.

"You okay?" Mac asked.

I wasn't sure how to answer. I wasn't okay in the slightest, and I was worried about Christina. *Did Logan touch her? Or do something to her without her consent?* I needed to make sure she was all right.

"Go get her already," Chance smacked me on the back and gave me a little shove.

"Seriously, what are you waiting for? A hand-engraved invitation?" Mac added with a grin.

"Thanks," I said before shooting off like a bat out of hell, keys in hand, heading toward my truck in the driveway.

Just One More Chance

Christina

M Y CELL PHONE vibrated against the coffee table. I leaned forward from the couch and looked at the number and face flashing on my screen.

Cole.

I debated not answering, but the warm buzz of emotions from the night left my self-control weaker and more vulnerable than usual.

"Hello?" I answered, and his breaths came out fast, like he'd been running.

"Can you let me in?" he said, and I looked at my front door like he might magically appear there.

"Let you in where?"

"I'm here. I'm outside your building." He sounded upset, and I wondered if he was mad at me for showing up with Logan to the party even though he had no right to be.

"I'll be right there," I said.

"Who's here?" Lauren poked her head out of her room and asked as I made my way toward the front door.

"Cole."

"Interesting," was all she said in response before disappearing back into her room.

I walked down the hallway, and when I turned left toward the front entrance, I saw Cole standing behind the glass door with his head down. As if on cue, he looked up, his eyes locking with mine. A small smile formed on my lips, and I tried to make it go away, but my mouth refused to listen.

When I reached the door, I pushed it open and held it as he walked inside, and it slammed behind him, making me jump.

"Are you okay?" he said, looking me up and down, like he was checking for battle wounds of some sort.

"I'm fine. Why?" I cautiously asked him, the look on his face giving me pause. "Are you okay?"

"Fuck no, I'm not okay," he said before reaching for me and pulling me into his arms.

I struggled against him, but he only held me tighter, so I relented, knowing that I was no match for his strength. I melted against his hard chest, hating the way I always fit into his body like we had been molded for one another. We stood that way, our breaths synchronized in the too-bright hallway of my building, neither one of us moving or breaking contact until someone cleared their throat.

"Didn't want to interrupt," the guy said as he moved around us and headed out the door.

"We should probably go inside," I suggested, and Cole nodded.

He looked awful, but I still had no idea why. Any anger I

had felt toward him earlier had diminished the second he showed up, looking so devastatingly broken. He had always had that affect on me. And that was how we always ended up like this, year after year.

Opening up my apartment door, we walked inside, and I closed and locked it behind us, knowing that Lauren would be paranoid if she didn't hear the dead bolt click into place.

"Hi, Cole." She popped her head out and looked at us. "Twice in one day. How lucky for me."

Twice? I looked between them, not knowing what they were talking about.

Cole read the confusion on my face and answered the unspoken question, "I stopped by after the game."

"You did?" I asked him before glaring at Lauren. "Why didn't you tell me?"

" 'Cause you were On. A. Date," she clarified.

"You still should have told me," I argued.

Lauren only shrugged. "Looks like it didn't matter. You're ending the night with him instead of that other asshole."

Cole's head snapped toward me. "Did he hurt you?"

"Hurt me how?" I cocked my head and stared into his blue eyes. They looked so pained, and I realized that he was suffering for me.

His hand reached for my arm, and he moved it up and down, as if to comfort me when he was so clearly the one in need of comforting. "Did he try anything with you after he took you home? He didn't force you to do anything, did he?" Cole stumbled on the words, asking the questions through clenched teeth, as if to hold back the emotions it made him feel.

"After he took me home?" I realized Cole didn't know that Logan had left me in the dark driveway. "He didn't take me home, Cole."

"What do you mean? Where did he take you?" he asked before he started pacing, like my answer might be too much for him to stomach hearing.

"Cole," I said, but he kept moving. "Cole!" I reached for him, and he stopped, his expression distressed. Pulling him by the hand, I led us to the couch and sat down. "Logan didn't take me home. He told me to find my own way. I called Lauren, and she picked me up."

Cole shot straight back up. "He did what?"

"He's a real asshole," Lauren shouted from her room.

"Can I get some water?" he asked as he moved into the kitchen and helped himself before I even answered. He downed an entire glass before filling it up again and doing the same thing. "Okay. He left you. Why?"

"He wanted to know why I believed you over him," I started to explain.

Cole gently sat down, his body angled toward mine as he rested his hand on my thigh. "What did you say?"

"I told him that I knew you better. And that I didn't trust him." I placed my hand on top of his, and he quickly switched our positions so that his hand covered mine as he squeezed it tight.

"And he left you out there? Alone?"

"I thought you knew. I figured he walked right back

inside." I shook my head because it was the only logical explanation I had.

"He didn't come back in until enough time had passed that I had lost my damn mind."

"Why would he do that?"

"Because he wants me off my game. He wants my position. He knew this was the only way to get it. Through you," he explained, and my heart started pounding.

What did I have to do with any of that?

"I didn't mean to say what I did at the party about him using you. I mean, I meant to say it, just not in front of everyone. I'm sorry if I embarrassed you," he apologized, but I wasn't mad about that. At least, I'd stopped being mad at him once I realized that he was right.

"I was a little embarrassed. But I'd never seen you like that before, so I knew there was something serious going on."

"I shouldn't have done that though. Not in front of everyone, but it was killing me to see him touching you. I wanted to rip his limbs off, so he couldn't ever do it again." Cole sounded so sincere that I couldn't help but believe him.

"Why was it killing you?" I asked, so desperate to hear the answer that I could practically taste it on my tongue.

"Because you're mine, Christina. You've always been mine. And everyone knows it." He squeezed his eyes closed before staring at our hands.

"But I'm not yours. You won't let me be," I started to argue, but he leaned over and stopped my words with his mouth.

His tongue pressed against my bottom lip, and I hesitated

before letting him in. His lips apologized, his kiss spilling all of his feelings and emotions into me, and I took them without hesitation. I wanted everything Cole was willing to give in this moment even though I shouldn't.

"You're mine," he whispered against me, his breath warm. "At least, I hope you are. Because I'm yours. And I always have been too." He looked into my eyes like he was searching for a truth hidden in there. "It's only fair that we belong to each other, don't you think?" he asked with an unsure smirk.

My heart leaped into my throat, begging for me to say yes, but my brain flashed warning signals like a train was coming.

"Is this a game? Some sort of trick?"

He leaned away from me, his expression revealing that he had expected me to ask exactly that. "No. I mean it. I mean every word. I have so many things I need to say to you. So many things to apologize for. I don't know where to start." He looked so frustrated, his brow creasing. "I knew I should have made a list."

I laughed. Because I wanted to ease the tension that was building and because it was so damn cute to see him so flustered over me for once. "Lists are always helpful."

He looked me in the eyes and asked, "What are you thinking?"

I sucked in a breath and chose honesty. "I was just wondering, why now? Nothing's changed," I asked because the cold, hard truth was that nothing about our situations had altered in the slightest. It made no sense for his mind to have switched.

His head shook like I couldn't be more wrong. "Everything's changed. I've been living my life for one thing for so long that I didn't know any other way to live."

"But you do now?"

"Not even a little bit." He let out a guttural laugh. "But I want to try with you."

I folded my hands in my lap. "But why? Why now? Why me?"

He wasn't offended by my questions, but he looked unsure of how to respond to them. We both stayed quiet, soaking in the moments while I waited for him to say something.

"I realized that nothing works if you aren't with me. My hitting didn't start to really suffer until I tried to force you out of my life for good. It was stupid. It was wrong." He pushed up from the couch again and started slowly pacing in front of me. He tossed his hat to the floor and tugged at his hair. "I thought I was getting some kind of balance by concentrating on only one aspect of my life, but it was the exact opposite. Focusing all of my time and attention on baseball created an unevenness inside of me. But I couldn't see that. I didn't put it together until today."

"The game," I said as the realization hit me like a fast ball. "That's why you looked in the stands and pointed your helmet at me." He nodded as another question popped into my mind, "So, you're using me for your batting average?" I asked, half-joking and half-serious.

He had just said that his hitting suffered once he left me.

What if he only wants me around to get it back on track? What if I'm basically just good for business?

"No, Christina. I'm not using you. I didn't mean for it to come out like that. I want you."

"What are you saying, Cole? I need to hear it. I need to hear you say it out loud."

"I do too," Lauren shouted from her room.

I yelled at her to close her door. She grunted before slamming it shut, and Cole and I both smiled.

"I'm asking for a chance." He lowered himself in between my legs, his large frame sitting right in the dead center of my universe. "I sure as hell don't deserve it, but I promise I won't ruin it. I won't be perfect, but I'm going to try. I have a lot to learn, but please don't give up on me."

Part of me knew I should make him beg harder or grovel more, but nothing erased the fact that we deserved a chance at being together. It was the one thing I'd always wanted ever since I first met him during our freshman year. And I refused to throw away the opportunity because of my pride or to prove some sort of moot point.

"You really want to do this?"

"If you'll have me," he said, sounding unsure of what I'd say in response. When I didn't say anything, he added, "I am sorry it took me so long."

I leaned forward and shut him up with my lips this time. Kissing Cole was something that was way too easy to get used to. I could get lost in those lips if I allowed myself … but first, logic.

I pulled away, breaking the kiss. "I need you to leave."

"Wait, what?" He pushed to his feet, his full frame towering over me.

"It's just …" I formulated my thoughts. "I need to make sure this isn't some heat-of-the-moment kind of thing because of Logan. I need to know that you'll still mean all this in the morning."

He reached for my hands and pulled me up. "I will still mean all this in the morning."

"Good. Then, you can tell me all this again then." I held a hand toward the front door, expecting him to take the hint.

"You're serious?"

"I am," I said. "I need to make sure you still feel the same way when you open your eyes tomorrow."

"I will," he said, his tone filled with determination as he leaned down to pick up his hat before heading toward the door.

"Okay," I said, my tone clearly skeptical. "I'll talk to you tomorrow."

"No." He stopped walking. "I'll see you tomorrow." He pulled out his phone and looked down at it. "Be ready by eleven."

I eased my head back in surprise. "Ready for what?"

"I'm taking you out to eat, for starters. In a real restaurant. On a real date." He pressed a kiss to my forehead before shoving his phone back in his pocket.

"At eleven?" Lauren pulled her bedroom door wide open and rolled her eyes. "Give me a break, you guys. Like I wasn't going to eavesdrop."

Cole laughed before focusing his attention back on me. "I

know that dinner is more romantic, but I don't want to wait that long to see you again. I never get days off. I'll be here at eleven. That's only eight and a half hours from now."

"I guess we'll see," I said with a little more snark than I had meant, but I wasn't sure that all this wouldn't go away.

"I know you don't believe me, and that's okay. I'll show you, Christina. I meant every word I said tonight. I'll see you soon." He pulled open the door and stepped out before leaning his face back in. "And don't worry, Lauren; we'll bring you a doggie bag," he added with a laugh before shutting the door behind him.

I immediately turned to face Lauren, a million questions racing through me. "What do you think? Is he being sincere? Does he mean it?"

From my perspective, Cole had seemed genuine, but I didn't trust myself to read him correctly. People convinced themselves all the time that they felt certain things when they really didn't. Humans were masters at lying—and not only to other people, but to themselves the most. I needed an outside opinion.

She walked into the living room, her head shaking and her eyes wide. "I totally think he means it. That boy is going to be here at eleven. The same way he showed up here after his game today," she said.

I had forgotten all about that. "Oh, yeah. What happened? He came over here? I can't believe you didn't tell me."

"He was looking for you, and I told him to leave you alone. I said if he cared about you at all, he'd let you be happy for once." She reached for me and pulled me into a hug before letting me go. "I didn't know Logan was such a jerk. I didn't see it. And I'm sorry."

"That's not your fault. I didn't see it either," I said, annoyed that I seemed to be so freaking awful at reading guys.

Either that or they were really good liars. Maybe it was a combination of both, I decided.

"Cole tried to tell me," she argued. "But I didn't believe him."

"Why would you?" I asked, trying to make her feel better about the situation. "Anyway ..."

"Anyway," she repeated. "Better go get some beauty sleep."

"You really think he'll show up?" I asked again because I wasn't convinced. At least not a hundred percent. I didn't think I'd believe Cole meant it until he was standing at my front door, picking me up.

"I do. And if he doesn't, I'll cut his nuts off and sell them online."

"Too far," I said with a laugh before I headed toward my room. "Night, weirdo."

"Night."

I could have stayed up for hours, talking to Lauren and asking her more questions, but there was no point. Whatever was going to happen with Cole tomorrow was going to happen whether or not I overanalyzed it. If he'd truly meant what he said, then he'd follow through. And if it was just some spur-of-the-moment emotional response, then I'd finally know the truth. We both would. And no amount of sweet-talking could ever get him to convince me otherwise.

No matter how much I wanted Cole to show up tomorrow and mean what he said, I wouldn't believe it until I saw it. And I refused to feel hopeful about his promises or hold my breath in regard to them. I wasn't willing to put my heart on the line for him again if he wasn't serious.

I guessed I'd find out in about eight hours from now.

First Date Nerves

Cole

CHRISTINA DIDN'T TRUST me, and I'd given her every reason in the book over the years not to. I wasn't deterred because I had every intention on fixing this. I would do right by her, make it up to her, and sweep her off her damn feet.

God knows she deserves it.

Once I got home, the house had already been cleared out, and only a few party stragglers remained passed out on the couches and the floor. There were messages from both Mac and Chance, telling me good luck and that they hoped I'd gotten the girl. I smiled before locking myself in my room and thinking about plans for tomorrow. I knew exactly where I wanted to take her to eat, but after that, I wasn't entirely sure. My days were typically so planned out that I didn't have that much free time. I almost didn't know what the hell to do with it all.

Reaching for my phone, I set my alarm. If I didn't, I knew I'd sleep until mid-afternoon and screw everything up without even meaning to. I'd promised her I'd try. For her,

I'd try to pretend like I knew how to be a boyfriend when the truth was that I'd never done it before. Not really. I wasn't worried about being faithful or messing around with other chicks; that was not going to be an issue. My main concern was letting her down. I'd done so much of that already. I wanted to make sure I didn't do it again.

When a yawn escaped, I laid my head against my pillow, excited for tomorrow. I couldn't wait to show Christina that I was a man of my word.

AFTER TEXTING BOTH Mac and Chance so they would stop acting like chicks, asking me for an update, I headed to the florist. I could have gotten Christina a bunch of roses from the grocery store, but for whatever reason, that seemed cheesy. It was stupid, I knew that much, but I was still going to a flower shop. I wanted that extra personal touch. And God knew I needed all the help I could get.

When I walked inside, my senses were overwhelmed with the scent. I almost turned right back out the door I had come in but stopped when someone shouted, "Welcome in. I'll be right out."

I'd literally never stepped foot in a flower shop in my entire life, so I had no idea what to expect. I'd naively thought that there would be maybe five flower types to choose from, but boy, was I wrong. Wandering around the refrigerated glass, I looked at all the water-filled buckets overflowing with various kinds of flowers. Some I recognized and some I had never seen before. With all the colors surrounding me, it looked like I'd stepped into a life-sized box of crayons.

"Hi." A middle-aged woman stepped out from the back, wiping her hands on a towel. "I'm Maggie." She looked so happy to be here, surrounded by flowers as she greeted me.

"Hi, Maggie. I'm Cole."

"What can I help you with today?"

"Well, it's my first time buying flowers for a girl," I admitted, and she clasped her hands in front of her face in excitement.

"Is this girl special?" she asked with a grin.

"Very."

"Do you have any idea what you're looking for or want to get for her?"

"I was thinking roses. Is that too cliché?" I asked, suddenly feeling ridiculously uneducated on the subject.

"Honey, roses are never cliché." She eyed me before walking away, and I realized that growing up with a mom, or at least some female inspiration, might have been helpful. "Come look at these." She stopped in front of another glass case and opened it as I did as she'd asked.

"Wow. They're huge," I said as she pulled a purple one out for me to hold. The actual flower itself was the size of my fist.

"These are premium long-stemmed. They come in all kinds of colors. But you know, that each color means something different, so you don't want to get the wrong one," she said.

I swore I felt myself starting to sweat even though the store was damn near freezing.

"Um, Maggie?" I said, and she pulled her head from the case and looked at me. "I haven't done this before. I have no idea what the colors mean or if I'd be messing up by getting my girl some of those really pretty yellow or pink ones," I said, pointing at the giant blossoms, and she laughed.

"You are sweet. And yeah, if you want to confuse her, those colors might do it." She gave me a funny expression before she explained. "Yellow means friendship."

"Forget yellow. I never want to see another yellow rose again."

"And pink is more that you're saying the person is sweet. Or you're thanking them for something."

"That doesn't sound romantic," I said, feeling annoyed, and she laughed again.

"You want romance, then you go with a classic," she said, pulling out a deep red rose, and a flash of white caught my eye.

"What about white?"

"White roses signify new beginnings. Unity. Purity," she continued talking, but I zoned out a little and stopped listening.

"The red ones are really pretty, but I feel like everyone gets red. I've never seen anyone get white. And to be honest, Maggie, you had me at new beginnings," I said, knowing that she would love that answer.

"White it is. A whole dozen or half?"

"Do I look like a half kind of guy to you?"

She propped out her hip and said, "You look like a poor college student, so maybe."

"I'll take a dozen. Make them pretty. I won't get a second chance to do this right," I directed, like I had any idea what the hell I was talking about.

Maggie promised I wouldn't be disappointed as I put the charge on my credit card and she went to work, cutting a bunch of green stuff she called filler.

I typed out a text message to Christina, letting her know that I would be there soon and I hoped she was awake. She responded a few minutes later with a bunch of food emojis, and I laughed, thankful that she was as hungry as I was.

"Okay, all done," Maggie said with a satisfied grin as she handed me the most stunning bouquet I'd ever seen of white roses and a bunch of green shit.

"This is a work of art," I said, studying it.

"I'm glad you like it."

"I hope she does."

"She will. If she doesn't, come back and let me know."

"No way. If she doesn't like it, you're definitely fired," I said with half a grin, and she shook her head at me.

"Yeah, yeah." She waved me off, and I walked out, suddenly fucking paranoid that I was overdoing it or trying too hard.

Placing the roses on the passenger seat, I realized that I seemed to second-guess every single thing I did when it came to this girl. Nothing seemed good enough, and in the same vein, it also seemed like too much. I'd gotten used to screwing up so many times without even trying that I wasn't sure I knew how to stop doing it.

When I pulled up to the privacy gate in front of Christina's complex, I typed in the numbers and laughed as the large thing swung open. Lauren must not have forced them to update the passcode yet. Driving around the lot nearest her building, I pulled my truck into a spot, grabbed the flowers, and hopped out.

Instead of texting to let her know I was outside, I dialed the numbers on the security box and waited for one of the girls to grant me entrance. The buzzing sound came without even a hello or anything, and I reached for the glass door and pulled it open as soon as I heard it unlock.

As I walked down the hallway, flowers in hand, my heart started racing in my chest. *What if she hates the white? Should I have gotten her red?* Everyone got red roses for a reason—because they were classic and classy. Blowing out a long, dramatic breath as I reached her front door, I lifted my hand and knocked, praying to whoever was up there that I wasn't sweating through my shirt. I was more than just a little nervous. The door flew open, and the sight of Christina standing there in tiny jean shorts and an off-the-shoulder sweater almost knocked me on my ass.

When her eyes moved to my right hand and her jaw fell open, I remembered the roses and handed them to her with a smile. "These are for you."

"Wow." She took them, turning them around so she could study them from every angle. "These are the prettiest roses I've ever seen in my life. They're so big," she said and instantly buried her nose in the center of the bouquet and inhaled.

"I did good?"

"You did good." She smiled before telling me to come inside and closing the door behind us. "I'm going to put these in water"—she stopped short—"I think."

"You think?"

"I'm not sure we have a vase," she said with a shrug. "I'll figure something out."

"Wow, Hat Boy," Lauren said, appearing out of nowhere and standing next to Christina in the kitchen, "I'm impressed."

"Picked 'em myself and everything."

"Did you?" Christina's head shot up, her blue eyes meeting mine, and I gave her a confident smirk.

"I did. You can even call Maggie and ask."

Her brow furrowed. "Who's Maggie?"

"The owner of the flower shop," I said even though I wasn't sure if she owned it or not. I just assumed she did.

"You got these at an actual flower shop?" Lauren sounded shocked, and I knew I was scoring some serious brownie points. Which I desperately needed.

"Nothing but the best for my girl," I said the words a little too cocky.

Christina gave Lauren a quick side-eye glance. I had no idea what it meant, but it took my confidence down a notch or two. Maybe this wasn't going to be as seamless as I hoped.

After some rustling and giggling, Christina presented the

roses, sans paper, stuffed inside an oversize water bottle that you'd bring to the gym. "It was either this or go buy a thirty-two-ounce Big Gulp from 7-Eleven for the cup," she said with a shrug as she set them down in the center of the kitchen table.

"I didn't even think about the vase part. I blame Maggie," I said, and I did. *Why didn't I get her a vase instead of wrapping them in paper?* Maggie should have told me—or at least mentioned that part.

"I kind of like the look of it, to be honest." She stood, staring at them, hands on her hips.

"Bullshitting me?" I asked because I wasn't sure if this was some sort of trick or not.

Christina turned to look at me, a gleam in her eye. "I mean it. The roses are so perfect. I like that they're living in something they're not really meant for."

I shifted my weight to my other leg and considered my words. "I feel like that was a metaphor somehow, but I'm not getting it." My stomach growled, and both girls stared at my covered abs. "I'm starving."

"Me too," Christina breathed out, her eyes still locked on my midsection.

"We should go." I held out my hand, and she scurried away.

"Let me grab my purse," she said before coming back and walking ahead of me, ignoring the hand I held out for her to grab.

Apparently, we were going to be taking this slow. I had to earn my way back into her heart, and I was okay with that.

I had to be.

Show Me Off

Christina

TWO THINGS HAD surprised me this morning.

The first was that Cole had actually followed through on what he had said the night before. I had gone to bed, hoping that he had meant every word, but I wasn't counting on it. I had fallen asleep, knowing that today would either be a day of extreme disappointment or hope. So far, the latter was winning out.

The second surprise was the roses. Cole showing up was one thing, but coming to get me with a handful of the most beautiful white roses I'd ever laid eyes on was another. I hadn't expected it. Hell, I'd barely expected him. The roses were a gesture that added to the fact that Cole was truly trying. He wanted me to believe his words, but he was backing them up with action. I'd realized the moment I saw him outside my front door this morning that I needed both.

When he reached for my hand as we left, it took every ounce of willpower to not intertwine my fingers with his and give in to him. The last thing I wanted was to jump in headfirst and pretend like everything was totally perfect when nothing between us had ever been. Cole had to work a little bit harder to break through the walls I'd put up. The walls that he'd helped build.

"So, where are we going?" I asked as he opened the passenger door for me, and I hopped in before pulling my sunglasses out of my purse and putting them on.

"You'll see," he said as he shut the door, and I wondered where he would take us to eat in this time between breakfast and lunch.

"Please tell me if we're going to a breakfast or a lunch spot. I need to get my head right about which meal I'm getting," I practically whined, and he laughed, but I was serious. Eleven meant that you could get totally screwed if you wanted breakfast and the place stopped serving it at ten. Or if you wanted lunch and they didn't start serving until noon. It was a serious subject.

"I'm taking you to a dope brunch spot. They have the best Belgium waffles in the area," he said, and I swore he almost started drooling.

"Thank God," I breathed out in relief as I lowered my window down partway. "I wanted breakfast so bad but didn't want to say anything if you had plans for lunch."

"I've been dreaming about these waffles all night." He quickly glanced at me before looking back at the road. "Well, waffles and you."

"Don't do that," I said, looking away from him, my hair blowing.

"Do what?"

"Don't say things just to say them. It's cheesy, and I

don't need it."

"That's fair," he agreed, and I was surprised. I'd half-expected him to argue back, insist that he had meant it or that he wasn't being corny, but he didn't. "What do you need?"

I swallowed hard, my throat suddenly feeling thick at being put on the spot. "Just the truth."

"Okay. Me too." He nodded. "So, if you ever want breakfast when I want lunch, tell me. And we'll find a place that serves both at the same time."

I smacked his shoulder with my hand. "Smart-ass."

"I mean it. Food's important. Especially waffles."

"I never knew this about you," I said with a grin as he kept his hands firmly on the wheel. "About your love for waffles, I mean. How have you kept this from me for so long?"

"I think I told you once." His voice sounded almost wistful as I searched the recesses of my mind for memories with him, looking for the one with the waffles.

It suddenly hit me.

"You did. Oh my gosh, you really did," I said, remembering one rare afternoon when we had studied together for finals.

He'd mentioned waffles that his mom used to make and how this one place in town made them just like she had. He'd wanted to go right that second, but they weren't open.

"Your mom," I added, and he gave me a slight nod.

"Yeah. I'm not sure why I've held on to that memory so hard. It's almost like she took every other one with her when she left."

"You haven't talked to her lately?" I asked, knowing that the relationship he had with his mom was strained, at best.

He had offered up a few details over the years, but anytime I started to dig in too deep, he'd cut me off and slam the door shut.

"Nah." He tried to sound like he didn't care, but I knew it was the opposite.

"You don't have to do that." I reached for his thigh and gave him a squeeze but didn't leave my hand there.

"Do what?"

"Pretend like her leaving didn't hurt you. Or keep those kinds of things to yourself. If we're really going to give this a shot, we have to talk about the stuff that haunts us. Because those are the things we carry. They affect everything else," I said like I was an expert on the subject.

"What haunts you?"

I said the first thing that popped into my mind even though it felt sort of small in comparison to his inner demons, "My no-alcohol rule."

He visibly stiffened, his back straightening. I watched as his knuckles started to turn white as his grip on the wheel tightened.

"You never told me where that came from," he said, trying to sound calm but I could tell that it was eating him up inside. Cole sensed that the rule had been born out of a bad situation, and he wasn't wrong.

"I know."

"Will you?" he asked as the truck slowed, and I looked up, noting the line out the door of a restaurant I'd never been to before.

"Not right now, but yes, I will," I said, and he calmed.

"Okay. Have you been here before?" He pulled the truck to a stop and cut the engine.

I rolled my window up. "Never," I admitted, wondering how the heck I'd missed this on my food radar the entire time I'd lived here.

"How is that even possible?" He looked at me like I'd grown two heads.

"I have no idea," I said as I turned to reach for my door handle.

"Don't move," he directed.

I did as he'd asked, knowing that he wanted to open the door for me. I waited for him to reach my door and smiled when he did. Pulling it open, he extended his hand and helped me out. He placed his hand on my lower back, and I felt myself instinctively lean into it.

"I like this side of you."

"What side? My backside?" he teased, and I shook my head.

"No. Your gentlemanly side," I said with a smile. "It's nice."

"I'm sorry I kept it from you for so long." He winked, and I wondered if he turned things into a joke whenever he was uncomfortable. It wouldn't surprise me in the least if that was one of Cole's defense mechanisms.

We walked toward the waiting crowd of hungry eaters, and Cole excused himself to head inside and put our name in. I stood alone for only a few seconds before I heard the familiar sound of whispering. I was thankful I had my sunglasses on as I tried to stealthily find whoever was doing the talking. That was when I realized that there were a lot of students here, and it wasn't just one girl staring at me but quite a few.

Cole reappeared at that moment and wrapped one arm around my waist. I pretended not to notice the phones pointed in our direction, most likely taking pictures to share online or text to friends.

"There are a lot of students here." I wondered if he had known how full this place would be and how many people would see us together in public.

"I know," he said matter-of-factly. "Does that make you nervous?"

"I'm not nervous," I said. "Just surprised, I think."

"Surprised by what?"

"I guess I just didn't think you'd want to be so public on our first outing together," I said, hating how unsure I sounded and that I'd used the word *outing*.

"*Date*. It's our first date. And hell yes, I want to be in public with you. I want everyone to know that you're here with me. I want to show you off."

I laughed, feeling a little embarrassed and excited at the same time. "You want to show me off?"

He turned my body, so I was facing him straight on as he looked down at me. "You told me once that I never took you out in public. You felt like I kept you in the dark. And you weren't wrong about that. All I want to do now is put you in the light, where everyone can see us together."

I swallowed hard, that ball back in my throat. "Really?"

"Really," he said as he leaned down to kiss me, tentatively at first, as if he was testing the waters and making sure it was okay.

I deepened the kiss, forgetting that we were surrounded by people, and focused on my legs, which felt like they might give out at any second. I was convinced that Cole's kisses could cause knees to buckle across the globe.

We slowly pulled away from each other, my eyes still closed but shielded behind my sunglasses.

"Cole, party of two?" was being shouted from somewhere behind us.

"Already?" I said. I looked around at all the people still waiting as I reached for my glasses and dropped them into my purse.

He shrugged. "What can I say? It's my favorite place. They kinda love me here."

He reached for my hand, and I let him this time, our fingers locking together as he pulled me through a group of snarling girls who grumbled under their breath. I swore I'd heard one of them call me a name, and it took everything in me to keep walking and not cause a scene. They weren't worth it.

As we maneuvered through the large space, I couldn't help but smile at how it was decorated. It felt like we had legitimately stepped back into the 1970s. And even though you could tell the interior was dated, the restaurant still beamed with bright light, the immaculate white flooring giving off a glow as you moved across it. The dark wood paneling was accented with a plethora of puffy-looking orange booths and multicolored barstools. I actually appreciated the fact that they hadn't reupholstered everything to make it look brand-new. It would have lost some of its charm if they had.

"This place is so cool," I whispered toward Cole as the hostess pointed at a small two-person table, and we moved to sit in it.

She handed us each a menu before walking away.

"I bet I know why you've never heard of this place!" He sounded so excited and sure of himself that I decided to play along.

"Why?" I asked as I bounced in my seat, surprised at how springy and cushy it still was. I figured that after years of use, it might have been worn out, but I was wrong.

"They probably don't have any social media. How can they expect the queen to find them if their online presence isn't any good?"

I looked around again, noting how every single seat was filled with happy eaters. "Word of mouth is better than anything online. How have I never even heard of this place before though? How has no one told me?"

He only shrugged. "Obviously, you have bad friends. Time to trade Lauren in."

"If the food is as good as you say it is, I'll consider it," I said as I unfolded my menu, and Cole reached for it, taking it out of my hands.

"We're ordering brunch. No menu needed," he said, and I decided not to argue and actually be a good listener instead.

"And to be fair, I did tell you about it once before."

That day where he'd mentioned his mom. "You're right. But you never told me the name, I don't think."

"Probably not," he said as a waitress appeared, bringing us two waters and asking if we were ready to order. Cole ordered for us both, and I knew I shouldn't have enjoyed it as much as I did.

She pointed us toward the brunch station, and once again, I found myself shocked at how state of the art and trendy it all was. They had an unlimited mimosa station paired with a freshly squeezed juice bar, featuring ten types of juices. Ten! The waffles were made to order, not stacked and waiting for you to take one, like they were at other places. They featured eggs made five different ways, or you could order an omelet with whatever you wanted on it. The fruit was all farmed locally. And they even had a tea corner that showcased honey from all local beehives.

"This place is heaven, and I'm going to eat here every day until I die," I said to Cole as we walked back to our table, balancing our too-full plates in our hands.

He laughed out loud. People stared. "You haven't even tasted anything yet," he said with a smirk once we sat down.

I spread butter across my hot waffle and watched it melt into the deep squares. Cutting a small piece off, I took a bite and moaned. "Holy crap," I said around whatever blissful ingredients were currently melting in my mouth.

"Told you."

"But why? Like, I don't understand why it's so good. What's it made of, rainbows and puppy breath?" I asked seriously because I really didn't understand how a waffle could be so superior tasting to other waffles. *Don't they all have the same ingredients?*

"Honestly? I think it has something to do with the flour they use. They don't buy it in the grocery store. It doesn't have any of the extra crap in it to make it last on a shelf. At least, that's what they told me after I came in here, asking once," Cole explained, but I was too busy chewing and living in food ecstasy to pay attention. Cole laughed as he watched me, and I knew that he'd realized he'd lost me to the waffle. "Tell me what's going on with work," he asked, knowing exactly how to bring me back to him.

"Work?" I scrunched up my face as I swallowed. I wasn't sure what he wanted to hear.

"Yeah. I know you took on Jason's band. How's that going?"

I smiled. "It's going so good. I've made a few changes and improvements to their accounts. I've already seen their follower numbers double on one platform, and their video views have tripled on another."

"I love watching you talk about this," he said, staring at me like I fascinated him somehow, but it was a little embarrassing. He was so focused on me, so mesmerized, that it was unnerving.

And suddenly, the last thing I wanted to do was shovel more food down my throat.

"What? Why?" I looked away, but Cole wasn't having any of it.

"Look at me," he insisted, and I slowly looked back up.

"You light up when you talk about this. That's how I know you'll be great at it. I mean, you already are."

"Thanks, Cole," I said quietly, a little taken aback by the compliment as I reached for my water and downed half the glass.

"Don't get embarrassed," he said, totally calling me out as he worked on one of the three waffles on his plate.

"I'm not. It's just …" I paused for a second. "I'm not used to having someone be so supportive." I started shaking my head because that wasn't it at all. "That sounds wrong and isn't what I meant. I just … I think I'm more comfortable with encouraging you to chase your dreams than talking about mine."

"Why the hell would you be more comfortable with encouraging me than yourself?" He sounded as bewildered as I felt.

"I don't know." I started to work out the reasoning in my mind. "I think because my goals feel so private, and talking about them out loud makes them really real. And then if I fail, I won't be the only one who knows it."

He chewed on his food, nodding, like what I'd said made complete sense to him. "I get it."

"That doesn't sound stupid?"

"Not at all. Our goals are private. They're personal as hell. I mean, everyone knows that I want to get drafted. I never got to keep that to myself. And you're right; if it doesn't happen for me, everyone will know. But the flip side is, if it does—"

"*When* it does," I interrupted because I refused to sit here and listen to him talk about his future as if was an option.

He cleared his throat and took a drink. "Okay. *When* it does, everyone will know."

"And they'll celebrate with you," I added with a knowing nod.

"Yeah. Same thing goes for you," he said, but I wasn't convinced.

People wanted to be a part of other people's successes, especially when it came to athletes and anyone in the celebrity spotlight, but I wasn't so sure that applied to someone like me and what I wanted to do.

"You know how good you are, right?"

"You know how good *you* are, right?" I fired back before giving my waffle attention.

"I mean it."

"So do I."

"You've always believed in me," he said, and I knew he was thinking back to some specific moment we had shared over the years. "You told me I'd get drafted. You told me I could do anything I wanted."

"I meant it. I still do. I want you to get drafted, Cole. I always have. Even when I hated you. Even when you didn't deserve it. I've always wanted you to succeed."

"Why?" he asked, and I knew he was truly wondering how someone who hated him could still root for him.

"Because it's important to you. And because I believe in you. And I want you to succeed."

"I'm so mad right now," he said as he chewed on his food like it was in trouble in his mouth.

"Mad? Why are you mad?"

"I feel like I wasted so much time convincing myself that I couldn't have this." He waved his arm in my direction. "And we could have. We should have been together this whole time, and it's my fault we haven't been."

I sucked in a quick breath, hoping my next words would help calm him down. "We can't change the past, Cole. You know that, right?" I asked, and he nodded even though I could tell that he didn't want to agree. "Let's make a decision right here, right now," I insisted as I put my fork down and leaned toward him, my elbows on the small table between us.

"I'm listening."

"We don't go back. We don't spend our time focusing on what we could have done differently or what we should have done or how we could have been better to each other. We only look toward the future. And we live there. Deal?" I asked as I extended my hand toward him.

"Deal," he said as he reached for my hand, shook it, and then kissed the top as a soft grin appeared.

Best First Date in the History of First Dates

Cole

I'D BEEN RIGHT about the waffles. And the restaurant's lack of social media presence. The owner didn't see the need, claimed that business was plenty busy without it. And while Christina didn't argue that particular point, she did appeal to his other senses when he stopped by our table to say hello. She told him that the goal didn't have to be about getting new customers, but more about showcasing the restaurant's history, staff, and menu.

He loved her idea, claimed it was something that no one had explained to him before, and then he kissed her on the cheek without warning. I allowed it, considering he was about a hundred and five years old. Christina walked out of brunch with a full stomach and a new client.

"You're incredible, you know that?" I pulled her hand to my lips and pressed a kiss there. I'd found myself doing that a lot with her. It seemed safer than constantly trying to maul her face, which, trust me, I wanted to do.

"Thank you." She looked down for a second before

lifting her head back up.

"How did you do that back there?" I asked.

Watching her in action was thrilling. She was so damn good at what she did. It was fun to see. I wondered for a second if that was how it felt for her to watch me play baseball.

"I listened. Being a good social media manager is about hearing what your client wants to sell or offer the public. What's their angle? Mr. Barlow has no interest in advertising. And he's right. He doesn't need to. But I think it's a shame to not let people know this place exists. There's so much history. Did you know that Frank Sinatra ate there? More than once!" Her voice was ecstatic, and it was fucking adorable.

"I heard him say that," I said with a grin as I pulled her door open, and she got inside.

She waited for me to get in the truck before she finished talking. "I'll use the platforms to showcase how the restaurant has changed throughout the years. And how it hasn't. Show old pictures, original menus, things like that. But also, the food. Because you wouldn't expect food that tastes that good to come from a place that looks like that."

"Told you," I said, sounding more than a little smug.

"You were right." She nudged me with her arm.

I sucked in a breath before asking if she was ready for the next part of our date. She nodded with a beautiful smile, and I drove off with one place in mind.

I DROVE ALL the way to the top of the parking structure, which was thankfully empty, before cutting the engine.

"You brought us here?" she asked as she looked around, her voice sounding more than a little shocked.

"Yeah. It's kind of our place, right?" I said because I had always associated this structure with her. It was where we'd stayed up all night together and talked about the kinds of things that I never talked about with anyone. "It reminds me of you," I added, and she looked at me, a soft half-smile appearing. "I come here when I need to get away from it all."

"I honestly figured you brought all the girls here."

"All the girls?" I asked, thoroughly confused. "What girls?"

She rolled her eyes and gave me an annoyed huff. "Don't act like you've been some sort of saint this whole time. I know you've slept with other girls besides me."

It was a subject I really didn't want to talk about but only because it led to knowing what other guys she had slept with, and I couldn't fucking stomach hearing that answer. Not when I had tried so hard to keep that stuff out of my head. Not when I wanted her to only be mine.

"I've never brought any girl here. Hell, I've never brought any girl anywhere. Only you." I reached out to cup her face and was grateful when she leaned into it instead of away from it. "It's okay that we're here?" I asked because, now, I was suddenly unsure.

She let out a slight laugh. "It's okay. Maybe I'll stop hating it now," she said, and I opened my mouth in shock.

"You hate our parking structure?"

"Uh, yeah. You broke my heart, Cole. I had to hate anything that reminded me of you," she said as if that explained it all, which, in a way, I guessed it did.

It was just that I had never hated anything that had to do with her. And this parking structure, which held memories of us, had become my solace. It was where I went to when I needed peace and quiet. I found it ironic that she'd avoided the one place that I kept coming back to.

"Time to make you love it again," I said before reaching around into the backseat and pulling out some blankets and pillows I'd stashed there.

"What's all this?" she questioned as I got out and went to work on setting up the blankets and pillows in the bed of my truck.

She quickly joined me, and I lowered my tailgate and hopped up, reaching for her hand. When she gave it to me, I pulled her up with little effort.

"Sit with me?" I said as I pressed my back against the pillows, propping them up and moving them to get comfortable.

She sat in between my legs, scooting until her back was flush with my front, and leaned into me.

"Your hair smells so good," I said as I breathed it in. I almost couldn't believe that I had her in my arms again.

"This is nice," she said as her body relaxed.

I was hard as a rock and only getting harder. I wanted Christina in more ways than one but knew it wasn't the right time. My dick really needed to get the memo and take it down a notch.

"Thank you for giving me a chance."

She turned, her body angled awkwardly toward me, and I knew she wanted to say something, but she stopped herself. Cupping her cheek, I pulled her toward me, my tongue instantly searching for hers. She moved into me, turning all the way around so that her legs were wrapped around my waist. It definitely didn't help in the dick-hardening part of things.

"You're killing me," I said as I continued kissing her, loving the way her lips felt against mine, grateful that she hadn't tossed me out of her apartment when I showed up there last night.

Has it really only been a handful of hours since I declared my feelings for her? It felt like so much longer, and I knew it was because we had years of history lingering between us.

Breaking the kiss, I ran my fingers through her hair.

"What's wrong?"

I shook my head as I looked into her blue eyes. "Nothing. I was just thinking about how comfortable I am with you. How natural it feels."

She smiled, and it took up her whole damn beautiful face. "I feel the same way."

"You do?"

She pulled her legs back and crossed them, taking her

body away from mine, and I stopped myself from wrapping my hands around her waist and holding on for dear life. "Of course I do. We're not strangers. We didn't just meet an hour ago."

"So, this is normal then? To feel this way?" I asked because what the hell did I truly know about relationships and love? Nothing. I knew fucking nothing.

"I think for us it is. It's pretty logical that after three years, we'd feel this way."

"You know, looking back now, I see it all so clearly. But it was so muddled at the time," I started to explain what I had only more recently figured out and admitted to myself.

"What do you see?"

"How it's always been you. Well, you and baseball. I didn't think there was room for anything else. But you've always been there. I tried to outrun you for so long. I don't want to run anymore."

Christina's mouth opened slightly, and she blew out a breath. "You can't just walk around, saying things like that to a girl."

I looked around. "I wasn't walking."

"You know what I mean." She swatted my leg, and I knew that I had affected her by admitting the truth, but it'd felt good to say it out loud.

"I know we said we weren't talking about the past, but I need to say one more thing. I am sorry for how I treated you. After my mom left, my dad never dated or remarried. I don't have any idea what a normal couple looks like, realistically. I never learned, you know? And I'm not trying to make excuses. I just want you to understand that I'm a little messed up."

"We're all messed up. And our parents screw us up one way or another without ever meaning to. No one's perfect," she said, and I didn't fail to notice that she hadn't accepted my apology. She'd simply moved right past it.

"Can I ask you something?"

"Anything," she said, and I wondered if she'd take back that response once I asked the question.

"Will you tell me about the no-alcohol rule? It's been driving me crazy, not knowing."

Her body visibly tensed, and I reached for her, moving her so that her back was pressed against my front once more. I wrapped my arms around her middle and held on, wanting her to know that I had her and that she was safe with me.

"It isn't what you think," she started to say, but her voice said otherwise.

I almost told her that she didn't have to go on, that she didn't need to tell me, but I wanted to know.

"It was my first high school party. Everyone was drinking. I thought it was so cool to take shots and drink mixed drinks like a grown-up, you know?"

Her tone was a mixture of sadness and anger, and I mentally braced for what I was sure was coming next. How was I going to stay calm and composed if she told me that someone had put their hands on her without her permission? Touched her when she hadn't wanted them to? My mind raced, but her voice pulled me out.

"I was there with my best friend. I had a curfew that

night, but she didn't. So, when I left the party with a friend's older brother who had come to pick a few of us up, she stayed behind. I knew I shouldn't have left her, but she wouldn't leave with me. I'd tried to get her come, but she'd kept saying no."

I started rubbing the side of her arm with my hand, hoping to comfort her as she continued, "The next day, there were pictures of her passed out on the couch while guys lingered over her, making lewd gestures and stuff. They were all over the internet."

I stayed quiet as she took her time.

"Nothing physically happened to her, but the pictures told a different story, you know? They looked really bad," she said before moving away from me and turning so we could look each other in the eyes. "They made her look really bad."

"How did she know nothing had happened if she was passed out?"

I wasn't trying to sound accusing, but Christina's tone turned defensive. The memory was still fresh in her mind, still upsetting.

"Because she remembered everything up until that point. And when she woke up, all her clothes were on, she wasn't sore anywhere, and she was alone."

"Let me guess." I assumed what was coming next. "No one believed her that nothing happened."

"I did." She nodded her head. "But I was the only one. The pictures were eventually taken down, but by then, it was too late. Everyone had already seen them. And they had copies or screenshots. It was the ultimate example of how bad social media could be. How it could ruin someone's life."

I felt like a lightbulb had switched on inside my head. "And that's when you discovered your passion for it?"

"That's definitely where it started, yeah. I wanted people to be accountable for the things they posted online. To realize that everything wasn't a joke. That sometimes, real people were affected and got hurt. I wanted my fellow students to think about the messages their posts were sending. You have any idea how hard it is to get a teenager to think before they act?" she said with a slight laugh.

"I think most people don't think before they act. Especially online. It gives them some kind of power trip to be anonymous."

"I totally agree."

"So, is that where your rule came in?" I asked, still wanting to know.

"Well, yeah. The shots got me pretty drunk. It felt like all the logical and rational parts of my brain shut off. I didn't care about anything. They could have told me to jump off the roof and into the pool, and I would have done it without question. If I had stayed, it would have been both of us in those pictures instead of just her."

" 'Alcohol makes you stupid,' " I said with a nod of understanding, repeating the words she'd once told me.

"Exactly."

"Then, why'd you take the shots from Logan?" I found myself getting upset, but I wasn't sure why exactly.

"I'm older now. I think I can handle my liquor better than when I was in high school," she said. "But mostly, I did it to get back at you. To show you that you weren't the boss of me. To be rebellious," she rattled off the list like it was right there on the tip of her tongue the whole time, just waiting to be set free.

"Took shots with my enemy just to spite me," I started before she interrupted.

"I didn't know he was your enemy," she said seriously, as if trying to convince me of something I'd already known.

"But you do now, right? You know he isn't a good person. Tell me you see that," I pressed because I needed to hear her say that she saw through Logan's false front.

"I do see that. But it doesn't matter. I'm with you now. Logan's irrelevant."

I wanted to agree with her, but I knew Logan better than that. If he wanted to fuck with me more, I'd just given him the ammunition he needed to do it. He was only guessing before that Christina was my weakness, but all I'd done by pursuing her and making her mine was prove him right. This thing with him wasn't over, and I knew it.

Girlfriend

Christina

WE STAYED IN the parking structure—or "our parking structure," as Cole had called it—holding each other and talking until the sun started to set. Hours always seemed to fly by whenever we were together, and today had been no different. *How had a single day felt more like twenty?*

When he walked me to my apartment door, he shocked me for what felt like the hundredth time. "I don't know if people do this anymore, but I don't care. Will you be my girlfriend?" he asked, and I forced myself to hesitate instead of blurting out a resounding yes.

I thought I'd waited a little too long because he started shifting on his feet and dug his hands into his pockets.

"Look, I know that one day doesn't change the past three years. But it's just the beginning. We don't have to call each other boyfriend and girlfriend even though I want to," he said in a tone that left little room for questioning how he felt on the matter, "but I really, really, really don't want you to date other people."

"What about you?" I asked because it felt foolish to

assume anything without at least asking. We'd been through too much.

"I don't want to be with anyone else. Only you. But I get that I might be jumping the gun a little here even though it doesn't feel like it. Like you said, it's not like we just met."

It didn't feel like it was too quick for me either, but there was still a tiny part inside of me that wanted to encourage his suffering.

"Let's hold off on the titles but definitely yes to the exclusively dating part." It was my way of offering a compromise. Plus, I knew that I would never in a million years agree to be in this place with him again if there were going to be any other girls in the picture.

"Isn't that basically the same thing?" he asked with an uncomfortable laugh, and I realized that I was being stubborn purely for the sake of it. Trying to hurt him because a part of me still hurt and hadn't recovered.

"You're right; it is," I relented.

"So, that's a yes then?"

I tried to stop my smile when he asked the question but failed.

"Don't say no, Christina. Don't say no because you want to punish me or make me work harder. I mean, I'll do it. I'll jump through all your hoops. But don't make me if you don't really want me to."

He looked exhausted but sounded determined, and I knew that he meant every word. If I continued to keep him at arm's length just to prove a point, he'd let me do it and probably not complain. But that wouldn't be fair—to either of us. If I was going to give us a real shot, I had to do exactly what I'd told him we should during brunch—live in the future and not in the past.

"Okay. Yes."

The smile on his face was enough to tell me that I'd made the right decision. He reached for me, wrapped his arms around my waist, and picked me up into the air, planting kisses all over my face and neck. He was so damn happy. And all because I'd agreed to be his girlfriend.

I am Cole Anders's freaking girlfriend!

One Week Later

WHEN I'D WALKED through the front door that night after our first date, Lauren had been eavesdropping—or at least trying to. She said she couldn't hear a damn thing and insisted I fill her in. To my surprise, she was excited, encouraging, and hopeful. A part of me had thought that she might be more hesitant than I had tried to be, but she wasn't. It felt good to have my best friend on my side. It reassured me that I wasn't a complete idiot for giving Cole a real shot after everything we'd been through.

"It's because of everything you've been through that you should give him a shot," Lauren had said that night. And when I questioned her on what she meant, she finished with,

"You two deserve a real chance. He's never given you one before, and he's begging for it now. You would have always wondered *what if* and *what could have been* if you didn't get this opportunity. He would have haunted you until you were old and unhappily married one day, thinking back to the hot baseball player you should have ended up with instead of the guy by your side."

I'd laughed at her, but I remembered feeling a distinct ping of truth ricochet off my insides. Her words had struck a chord somewhere deep in me that I forced myself not to overanalyze because it was no longer relevant. I was his, and he was mine.

Being Cole's girlfriend was fun. I loved it. I hated that it had taken so long for us to get together, but all that drama felt like it was in the distant past even though it wasn't. We were in such a different place emotionally that it was hard to believe all we'd gone through to get here.

I savored it.

Adored it.

Loved the way it felt to be his and for him to be mine.

Things with Cole were effortless and, dare I say, almost easy. Being together was like snapping two puzzle pieces into place. We fit naturally. I'd had no idea that it could, or would, be this good. He was attentive and thoughtful. He was always texting and calling, and he FaceTimed me every night before bed. Baseball kept him busy, and I understood, making sure to never give him any crap for it. To be fair, I was busy with classes and my side work with The Long Ones and the new restaurant as well.

My mind thought about him as I stepped outside of class and ran straight into a set of rock-hard abs. Cole was standing there, waiting for me, a smirk on his gorgeous face, his baseball hat pulled down low.

"Hey, beautiful," he said as he reached for me, and I heard harsh whispering mixed with sweet coos from whoever was watching us as we kissed.

"What are you doing here?" I asked him even though it was a happy surprise.

Our paths on campus didn't usually overlap, so we had to make plans to see each other during the days when we could. Right now, outside my class, wasn't planned.

"My class was canceled, so I thought we could go grab lunch before I headed over to the field," he suggested, and as if on cue, my stomach growled loud enough for him to hear. "I'll take that as a yes."

Sometimes, it was hard to reconcile the guy whose hand I was currently holding with the one who had busted my heart open on more than one occasion, bringing me to tears. Cole had worried so much about the kind of boyfriend he would be to me, worried that he wouldn't do it right or that he'd disappoint me somehow. But he was so exceptional at it that it was hard to imagine how he hadn't been raised with three sisters or at least a mom who had been present in his life.

"Yes. Feed me," I agreed with a smile as I dropped a pair of sunglasses over my eyes and started walking across campus, his hand in mine.

I wasn't oblivious to the stares, but I didn't give them any extra attention. It seemed almost unbelievable that on a massive college campus, word could spread quickly about someone, but it did. And had it not happened to Cole and me, I probably wouldn't have believed it or thought the stories were exaggerated somehow. It had only been a little over a week since we went to brunch, but everyone seemed to know that we were officially together. And every one of those people had an opinion about it.

"Hey, Cole," some girl I didn't recognize said as she flashed him a smile and fluffed her hair.

I was literally standing right next to him, but she couldn't have cared less. Cole ignored her.

"Aren't you going to say hi?" I asked in a snotty tone.

"Wasn't planning on it," he fired back as we continued moving toward the campus commissary.

"Rude," I teased, and he stopped walking, causing my arm to jerk backward when I continued moving.

"Do you want me to go back?" He thumbed toward the Hair-Fluffer, and I stuck out my tongue at him and called him a brat. He laughed. "Didn't think so."

I was hit with a sudden thought, and instead of keeping it to myself, I blurted it out, "Do girls hit on your more or less now that they know about us?"

He glanced at me and gave me that famous panty-dropping smile. "Do you want the truth?"

"Always."

"More," he said, sounding bored.

"Really?"

"Yeah. I don't know why you girls do that kind of shit."

"Uh, I don't do that kind of shit," I said slowly, throwing

his words back at him as he gave me an obvious glare.

"I didn't mean you but your gender."

I thought about it for a second before realizing that guys had been talking to me far more this week than they ever had before. They hadn't necessarily been hitting on me, but they had been chattier.

"What?"

"I was just thinking about your gender and how they talk to me more now that we're together."

His grip on my hand tightened, and I wondered if he even knew he was doing it. "Talk how? Like, ask you out?"

I couldn't stop the laugh that escaped. "Not so fun when the shoe's on the other foot, is it?" I teased, and he stopped walking again even though we were almost at the doors.

"Christina," he practically growled.

"Cole," I growled back.

"Are they asking you out? Hitting on you when they know you're with me?" He was being serious, and he was actually getting upset.

"No." I leaned up on my tiptoes and kissed his nose. "They're just friendlier. Talk to me more. They aren't even flirting, I don't think. I think they just want to be my friend now that they know I'm yours."

"We're not friends," he bit back as he messed with his hat.

"We most certainly are."

"I meant," he stumbled, and it was downright adorable to see this cocky, arrogant guy searching for the right words, "we're more than friends."

"I know that. And they all do too. Promise," I reassured him because I didn't want him worrying over nothing.

"You'll tell me if anyone's inappropriate with you, right?" he asked.

"Um"—I looked around, my eyes hidden by my shades—"I guess? I don't know. I think I can handle guys talking to me."

I could tell he didn't like that answer. His weight shifted, and he pulled his hat clean off his head to run his fingers through his hair. It was something he did whenever he was frustrated.

"It's not like I expect you to tell me about every girl who hits on you."

"I will. You want me to?"

"No, I don't actually," I said, stunning even myself with that answer. I couldn't give all the other girls that much control or presence in our relationship; otherwise, they would affect it in a negative way.

"Okay." He put his hat back on. "Well, if anyone gets out of line or makes you uncomfortable, promise you'll let me know." It was his version of offering up a compromise.

"I promise."

He wrapped an arm around my waist and pulled me tight against him as we started walking again, our steps in time with one another. "I'm not trying to be possessive and crazy, I swear. I just won't always be here, and I don't want guys thinking they can do things to you when I'm not around," he overly explained.

Then, understanding dawned on me.

The team had a road series coming up, and it would be the first time that we'd be apart since officially getting together. Cole was worried. He'd never been in this situation before—leaving a girl at home while he was away for days on end.

"I get it. It's the same for me. I don't want girls thinking they have a chance with you. Especially girls in another state," I said before my stomach twisted—and not because I was hungry.

I'd done my best in the past to not think about what life was like for Cole and his teammates whenever they traveled. But now that he was my boyfriend, I was finding it harder to ignore the fact that the baseball team was a hot commodity— and that didn't only hold true within state lines.

"You okay?" he said as we reached the double glass doors. He pulled one wide open and allowed me to step through first as the sounds of people rushing, trays slamming, and orders being shouted out surrounded me.

"I'm good." I offered him a small smile, not wanting to get into it in the middle of the commissary where prying ears could overhear. And trust me, they were prying.

Cole reached for my hand. "Does the word *salsa* do anything for you?"

"Do I look like the kind of girl who would ever turn down a chance to eat Mexican?" I asked, not knowing what the hell that was supposed to even mean, but he laughed anyway and pulled us toward the small Mexican café.

We reached the line and stood there, preoccupied with each other as we waited for our chance to order. He reached for my chin and tipped it up, pressing a long kiss on my lips, and I almost forgot how to stand or where we were. Kissing Cole was as all-consuming.

In the past, I'd never known when I'd be able to do it again. Our kisses always felt desperate somehow, like my lips might fall off if I stopped. They were something that could be taken away at any moment, so the intimacy we shared had always felt temporary. And it had been.

These kisses were something entirely new. They lacked the frenzied rush. They were meant to be savored and appreciated. Our mouths moved in softer motions, at a slower pace, and were filled with more intimacy than should be allowed on a college campus.

"Ahem," someone cleared their throat, and the sounds of cheering and whooping filled the air.

My face burned as I saw a table of his teammates fist-pumping the air.

"Oh my God. Cole." I swatted his arm.

"Why are you mad at me?" He threw a fist in the air back, and they cheered more.

"You can't kiss me like that in public," I complained as I steadied myself.

"You can kiss me like that in public," a voice said.

I turned on my heel to face the female in line behind us, the nerve of her boldness fueling mine.

"What did you just say?" I tried to take a step toward her but was stopped by a pair of strong arms holding me back before he reached for my hand and held it tight.

"What? I think there's enough of him to go around. You

shouldn't really keep a guy like that all to yourself." She pursed her lips like she had made the most brilliant point in the history of making points.

"Do you see this? Are you blind?" He shoved our linked hands in front of her face.

"I see it. So what? It's just her," the girl said with a wave, discarding me as if I were a piece of gum on the bottom of her shoe, something she needed to clean off and get rid of.

"Have you ever seen me holding a girl's hand in public before?" Cole sounded a little too aggressive, but the girl didn't seem to back down or notice.

"No."

"Have you ever seen me kiss a girl in the commissary before?"

She kept her eyes firmly locked on Cole's. "No."

"Then, get it through your thick skull. This is my girlfriend."

"She's always been your girlfriend," the chick said.

I couldn't believe what I was hearing. Not only did she not care that I was standing right there, but she also thought I was his girlfriend, and she was still hitting on him?

"No, she hasn't been. But she is now. So, leave me the hell alone," he snapped before looking at me, all anger gone. "It's our turn."

I almost told him that I'd lost my appetite, but that wasn't true. Seeing Cole like that made me even more ravenous but not just for food. I was so turned on after that public display.

"Oh, you are so getting lucky for that later," I said under my breath, but his eyes lit up, so I knew he'd heard me.

"How lucky?" he asked, and with the look on his face, you would think I'd just told him he'd won a million dollars.

I gave him a wink before turning to place my order.

Getting Lucky

Cole

THE SECOND CHRISTINA had mentioned getting lucky, my dick got hard. Even though we were in the commissary, surrounded by hundreds of students in broad daylight, my dick still had a mind of its own. It wanted her, and it apparently didn't care who knew.

"Christina," I said as I carried our tray of food toward a table where Chance and Mac sat by themselves. The rest of the guys had already cleared out.

She looked at me, drinks in hand. "Yeah?"

"You can't say shit like that to me. Look what you did." I gave a gesture downward, and she looked at my pants and froze mid-step, her jaw slacked, open wide.

"I …" she stuttered, but I kept walking, needing to sit down and hide my bulge from prying eyes. Placing the tray on the table, I pulled out two chairs before I sat.

"I'm sorry," she whispered toward me once she was seated and scooted closer to me.

"It's okay," I said before reaching for the bottom of her jaw and closing it. "It's not like you haven't seen it before," I teased, and she blushed, her cheeks turning an adorable shade of pink.

"Hey," Chance said with a nod before he took a hearty bite out of a sandwich that looked to be about ten layers tall.

"You two can't ever do anything quietly, can you?" Mac asked, and my brain was suddenly back in the bedroom, thinking about all the sounds that I could get Christina to make. And how very not quiet we could be.

"What?" Christina asked as she dipped a chip into some salsa before crunching on it.

"Look around, sweetheart," Mac said, and I shot him a look, which only made his grin grow bigger. "You two are always causing a damn scene."

I glanced around, not in the least bit surprised at the number of people watching us or looking back and forth between their tables and ours. "You're one to talk, Mr. Can't Keep His Tongue Out of Random Chicks' Mouths at Every Party."

"Yeah, but I never cause a spectacle while I'm doing it," he said.

"Not our fault that we're more interesting than you are," I shot back, and his face fell for a second before he shrugged it off, basically agreeing.

"Was that chick hitting on you in front of Christina?" Chance asked even though he already knew the answer.

I nodded as Christina's face formed a small snarl, and I leaned in to kiss the corner of her mouth.

"It used to happen all the time to my dad, I guess, when he was here. My mom has told me some pretty fucked up stories. It amazes me how little college has changed since they were here and now."

"It's not that college hasn't changed," Christina chimed in. "It's that the people haven't. The girls, I mean. The way they feel about the baseball team and how they all want to be a part of it in any way that they can. It's been like that in one way or another since the dawn of time. It probably always will be."

She reached for her burrito and took a hefty bite, pieces spilling out all around her, but she couldn't have cared less. I almost dropped to my knees and proposed right there. Any girl who ate like that and actually enjoyed it I wanted to share every meal with until I left this earth.

When no one said anything in response, she looked up, almost unsure as she swallowed. "Don't you guys agree?"

"Sorry, I was too busy watching you eat to formulate thoughts that revolved outside of getting you naked," I said.

Mac laughed as she gave me a sweet look. I was being a total caveman, and she found it endearing.

"I think you're right. That basic kind of human nature, I guess, hasn't really evolved," Chance said.

Mac cleared his throat. "Let's be honest, and I'm not trying to be offensive." He looked at Christina, and she gave him a face that told him to continue. "Girls want to hook up with guys they think are going to be successful. Especially guys they think are going to be rich or famous. They want a part of that."

"You're not wrong. They do," Christina agreed. "Women are drawn to men they think are powerful."

"So, you think I'm powerful?" I asked, nudging her leg under the table with my own as I took a bite of my taco.

"Who said I was drawn to you?" she fired back, and Mac and Chance both laughed, fueling her on.

"You don't have to play hard to get. I already got you, remember?"

She playfully raised her eyebrows. "For now."

"Okay, I don't like what's happening. Let's get back to girls being cleat-chasers and you loving me," I said quickly, and she practically choked on the drink she had been taking.

"Love," she stuttered, and Mac and Chance both stood up at the same time.

"That's our cue," Chance said before Mac looked at the nonexistent watch on his bare wrist.

"Gotta go. See you at the field. Bye, Christina."

They disappeared in a fucking instant.

"You scared them away." I looked at her, pretending to be shocked.

"*You* scared them away with all your love talk," she mimicked, emphasizing that the blame was squarely on my shoulders.

I shrugged. "Oh well. Not my fault if they can't handle grown-up emotions."

Her face scrunched up like she wasn't sure if I was fucking around with her or being serious. And even though I was no expert on love, I thought about her all the time. When I looked to the future, my future, I saw her by my side. Or maybe I was by hers? Was that love? It sure sounded like it to me.

She dipped another chip into her salsa, watching me the whole time, before taking a bite and chewing it in slow motion. I grinned.

"You think I'm up to something, but I'm not," I said before she could say a word. And just like that, my mind was in the gutter again. I wanted to be all up *in* her something. Hell, I wanted to be all up in her everything. "I'm coming over tonight after practice. Unless you're working?"

"I can be done working by then," she said, still eyeballing me like I might pull the proverbial rug out from under her at any moment.

"I actually do need to head to the field though. I'll see you later?" I kissed her cheek first before turning her face and kissing her mouth, tasting the zing of hot salsa on her lips.

"See you later." She smiled, her eyes so soft and filled with so much emotion that it fucking melted my insides.

No one—and I mean, no one—in my entire life had ever looked at me the way she did.

PRACTICE HAD DRAGGED by at a snail's pace. I wasn't used to feeling bored and wishing I were somewhere else during those hours. I had always wanted to be on the field, in the cages, or working hard to improve my game and chances in the draft. But not today. Today, I had been officially, one hundred percent distracted. I couldn't stop thinking about my girl. Not even the sight of Logan and his piss-poor attitude fazed me.

The need to be with Christina consumed me like a fire with no help in sight. It raged, devouring everything in its path until there was nothing left to burn. We'd go up in smoke together, our ashes now one, and everyone else could go to hell.

In any other circumstances, I would have considered this moving too fast, but this wasn't a normal relationship. We had years of history under our belts, and we'd slept together before. More than once. But there had been no post-sex cuddles or sleeping over after it was over. Sex in the past had usually been a wham-bam-thank-you-ma'am type of deal that I suddenly wasn't very proud of.

Nothing about our situation now was the same as before. And even though it wouldn't technically be the first time that we shared our bodies with one another, a strange anticipation lingered like it was. Parts of this were completely brand-new. I almost wished we'd never done it before, so I could treat her the way she always deserved to be treated—with care, with reverence, with love.

I balanced the pizza, breadsticks, salad, and wings that I'd brought over in my hands as I pressed the call button, and knowing I was on my way, she buzzed me in. Her front door flew open before I had a chance to kick at it, and she yelped in surprise before taking some of the food out of my grasp.

"Thank you," I said as I closed the door behind me and followed her toward the kitchen.

"You bought enough to feed us for a week," she said, looking at the sheer amount of food that covered her countertops.

I wasn't sure if Lauren would be around, and I had no idea what Lauren ate if she was, so I'd bought a little of everything.

"Uh, you haven't seen me eat pizza. There won't be leftovers," I said, and she let out a nervous giggle.

"Are you hungry now?" she asked as she opened a cupboard, but her eyes were asking me something else entirely. They weren't talking about the food.

I wondered if she knew how easy she was to read. How every single emotion she felt was written all over her face, no matter what her words said.

I took a step toward her, wrapping my arm around her waist before kissing her senseless. Her body relaxed in my grip, molding against mine.

I pulled away for only a second to say, "I'm hungry for you," before I continued kissing her and moving us out of the kitchen and in the direction of her bedroom.

If I had expected Christina to hesitate or push me away, I would have been wrong. She practically climbed my body, wrapping her legs around my middle so I had to hold her up by her ass, like she'd been counting down the seconds for this moment to happen.

"Lauren's not here," she admitted once we reached her doorway, and I kicked off my shoes without breaking contact.

"Good," I breathed against her, my mouth fused to hers

once more as I walked through, closed the door behind us, and deposited her on top of the bed.

She scooted back, giving me room to join her, but I could tell something was on her mind. I climbed on top of the bed, my body hovering over hers, and she looked so vulnerable, so trusting.

"What's the matter?" I asked as her hand snaked around my neck, and she pulled me down.

Her tongue found mine as she teased, nipping at my bottom lip before kissing me deep. She was trying to distract me.

"Christina," I said, my breaths labored. "Is it too soon?"

"No. It's not that," she said, but her voice was soft, hiding something.

"What is it?" I asked as I rolled off of her but still stayed close. She hesitated, so I reached for her hand and kissed it. "You can tell me anything."

Her hand caressed my cheek, and I closed my eyes for a second before she started talking, "I just don't want this to disappear. I know we've had sex before, but it doesn't feel the same. This feels different. Does it feel different to you?" Before I could answer, she crushed me as she said, "I just don't want you to go away after. I don't think I could take losing you this time."

Her confession damn near broke my heart in two. To hear her be so honest and to know that I had hurt her so deeply in the past caused my chest to ache. I didn't deserve her. And I definitely didn't deserve another chance with her, but she'd given me one anyway, and I wasn't going to fuck it up.

"I'm not going anywhere. I'm here. Today. Tomorrow. And the next. I'm not leaving you," I said, hoping that she would not only believe me, but also find it in her heart to deem me worthy of having her. Although I thought that was my own insecurity rearing its ugly head and not hers.

She closed her eyes and breathed deep, as if she was giving my declaration time to sink in and become a part of her somehow. When her eyes opened again, she nodded before saying the sweetest words, "I believe you."

Emotion coursed through me, but I pulled myself together as I looked her dead in the eyes. "I want you to know how lucky I feel to be the one who is here with you right now. You didn't have to give me another chance, but I'll never make you sorry that you did," I said the words easily, but I was giving them to her as a promise.

"We all make mistakes, Cole." She looked at me with soft eyes. "Do things we aren't proud of or wish we had handled certain situations differently. You're worth the second chance. I need it as much as you do."

"Really?" I angled my elbow underneath my body and propped myself up.

"Yes," she said the single word like I was an idiot for even asking the question. "I would have always wondered what-if when it came to us. We never really tried. So, yeah, I needed this too."

I leaned down, moving my arm next to her head to brace my weight as I kissed her. "And just for the record"—I stopped before kissing her again—"you asked if this was different for me. The answer is yes. It doesn't feel the same as before at all."

She exhaled against me, her breath warm. "Thank God. I was afraid it was just me," she said before grabbing my lower back with needy hands.

Reaching for my shirt, she tugged at it, ripping it over my head and tossing it somewhere. I stopped paying attention as I helped her remove her top as well.

There was no stopping us now. We craved the connection. Needed it. And even though my hands had touched her body before, it felt like I was exploring new territory as I unbuttoned her shorts and tried in vain to get them off. She wiggled underneath me before kicking them free.

Her fingers worked at my zipper, but she hesitated when she felt the tip of my dick pressing against it. "Am I going to hurt it?" she asked, and I laughed.

"No. He's tough. But it will be easier this way," I said before taking them off myself. It took every ounce of my willpower to not plow into her. I felt desperate. I wanted to handle every curve, caress every soft part of her skin before committing it all to memory.

Christina's eyes widened as she stared at my boxer briefs. "I know what you're going to say," she groaned before adding, "that I've seen him before, so I shouldn't be so surprised."

I smiled because it was exactly what I was going to say.

"But how do you know I wasn't surprised all those other times too? And you just never knew because we didn't really talk before."

"Is that what we're going to do now? Talk? Because I'd really like to be inside of you if you don't mind."

"By all means, don't let me stop you." She narrowed her eyes like she was upset with me, and I reached down, my fingers easily finding her panties as I heard her gasp.

My hand moved down lower, her heat beckoning me, and I pushed two fingers inside, her wetness instantly surrounding them. She moaned and squirmed, her body writhing beneath me, and I almost had an embarrassing *American Pie* movie moment. I was as worked up as she was.

I pulled her panties completely off and sat on my knees to pull briefs down, my dick springing free with relief.

Standing up, I kicked them off as Christina asked, "Where are you going?"

Searching the pile of discarded clothes on the floor, I reached for my shorts and fumbled for the right pocket before pulling out a condom and holding it up for her to see. She smiled as I opened the wrapper and rolled the rubber down my length before positioning myself back on top of her.

"Ready?" I asked, and it was a stupid question, but I couldn't take it back now.

She nodded, and I lined up the head of my dick with her entrance and slowly pushed inside.

Christina gasped a little, her mouth forming a perfect little O as I moved all the way in, burying myself in her warmth.

"Jesus," I said before realizing my eyes were closed tight. Opening them, I found Christina watching me, her blue eyes glassy and gazing into my own. "You okay?"

"I'm okay." She gave me a teasing smile, and I lowered my mouth to hers, wanting to feel every part of her against every part of me.

Will it ever feel like she is close enough?

My hips moved back and forth, working faster than I wanted but I couldn't help it. My dick craved a release, and I wasn't stupid enough to ask him to stop. He might end up betraying me and never come again, and I'd have no one to blame but myself.

"You feel so good. I love being inside you," I confessed against the hollow of her neck.

"Look at me," she pleaded, and I did as she'd asked. I would do anything she wanted. "Don't stop." Her voice was breathy, her hips grinding against my own, creating a friction I knew she craved for her own release.

I sent up a silent prayer that she'd get there before I did.

Our bodies continued to move in unison, finding a rhythm that wasn't forced or unnatural. We'd had sex before, but I'd never allowed myself to feel the kind of emotions that currently ripped through me. But maybe that was just it—this wasn't simply sex. It felt like more.

The closer I got to coming, the harder I had to work to stop myself from blurting out that I was falling in love with her. I'd never wanted to say those words to a girl in my life, and now, I had to stop myself from shouting them every time my dick dived deeper.

"Christina," I said her name like it was my lifeline to staying in this universe as my pace quickened.

"Cole." My name on her lips was the sweetest damn

sound.

I took it from her. My name, her lips, her breaths—I took it all as my mouth covered hers, ours tongue tangling, and I couldn't hold back any longer.

By the time my body stopped jerking, I focused on her again. She was breathing fast, her chest heaving up and down as I stared at her in awe.

"Did you …" I didn't even have to finish the question. She knew what I was asking.

"You couldn't tell?" she asked, sounding winded.

I shook my head because, to be honest, I didn't know if she had gotten hers or not. But I was damn glad that she had.

Rolling off of her so I didn't crush her beneath me, I tried to steady my rapidly beating heart but to no avail. Beads of sweat dripped down my cheeks. I hadn't even noticed them before.

Reaching for her body, I pulled her against my chest, needing to feel her. "I'm not ready to let go. Hope that's okay."

"That was nothing like before," was all she said, and I knew exactly what she meant.

We had always shared a connection, but I'd ignored it, pretending it wasn't there and giving it no life. Now, it felt like I was living for that connection.

I couldn't stop thinking about how I'd almost told her I loved her and how, now that it was over, I knew I was definitely falling. Suddenly, her body tensed against mine, and I reacted in kind, wondering what the hell had just happened.

Her head moved up from my chest, and cold air swooped in. "Was that real, or an accidental, postcoital, in-the-moment, slip-of-the-tongue kind of thing?"

Shit.

Did I say the words out loud? "Which part?" I asked as I navigated my next move depending on her response.

"That you're falling in love with me?" She sounded more cautious than hopeful.

"I …" I stumbled, not wanting to scare her off and wondering if it was way too soon to feel that strong, even with all of our shared history. "I'm definitely falling for you."

I swore I'd never seen my girl smile so big before, like she knew a secret I didn't. "If it's any consolation, I'm pretty sure I started falling the first night we met," she said.

My heart felt like it might explode—in a good way, if there were such a thing.

"I'm pretty sure I did too. Sorry it took me so long to realize it."

"It's okay." She smiled and kissed my bare chest.

"Is it?" I asked with a laugh because *okay* was the fishiest word in the female vocabulary, and even a relationship rookie like me knew that.

"Yes. Because we're here now. Together. And it was worth the wait."

Forget playing it cool or trying to act like her words hadn't fazed me. I was all in. "I'm never letting you go," I said as I ran my fingers through her hair.

"Good," was all she said. Then, she shot up from my chest, looked me in the eyes, and shouted, "Pizza!" and my stomach instantly grumbled in response.

I'd forgotten all about the food. Can you blame me?

Road Trips

Four Weeks Later

Christina

BEING A COUPLE with Cole had become as natural as breathing. It was almost like we'd always been together. Sometimes, it surprised me how considerate he could be— which I knew sounded bad, but it was just that, for someone who had never been in a real relationship before, he sure was good at it.

He texted all the time, never making me wonder or guess where he was. It wasn't that I wanted to control his every move or needed to know his whereabouts twenty-four hours a day, but there was something extremely comforting in the fact that he kept me in the loop.

It was especially helpful when a girl I'd never met before tried to tell me that Cole was currently at her house, in bed with one of her sorority sisters, because I knew that he was at a training facility with Chance, working on his bat speed. He'd sent me two videos of him hitting in the previous ten minutes.

I remembered smiling at her and thanking her for the info before walking away while she screamed that she wasn't lying. And to be fair, maybe she wasn't. Her sorority sister probably had been in bed with someone at that very moment ... but that someone wasn't Cole, and I had known it.

We'd even survived our first road trip apart.

I had been more nervous than I had anticipated the night before Cole left my apartment and boarded the team bus, heading to the airport.

"How does this work?" I asked.

We were lying on my bed with my head pressed against his body.

"How does what work?" His abs tightened, and I knew he was straining to look at me.

I tried to dig and maneuver my head into his hard muscles like they were a fluffy pillow that might move around for me.

"What are you doing?" He laughed as he wormed out from underneath me.

"It's not really that comfortable, lying on your rock-hard chest, to be honest. Can't you make it smooshier?"

"Smooshier?" he repeated before grabbing a pillow and placing it on his stomach and pulling my head back down. "There. Better?"

"Actually, yes," I said because it was.

"Now, what were you asking?"

"How this works. While you're away." I swallowed

around the insecure lump in my throat, hating that it even existed in the first place. But I would have hated myself more if I'd never asked him and let him leave while I sat at home with a million questions in my head. It wouldn't have been fair to either of us.

"The same way it works when we're here. I'll text and call you and FaceTime you before I go to sleep. And I'll be back before you know it." He sounded so confident. Like he hadn't even realized that I was starting to spin out in my own head.

"Okay," I said, but it wasn't believable. It was the least believable okay in the history of okays.

"What are you thinking in that head of yours?" He tapped the top of my head with one of his fingers.

"Don't think I'm crazy, but I just got kind of nervous out of nowhere."

"Christina." His voice was so soft and comforting, like thinking I was crazy was the last thing that would ever enter his mind. He pushed up to a sitting position and lifted me off of him at the same time so that we could face each other. "You can tell me anything. What's going on?"

I blew out a breath, squeezed my eyes shut, reopened them, and then dived right into his sea of blue. "It's our first road trip as a couple. And I'm sure that, over the years, there have been girls in other places. I guess I just wondered if they would show up at your hotel or if you'd see them again? Do they know you have a girlfriend now? Would they even care? Do you have, like, a set girl in every state?" I asked before covering my face with my hands. I felt so dumb. Dumb for asking all these things and dumb for never thinking of any of this before.

"I'm not going to lie to you," he started.

My stomach clenched as I dreaded what he might say next. I'd asked the hard questions, so I had to be prepared for the answers.

"There are guys who do have girls everywhere we travel. You'd be surprised at exactly who. But I'm not one of them."

"You've never hooked up on the road before?" I asked.

I knew there was no way he hadn't at least made out with random girls while he was away. That seemed way too far-fetched for any single guy to resist, especially the guys on this team. They weren't just hot commodities in the state of California. They were known all over the country for being the best. Everyone wanted a piece of something like that, no matter how small.

"I didn't say that. But I've never brought a girl up to my room. And I've never left with a girl. It was never worth the risk."

"Okay. So, will there be girls on this trip?"

"There's always girls," he said. "They find out where we are and show up there. They hang out in our hotel and wait for the team bus. But ..." He stopped and reached for my hands, his thumb moving back and forth.

"But what?"

He smiled. In the middle of this sort of uncomfortable conversation about girls who waited in hotel lobbies, he was smiling!

"But it's my choice. It doesn't matter who shows up. I'm

not interested or looking or willing."

I knew I should have been satisfied with that answer, but clearly, it wasn't enough. "But what if it's someone you've been with before? Someone you know? And she's expecting it to be like last time?"

Cole looked at me like he would entertain my what-if scenarios all night long if I asked him to. He wasn't even remotely irritated that I needed more information. He indulged me.

"Let me put it to you this way. Any girl could show up at my door, naked, holding a six-pack, and it wouldn't matter. I'd slam the door in her face. Might take the beer first," he said with a grin, "but never the girl. You're the only one I want."

I wasn't sure whether to laugh or cry, so I think I did a little of both. "Really?"

"Yes, really. And while we're on the subject, it goes both ways, you know?"

"What do you mean?"

"I'm not the only one out of town."

"I'm not following," I said. I'm not going anywhere, so what is he talking about?

"You're here without me too. You could meet someone and fall in love while I'm gone," he said, and I laughed because just the idea itself was completely ridiculous. *"See, you laugh, but I worry too. You never know what could happen while I'm away."*

"But I'm not even looking for anyone else. I wouldn't even entertain the idea. I'm so happy with you, Cole."

"Exactly." He gave me a pointed look, and I knew that I'd just proven the point he was trying to get across to me earlier. *"We will be fine. I promise."*

And we were.

He texted me all the time, more than usual, and I knew he was doing it to make sure I was comfortable. I appreciated the messages and always responded right away to let him know I was thinking about him and missed him too.

JUST LANDED. MISS YOU.

CAN'T STOP THINKING ABOUT YOU. DON'T FALL IN LOVE WITH ANY WAFFLES WHILE I'M GONE.

HEADING TO DINNER WITH THE TEAM. CALL YOU WHEN WE GET BACK TO THE ROOM. P.S. I HATE THE TIME DIFFERENCE

He called before and after every game, and we FaceTimed each night. He shared a hotel room with a teammate I didn't know very well, and he made fun of Cole for being "whipped," as he called it. Cole never even argued with him. At least, not while I was on the phone to hear it.

And when miniature snow globes from various cities started appearing on top of my desk, I realized that Cole had been buying me one from each airport he landed in without telling me.

When I confronted him one night, he simply said, "So you know that I'm thinking of you, no matter where I am."

<Insert dreamy sigh here.>

LAUREN SNAPPED HER fingers in front of me. "Earth to Christina," she said.

"I'm right here," I lied, not even caring that she'd caught me daydreaming with my mouth half-open.

It wasn't my fault that Cole caused me to get lost in fantasies. There was something about most baseball players' upper bodies, but there was especially something about Cole's. Maybe it was because I was the one who got to run my fingers all over his biceps, tracing the curves of his muscles all the way up to his broad shoulders and then back down again.

"Well, pay attention. Your boyfriend's up."

Lauren and I had tickets waiting for us at every home game now, thanks to Cole. And even though we could get free tickets with our student IDs, those would put us in a particular section, higher up and farther away from the action. Basically, the seats that Cole got us were better and closer to the dugout. I'd only complained once, feeling bad that I was using his complimentary tickets, but he insisted, reminding me that his dad was swamped with work. We hadn't even crossed paths at a single game yet, which seemed crazy to me, considering the fact that he only lived about twenty minutes away. But Cole reminded me that when you were self-employed, you didn't really have days off.

"Let's go, Cole!" Lauren shouted into the air as Cole

stepped into the batter's box.

I was too nervous to cheer for him out loud, my stomach tied into knots every time he was up to bat.

My hands folded in my lap, and I whispered, "Come on," over and over. My silent mantra, if you will, to help my man get a hit. I knew how much pressure he was under, and I also knew how many scouts were watching him, wondering if he was going to head back into another slump or not.

When the sound of the bat making contact with the ball echoed in the air, I jumped to my feet and watched it fly hard into center field, smacking the ground before bouncing toward the wall. The crowd exploded, and Lauren and I clasped hands as we jumped up and down. Cole pointed at me from first base, and I decided that I would never get used to him doing that, but I also never wanted him to stop.

I knew I was blushing as I sat back down, and the crowd quieted enough that I could hear the girls in front of me talking. I hadn't meant to eavesdrop, but they caught my attention.

"Oh my God, I really think he's pointing at you." The girl leaned toward her friend, and she sounded so excited that I almost hated to ruin it for her.

Thankfully, the ruining didn't have to come from me.

"You think the guy on first base is pointing at you?" Lauren leaned down to ask, and the two girls turned to face us.

"Cole Anders, right? I wasn't sure, but he keeps looking over here, and I just thought maybe—" one of them started before Lauren cut her off mid-thought.

"He's looking at this one." She thumbed toward me, and I braced for whatever insult was about to be hurled my way. "She's his girlfriend."

The two girls' expressions both morphed into apology and mortification.

"We're so sorry. We didn't know."

I actually smiled because it was rare that other females weren't rude or snide toward me. "It's okay. You didn't know. And he *is* looking this way. I would have thought the same thing."

They both visibly relaxed.

"He's really cute. You're lucky."

"I know. And thanks."

They turned to face the game again, and Lauren gave me an incredulous look. "That didn't go the way I'd thought," she whispered, and I knew exactly what she meant.

I had been braced for an argument or for the verbal insults to start flying. I realized that I was so used to defending my relationship and myself at every turn, even before we were officially a couple, that I'd assumed it was always going to happen. It was so nice when it didn't.

As the stands cleared out when the game ended, Lauren gave me a hug before throwing her arms in the air for an exaggerated stretch. We had a game day routine—she drove us both there, and then Cole drove me home after.

"I'll see you at home," she said, heading toward the parking lot as her long blonde hair swished behind her with each bouncy step she took.

I headed toward the meeting spot where girlfriends and

family members waited for the boys to exit the locker room. We never knew how long the guys would take after a game ended. Between Coach's speech, hitting the showers, and sometimes food, it could be anywhere from twenty minutes to an hour. I usually used the time to my advantage, waiting farther away from where everyone else was so that I could work instead of socialize. I wasn't trying to be antisocial; it was just that once Cole was out of uniform, we tended to monopolize each other's time ... *willingly*.

I pulled out my phone and started scrolling through my emails, making sure to respond to each one before checking the latest social media insights for my clients. Reaching into my purse, I pulled out a tiny notepad and a pen and scribbled down notes that I needed to add to my spreadsheet at home for comparison. As I jotted down updated page view counts and searched for videos and pictures that not only had the most views, but also the most interaction, a throat cleared, and I instantly looked up. I had no idea how long I'd been lost in work, and my smile instantly fell when I realized that it wasn't Cole standing in front of me but Logan.

"Hi," I said to him, my tone coming out weird, but I wasn't sure what he wanted or why he was looking for me.

"Can we talk?" he asked before reaching for my upper arm and pulling at me.

I shook him off. "Sure, but let go of me first."

"Sorry." He started walking slowly away, distancing us even more from the waiting crowd, and I followed him, wondering what on earth we possibly needed to discuss. When he stopped, he turned on his heel and leaned toward me. "I really liked you, Christina. I still can't believe that you left me for him."

"Left you for him? What do you mean?" I asked because I was not only genuinely confused, but it had been over a month since Cole and I had gotten together, and Logan was coming out of the woodwork now, all upset about how things happened.

He started pacing in small steps back and forth, and I looked behind me to see if Cole was on his way, but there was no sign of him.

"What do you want, Logan?"

He stopped pacing. "I want you back. I want to try again."

A sick laugh tore from my throat. "You never had me. We were never together. It was one date."

"That's not fair," he said a little too loud before glancing up quickly and recomposing himself.

"But it's true."

"Only because he stole you from me." He pointed a finger at my chest like he wanted to poke me there to further his point but didn't.

Did Logan really forget how things ended that night at the party? How he left me outside and told me to find my own way back home? How it had been exposed that he was only using me to bait Cole?

"And you let him take you away. Like I meant nothing. Like he meant everything."

I could never belong to Logan because I'd always belonged to someone else, but guys like Logan didn't take well to coming in second place.

"Logan"—I tried to sound calm so that I didn't set him off any further—"Cole and I have a lot of history. No one was going to be able to compete with that," I said, hoping he would take the rejection less personally even though I hadn't rejected him in the first place.

"I still like you," he said.

"You never liked me," I argued.

He shook his head like my words were insane to him. "Cole broke code by dating you after me. I'm better than he is on every level, and he knows it. Tell me you're not attracted to me anymore." His tone grew more desperate by the second.

I found myself looking around to see if anyone, not just Cole, was watching us or not, but the other girlfriends were focused on the entrance, looking for their boyfriends. No one was paying attention to Logan or me. We were too far away.

I had no idea what to say at that point. Every response was only going to egg him on further. Logan seemed irrational and illogical. You couldn't win verbal battles when someone was in that frame of mind. He stepped toward me, more words on the tip of his tongue when his eyes caught something behind me and locked on. I watched as they narrowed into slits before he looked down at me one last time and walked away without saying a thing.

"Christina?" Cole's voice echoed through the concrete hallway, and I turned around to see him jogging toward me. "Was that Logan?" he asked, his temper already flaring as I nodded. "What'd he want? What did he say to you? Are you okay?" His hand cupped my cheek as he searched my eyes for answers.

I tried to navigate the situation in my head before I answered, not wanting to lie to Cole, but also not wanting to tell him anything that could make him want to confront Logan and get in trouble.

"Christina, just tell me everything. Don't keep things from me to protect me," he demanded as if reading my mind.

"He said you stole me from him. And he wants another chance." I tried to sound like it wasn't weird at all, but we both knew that it was.

"What else did he say?" Cole didn't seem all that shocked.

"Um, that you *broke code* by dating me after him," I said, emphasizing the words *broke* and *code*.

Cole shook his head. "He's the one who broke code by going after you in the first place, and he knows it."

"What do you think he wants?" I asked.

While Cole didn't seem surprised by what Logan had said to me, he did seem a little concerned.

"To mess with me. That's always been his goal. To get me so rattled that I choke again at the plate. He knows you're the only way to do it."

"But why now?"

Cole's face looked like a lightbulb had gone off as he inhaled a quick breath. "Because he's running out of time," he said, and I knew exactly what he meant.

Their season was winding down, and it was Logan's last one too. Cole wasn't the only player trying to ensure he got drafted when it was all said and done. And even though it was obvious that Logan didn't have what it took to make it to the big leagues—otherwise, he would be starting over Cole instead of sitting on the bench—Logan clearly didn't agree. The only way to prove that to everyone was to get Cole out of the way so that he could take his place on the field. And he wanted to use me to do it. Too bad I'd never let it happen. I would never be used as ammunition against Cole.

We drove back to my place in silence with the radio playing low in the background and our windows down a crack. It wasn't awkward or uncomfortable even though I had a handful of questions running through my mind that I wanted to ask. The way Cole gripped the steering wheel of his truck, his knuckles turning almost white, told me that he was working things out on his own, so I didn't push him.

He exhaled, reached for my hand, and gave me a squeeze. "Sorry. I was in my head there for a minute."

"I noticed." I smiled. "You okay?"

"Yeah. I just really don't like Logan confronting you like that."

I knew what he meant. I hadn't particularly liked it either.

"It was weird," I admitted.

"Was that the first time he's talked to you since we've been together?"

Nodding, I said, "Yeah. I don't even think I've seen him since that night at the party."

"You'll let me know if he reaches out, won't you?"

"Of course," I said, hoping to comfort him. "But he probably won't."

Cole smiled, and it was downright devilish. "That's too bad. I'd love a reason to kick his ass."

I laughed. "Then, you'd get kicked off the team."

"Worth it."

"It's not," I argued because I'd never forgive myself if Cole got kicked off the team for fighting because of me. "He's not," I emphasized.

Once we stopped completely at a red light, he turned to face me. "Then, he'd better not touch my girl. Or come anywhere near her. I'm done being patient with him, Christina. You're where I draw the line."

"And he knows that. We can't let him win." I ran my fingers down the stubble on his cheek, and he grabbed my hand and starting planting kisses all over it.

"The bad guys don't win in our story. I'll make sure of it," he said, and I believed him.

With every fiber of my being, I believed that Cole would make sure nothing and no one ever came between us. I smiled so big that it actually hurt my cheeks. I was the luckiest girl on the planet, and I knew it.

Accidents Happen

Cole

I WANTED TO confront Logan in the locker room the next day, but I was worried that I wouldn't be able to keep my temper in check, and I'd do something stupid. Like break his fucking jaw. So, as much as it pained me to let him walk around like he hadn't talked to Christina and said some crazy shit to her, I kept my distance.

It didn't last long.

Coach Jackson had us doing hitting and base-running drills when Logan came up to bat. I was already on second base after crushing a double against the wall. Logan swung and hit a nice hard ground ball between short and third, but our shortstop nabbed it. The catch was pretty spectacular, but the throw was wild.

I watched as Mac maneuvered his body in the runner's base path in order to catch the ball. Logan lowered his head and ran even faster as he tried to beat out the play. They were going to collide if Mac didn't get out of the way. Mac scrambled to reach for the wild throw while he also twisted his body in an unnatural angle to avoid getting hit by Logan.

I looked away for only a second, but when I looked back, Logan was on the ground, yelling at Mac as he pushed himself back onto his feet. I bolted in their direction along with my other teammates. A group of us crowded around them, making sure they didn't come to blows.

"You tripped on the bag," Mac shouted as Logan lunged for him but failed, his ankle giving out underneath the weight of him.

"Because you were blocking it. You did it on purpose. You want me hurt. Cole probably asked you to do it," he accused as he searched me out, his eyes glaring. He didn't have to look very far since I was standing right there, ready to defend Mac and anyone else he tried to physically attack.

Give me another reason, pretty boy.

"I was trying to make the play," Mac ground out, his teeth clenched.

"You were trying to break my ankle," Logan yelled back.

"Why would I do that?"

No player liked being accused of playing dirty, least of all against one of your own.

"You and I both know why!" Logan gave one last push, and I worried for a split second that someone might believe him.

"Break it up. What the hell is going on here?" Coach Jackson said as he speed-walked toward us, his features hard and irritated, his face beet red. He was pissed as he separated Mac and Logan, pushing them apart before releasing the grip he had on both of their shirts.

"Nothing, Coach." I tried to defuse the situation and take

the lead, but Logan was out for blood.

"Stupid sophomore doesn't know how to play first. He should be benched."

"That's enough. I saw the play, Logan; it was clean. Shitty throw from Balmsy, but that's about it."

"He could have moved. He could have cleared the bag. He knew I'd run hard. He wanted to hurt me."

"Accidents happen. Go get your ankle looked at," he said, but Logan didn't move. "Now!" Coach yelled, and a couple of guys scrambled to help him hobble off the field.

I took a few steps toward Mac, who looked visibly distraught before letting him know it would be okay. "No one blames you."

"It was a fair play," Chance added, his catcher's helmet fisted in his hand.

"Thanks, guys," Mac said, but he didn't look or sound convinced.

"Get back to your positions," Coach hollered before waving a finger in my direction. Without another word, I hustled over as he reached for my shoulder and gave it a firm squeeze. "Everything okay, Anders?"

I couldn't tell Coach that Logan and I were having girl issues. He had no tolerance for that kind of shit and had told us on numerous occasions to keep our personal lives off the ball field.

I told him the only truth that mattered, the only truth he'd care about, "Logan's pissed I got my swing back."

Coach Jackson nodded and let out some sort of grunt. "He should be more pissed that his sucks."

I knew better than to respond or say anything disparaging about a teammate, but I couldn't believe Coach had just said that to me.

"You're a leader on this team, Cole. They look up to you. Don't let me down."

He gave my back a pat, a signal that our conversation was over and that I needed to get back to work, so I did just that.

THERE WAS NO sign of Logan once practice ended. He wasn't in the locker room or in the trainer's facility. I wondered briefly how his foot was before slinging my bag over my shoulder and heading out alone, the rest of the guys still showering and getting dressed.

The sun was starting to set, but Coach Carter was still working with the pitching staff. When he saw me, he shouted my name and started jogging over. "Hey."

"Hey, Coach."

"Don't get pissed, but Chance told me a little about what's going on between you and Logan."

"Okay." I wasn't pissed at all. Actually, I felt relieved that someone in an authoritative position knew what was happening. That way, if shit hit the fan, it wouldn't just be my word against his.

"Is he messing with your girl?"

I nodded. "A little bit, yeah."

Coach Carter cleared his throat. "You gotta stay out of it. Let *me* know if he does anything else. This is the kind of shit that tears teams apart from the inside out and can get you into real trouble with the big dogs."

"I know. You're right." I knew he was talking about the department that made all of the regulations for athletes across the nation. There were rules that each athlete at every school was required to follow, and if anyone was reported for breaking one of them, whether it was a valid claim or not, a case was usually opened.

"By the way, Logan's out for a week," he said, telling me all I needed to know without saying another damn word.

Logan wouldn't be cleared to travel with us for our next series of away games. Which meant that he'd be here, alone, with Christina, while I was in another state.

A Problem of the Sake Variety

Christina

STRETCHING MY ARMS over my head, I glared at the cell phone alarm blaring from my nightstand, hoping that my eye contact alone would make it stop. Cole was already moving toward it, taking all his body heat and warmth with him. I snuggled deeper into the covers and pulled them up to my chin.

The horrible beeping stopped, and Cole was back, his body wrapping around mine like a human shield. "I hit snooze. We have ten more minutes."

"Ten more minutes of sleep?" I asked as I scooted my butt deeper against him, realizing that not all of his parts were asleep.

"Well, I *was* thinking sleep," he said before reaching around and palming the outside of my panties. "But not anymore."

His fingers rubbed me from the outside, alternating between making little circles and moving up and down. I moaned, and I swore he grew even firmer behind me as his lips pressed against my shoulder before his tongue followed.

I turned around, making sure to maintain skin contact as I found his mouth, our tongues touching, tentatively at first. We deepened the kiss, and both started grinding in unison, thin cotton separating our most intimate parts. I needed him inside of me. Craved it actually.

I must have said the words out loud because Cole said something like, "Your wish is my command," before taking his boxer briefs off and reaching for my panties, which I knew were already wet.

He rustled around. Then, the sound of the condom wrapper tearing filled my ears, and I knew what was coming next. His hand became a barrier between us, his fist separating our parts from touching as he rolled the condom onto himself.

"I can't go slow. We don't have time."

"I don't care," I said because I didn't. All I cared about was having him in me and feeling that connection.

We lay there, facing each other on our sides as he worked to get inside of me. We hadn't done it that way before, and I gasped once he was all the way in, loving the way the pressure and the angle felt inside of me. Cole tossed the covers off before he reached for my leg and threw it over his hip, the grinding continuing.

"Is that okay?"

"Yes. It's amazing," I breathed out as I continued to work my hips.

"You feel so good, Christina. So fucking good," he said before pushing my body down so I was on my back.

He took over. He fucked me hard and fast, like he

couldn't get deep enough, and I welcomed it, loving the way our bodies slapped together in the dark.

He picked up speed, and I knew that meant only one thing—he was about to come. Suddenly, his tongue was in my mouth, and he was kissing me like I was his air and he needed me to breathe. I dug my nails into his back as he thrust hard inside of me with jerking motions.

When he finished, his breathing labored and his stupid cell phone blaring for us to get up, he said, "Your nails in my back did me in." He turned off his phone and sat up on my bed.

I laughed. "Really?"

"Oh, yeah. I don't know why, but that sent me over the edge. So, basically, it's your fault."

"My fault for what?" I asked as he pushed up from the bed.

"Your fault that I came and you didn't." He leaned down and kissed me again before flipping on the lights.

"Hey!" I complained as he headed into my bathroom.

Unlike Cole, I didn't come every time we had sex, but there was no point in mentioning that now. He had a bus to catch. The team was heading out of town for a weekend series away.

I was out of bed but still in my pajamas when Cole came out of the bathroom, wiping his mouth with the back of his hand.

"You know that Logan will still be in town," he said as he grabbed his duffel bag from my bedroom floor and slung it over his broad shoulder.

"I know. You told me already that he isn't traveling with the team," I said because Cole had randomly brought up the subject more than a handful of times last night. We walked out of my bedroom and into the living room. "Are you really that worried?"

"I'm not worried. I'm just," he stumbled, "uncomfortable. I don't like that he'll be here and I won't be. What if he harasses you or bothers you because he knows I'm gone?"

"You're starting to sound like Lauren," I teased, hoping to ease his fears because Logan seemed harmless.

"I heard that," she shouted from her bedroom.

"I can't even make sure she keeps an eye on you since *SHE WON'T BE HERE*!" he yelled the last part in her direction.

Lauren was going home this weekend. It was her mom's birthday, and even though she'd invited me to go with her, I'd declined. I planned on using the distraction-free time to focus on work. Plus, The Long Ones were performing at The Bar again, and I needed to get more live footage and still shots for their socials before graduation.

"I'm going to work and then film the guys on Saturday night, so I'll be fine." I reminded him, and that seemed to ease him slightly, but it wasn't enough.

He reached for my face. "Sorry if I sound a little crazy. I just hate the thought of Logan bothering you when I'm not here to stop him. It's my job to protect you."

"It's your job to hit balls," I said with a smile. "So, go do that. Don't worry about me. I'll be fine."

"Okay," he said before giving me a good-bye kiss that erased all others. He reluctantly headed for my front door. "Christina?"

"Mmhmm?" I said, still in a kiss-induced haze as he turned around and smiled.

"I love you."

My heart stopped, and the haze instantly cleared. I'd been dying to say those three words lately, but I didn't want to be the first to say them. "I love you too." I ran into his arms and hopped up, my legs wrapping tightly around his waist as he held me up by my butt. I couldn't believe we'd just said that to each other, and now, he had to leave.

He put me down and swatted my backside. "Be safe while I'm gone."

"I will."

"Love you too." Lauren stood in her doorway, her cell phone in hand as she smirked at us.

"I'd love you more if you didn't leave this weekend," Cole said before leaning down to give me another kiss before closing the door behind him. "Text you when I land."

When I turned around, Lauren practically squealed before exclaiming, "You're going to love that I eavesdrop."

I rolled my eyes. "Why?"

"Because you wouldn't have these otherwise." She turned her phone around and handed it to me.

Pictures of me running into Cole's arms, leaping up, him holding me, and us kissing all flashed past me. She had gotten pictures of the moment we said we loved each other and our immediate reactions after.

"You're right. I love it. These are amazing. Send them all to me. Print them everywhere. Turn them into wrapping paper," I suggested with a laugh before wondering if I could really do that or not.

"Already sent." She grinned. "You're welcome."

"Thank you," I said before attacking her from behind in a giant bear hug.

"Are you sure you don't want to come home with me this weekend?" She turned around to face me even though she knew the answer.

"Are you sure you don't want to stay here and go to The Bar with me and watch Jason bang on his drums?"

She sighed. It was long and drawn-out and dramatic. "I wish. But my mom would kill me. I can't miss her birthday, or she'll think I don't love her."

"I know. I'll give Jason your regards," I told her, and her face scrunched.

"My regards? Are you offering him my hand in marriage too?" she asked with a laugh.

"Fine. I won't tell him anything." I stuck out my tongue.

"I can tell him myself." She waved her phone in the air and pretended to punch buttons on the screen.

"I'd love to stay out here and banter with you, but I need to get ready for class," I said before disappearing into my bedroom to shower, the smell of Cole inundating my senses when I walked into my room. I hoped it would linger all weekend long until he got back home.

LAUREN LEFT THE next day, and even though I knew our apartment was going to be way too quiet without her here, I was grateful for the alone time. I had a checklist of tasks I needed to accomplish for my clients, and having no one around to distract me or allow me to procrastinate was just what I needed to get them all done.

Cole and I talked and texted often while he was away. Except, now, all of our conversations ended with *I love you*. It was like once the emotion was out of the bag, it refused to be contained. It was freeing ... to not only feel that way about Cole, but to also be able to say it out loud and have it feel so incredibly good and right each time that I did. The fact that Cole felt the same way back and wouldn't stop saying it to me first probably didn't hurt either.

By Saturday morning, I was wrapping up all of my notes to present to The Long Ones at The Bar later. I was excited to see them, not just for the new content I'd get to upload online, but to also let them know that their follower counts had doubled on every platform among other things. Their growth was almost unprecedented and definitely unlike anything I'd ever seen since I started doing this. I knew it was a combination of steady posting, fresh content, and their overall talent.

HAVE FUN TONIGHT.

YOU TOO. KICK ASS. HIT ME A HOME RUN.

HA-HA. I'LL TRY.

Before I could reply with something witty to Cole, he sent another text.

I LOVE YOU. BE SAFE. TEXT ME WHEN YOU GET HOME, OKAY?

I WILL! I LOVE YOU TOO. HAVE A GREAT GAME.

When I got to The Bar, it was relatively quiet, but it was still early. I knew that things would get hectic the later it got and the closer we got to them going onstage.

"I have some news," I said as the group of us sat around the bar.

"Well," Jason, the drummer, asked, "are you going to tell us?"

"You guys passed a hundred thousand views on your latest video!" I shouted, completely excited because it was a big deal to have that many views for a virtually unknown band. Two other videos weren't far behind.

"What?" They all threw their hands in the air and gave each other high fives before getting out of their stools and grabbing me.

I swiveled around in my chair before getting up and giving them each hugs.

"This is insane! You did this. Thank you," the bassist, Aaron, said.

"You guys did this. All I did was post the content. But it was your talent that got the views."

They weren't having any of it, arguing with me that I was the reason they were taking off. I groaned as Charley, the lead singer, yelled for the bartender to come over.

He introduced me to bartender David before instructing that he take care of me all night and get us started with, "Sake bombs all around."

I must have made a weird face because Charley asked me if the drinks were okay or not.

"I've never had one before."

"Really? You'll love them. You love beer, right?"

"Beer's my jam," I said with a grin.

Then, bartender David appeared, balancing five full glasses of beer and five shots of sake—whatever the hell that was. He distributed them, and I stared.

"How do we drink them?" I said, sniffing the sake shot. "It smells kind of like vodka." A hint of worry filtered through me before I waved it off, knowing that I wouldn't get drunk while I was trying to work. Beer was one thing. Beer I could handle.

"It's technically a rice wine," Jason said as he reached for his shot glass and held it above his beer.

Charley explained, "Normally, we'd balance the sake on top of chopsticks that we put over the beer. Then, we'd hit the table with our fists so that they crashed into the beer, but there are no chopsticks, so we'll just drop them in."

"Drop it in? The whole thing?" I asked.

They all took their shot glasses and dropped it, glass and all, inside the already-full beer. The contents spilled out, making a huge mess as they reached for their beer and drank it all like it might disappear if they took too long.

I dropped my sake shot into my beer, but unlike the guys, I sipped the contents, making sure I liked it and not wanting to get in over my head. Lauren wasn't here, and Cole was away. I knew it wouldn't be smart for me to get drunk while I was out alone ... what with the kidnapping cartel and everything.

"Like it?" Charley asked.

I nodded. "It tastes like"—I looked around at the rest of the band, who was all waiting for my response—"beer," I said.

They cracked up like I was the funniest person on the planet, but I'd meant it because I couldn't taste the sake at all.

Throughout the evening, bartender David made sure that I never had to ask for a cold beer. If my glass was half-empty, a new, fresh one would show up from one of the servers. Although I knew that I could handle my beer consumption better than most, I still made sure to sip it, not wanting to get in over my head. I also kept count—or at least, I tried. I left half-filled glasses in my wake as I filmed the band, taking videos and at least a hundred new pictures of them dominating the stage, a rambunctious crowd in the foreground.

Somewhere into the band's second set, my head started to spin, and the ground grew fuzzy. A minute earlier, I'd been sober, and now, I was way beyond being simply buzzed. I'd gone from feeling in control to feeling like I had none in the span of a breath. I wobbled on my feet before bracing against a chair for balance. I couldn't believe I'd gotten so drunk and seemingly out of nowhere. *How did that happen from drinking beer?*

I needed to leave.

"Need a ride home?" a deep voice asked.

I looked up, meeting Logan's eyes as he jangled his keys in front of me.

When did he get there? I wondered before my whole world went dark.

Blacked Out

Christina

I WOKE UP the next morning, my head pounding like a hundred drummer boys lived inside of it and my stomach turning. Glancing down at my body, I noticed that my shoes were gone, but my socks were still on. Aside from my top being on inside out, I was fully clothed, lying on top of my comforter.

I had no idea how I'd gotten home last night. The last thing I remembered was ... I searched my mind for the last piece of information it would give me ...

Logan?

Logan had been there, and he'd offered me a ride home, but there was no way I would have said yes. Even in my drunken state, I had known better than to leave with him.

Didn't I?

My phone flashed, and I reached for it, noticing the handful of unread texts and number of missed phone calls. I must have been dead to the world to sleep through all of those. Unread messages from Cole sat there, and I pressed his name first. As I read them, my stomach twisted.

I'M STARTING TO GET WORRIED. YOU'RE JUST BUSY
WORKING, RIGHT?

HAVEN'T HEARD FROM YOU IN HOURS, AND YOU AREN'T
CHECKING YOUR MESSAGES.

I'M HOPING IT DIED. NOT YOU. THE PHONE. HA.

OKAY, CHRISTINA, PLEASE CALL ME WHEN YOU GET THIS.
I'M FREAKING THE FUCK OUT. I LOVE YOU.

I AM OFFICIALLY LOSING MY DAMN MIND.

I DON'T KNOW WHAT TO DO. WHERE ARE YOU?

I felt awful as I continued scrolling through my unread
texts. A single message from Lauren appeared, letting me
know that she was on her way back home this morning, but
my heart stopped beating completely when I saw Logan's
name.

HAD A GREAT TIME LAST NIGHT. YOU'RE A REAL TIGER IN
THE SACK. NO WONDER COLE COULDN'T LET YOU GO. SEE
YOU SOON.

What. In. The. Actual. Fuck?
No, no, no, no, no.

I said the words like a prayer ... like a chant ... like
something that would make this all some sort of sick and
twisted joke. *I wouldn't do that. Would I? God, why can't I
remember anything?*

I dropped my phone like it was on fire and sprinted for
the bathroom. I threw up my shame, my embarrassment, and
the sake and beer I'd drunk the night before. But still,
nothing was clear. My mind was as empty as my stomach. I

couldn't remember anything after I had seen Logan.

I looked at my reflection in the mirror and shuddered. My hair was unnaturally ratted, and my mascara had smeared around my eyes. There was no way that I would have slept with Logan. But I couldn't be sure. At least, not a hundred percent because I had no memory of last night past a certain point. I'd never blacked out before, and I was scared. I didn't like the way it felt to have no recollection of my own actions.

Where is my car? I suddenly wondered.

I continued staring at myself, like all the answers would magically appear and my head would fill itself with the truth, but nothing came. It was blank, and the harder I tried to grab on to answers, the more they eluded me. Squeezing my eyes shut, I opened them again, and they went straight to my top, which was still on inside out.

That couldn't be a good sign. *Why the hell is my shirt on inside out unless I took it off at some point?* I pulled it off and then put it back on the right way as my phone pinged again. I slowly walked toward it, dreading what I'd find waiting for me there. It was Cole, asking if I was okay.

I couldn't call him or FaceTime him right now. Looking into his eyes or hearing his voice would rip me apart while I struggled to put together the pieces of last night. I had to try to figure out what the hell had really happened before I talked to him. I sent him a text back, telling him that I was so sorry for worrying him but I was home safe and jumping in the shower. He called me immediately, but I ignored it, knowing full well that I was only delaying the inevitable. Eventually, I'd have to tell Cole. I'd have to admit to him that I had no memory of the end of the night ... about Logan being there ... and what we'd apparently done.

Shaking, I sat back down on my bed and cried, wishing it were all a nightmare I could wake up from. I pinched my arm, but the pain alerted me that I was already awake. I hated the fact that I wasn't dreaming. I was so confused. And so ashamed. I loved Cole. *How could I do that to him, to us?* I hated myself.

I cried until my pillowcase was soaking wet against my cheek. And when I heard the front door slam, I sat up and tried to wipe at my face, but it was too late. Lauren bounced into my room, her expression falling as she ran to my side and sat next to me before wrapping an arm around me.

"What happened? What's wrong?" she asked, and I shook in her arms, my body convulsing with remorse. "I wasn't sure you were even here. Your car isn't outside."

"It's not?" I asked even though I had known deep down that it wasn't. It was further proof that I'd gone home with Logan last night.

"I didn't see it anywhere. What's going on?"

"I fucked up, Lauren," I said through my cries.

"What do you mean? What happened?"

"I think," I stuttered, "I think I slept with Logan last night."

Lauren leaned her body away from mine and looked at me. "You what? No way. No."

I rested my hand on my stomach, which, even though it was empty, it still threatened to empty itself again. "I don't remember."

"What do you mean, you don't remember?"

"I drank too much."

"That's not like you," Lauren said, and I knew how out of character it sounded. "What were you drinking?"

"I had some sake-bomb thing with the guys, and then I drank beer the rest of the time." I sounded argumentative because it didn't make any sense. I'd never blacked out from drinking beer before. "That's it."

"How many beers did you drink?" she asked.

"I'm not sure," I admitted, my shame engulfing me like a wet blanket.

"Where does Logan come in?"

"He's the last thing I do remember." I looked at her through watery eyes, and she looked sympathetic.

"That doesn't mean anything."

I reached for my phone and pulled up his text. "He sent me this."

She read it, her face telling me everything I needed to know. It was bad. "Okay. Well, he could be lying?" she asked, and I wondered the same thing too.

"He could be." I shrugged. "But I have no idea if he is or not."

"We'll just call him and ask," she suggested before adding, "but then again, he could still lie to us on the phone."

"I thought the same thing. But also, if Logan is lying about us hooking up last night, he has no idea that I don't remember anything." My thoughts started coming together more logically. "Do you get what I'm saying? Logan doesn't know I blacked out. It's a big risk for him to say we slept together if we really didn't." The words came out of my mouth, and I wanted to spit them on the ground and stomp on them with dirty shoes until they died a horrible death, never to be brought up again.

Lauren was shaking her head. "Not if that was his plan all along. Even if you did remember and nothing happened, it would be your word against his. Not saying that Cole wouldn't believe you, but by then, the damage would have already been done."

"How so?" I asked because I'd stopped following her train of thought.

"Meaning that Logan's already started something. And whether or not it's true might not matter. Because he's hoping for a fallout of some sort. At the very least, he's done this thing that will make Cole question you. And now, Cole will be rattled every time he leaves for an away game because he'll be worried or concerned about you. You follow?"

"Yeah," I said, my voice still clogged with emotion. "I see what you're saying, but none of it matters."

"Why not?"

"Because I don't remember."

"So, what are you going to tell Cole?"

My stomach twisted again. "The truth."

I couldn't—no, I *wouldn't* lie to Cole to make this go away. And this also wasn't something that I could talk to him about over the phone while he was getting ready for the last game of the series. I had to wait until he was back home and we were face-to-face.

Just as the thought entered my head, my phone beeped with another text alert. Reaching for it, I saw Cole's name, and I exhaled before opening it up to read it.

WHAT IS THIS?

Attached to the text was a picture of me and Logan, his arm wrapped around my shoulders as I stood there with the biggest damn smile on my face, my head dangerously close to resting on his shoulder. I had no recollection of that picture. It felt like I was watching a scene from someone else's life, a moment captured between two people I'd never seen before in my life—that was how disconnected I felt from the photo even though it was me in it.

"Lauren," I whispered like the air had been stolen from my lungs before shoving the phone at her.

"Crap. Do you remember taking this?"

I shook my head and focused on steadying my breathing.

"Looks real bad," she said, and my eyes started to water once more.

"What do I write back to Cole? What do I tell him?"

"Tell him it's not what it looks like. Or it's a long story. Or I don't know," she said, sounding flustered because this was something she knew she couldn't fix. "Tell him you'll talk when he gets home."

"What if I really did sleep with Logan and he has more proof? What if there are more pictures from last night and he's just holding out until the right time to use them?" I asked, but Lauren didn't respond. There were too many what-ifs and not enough answers.

How the hell did I do this to myself?

I hated not knowing. It was the most helpless and horrible feeling ever. I couldn't even defend myself when it was all I wanted to do. I sat, staring at my phone, my fingers hovering over the screen as I tried to figure out exactly what to say to Cole. The last thing I wanted to do was ruin his game, but it was too late for that now. Logan had already crashed the cars head-on at full speed. All I could do at this point was hope we walked away from the wreckage, intact.

LAUREN HAD DRIVEN me earlier that afternoon to pick up my car. It had been sitting all alone in the parking lot, the last reminder of a night I couldn't remember but also wanted to forget.

I paced around the apartment until Lauren begged me to stop. But I couldn't sit still. The second I sat down, I would hop back up again. Stillness allowed my nervousness to fester and multiply. Walking around kept it at bay even if it didn't look like it from the outside.

Lauren peeked around her bedroom doorframe and asked, "Do you want me to leave before he gets here?"

"It doesn't matter," I said before changing my mind. "No. You should stay. Can you stay?" I knew that when it was all said and done, I was going to need my best friend.

"Of course I'll stay," she said, trying to sound reassuring

and calm. "It's going to be okay."

"It's not. It's not going to be okay. There's no way that Cole can get past this. Especially when I don't have any answers for him." I continued walking as I waited for him to arrive and put the final nail in the coffin of our relationship. It had been fun while it lasted.

The team had landed at the airport an hour earlier. I knew that Cole had to wait for his luggage and get on the team bus to the baseball field before he could get his truck and come here. It seemed so unfair that, only a few days ago, I had been saying *I love you* for the first time, and now, I was awaiting our fate, knowing in the back of my mind that it wouldn't be good. The weight of it all sat in my lungs like bricks. Heavy and concrete, making it hard for me to breathe.

My phone rang, and I knew that Cole was here. My legs started shaking, and I felt like I might have a panic attack even though I'd never had one before. I pressed some buttons on my screen, and I knew he was on his way inside. *How the hell am I supposed to face him?*

The door opened slowly, and Cole walked in, looking distraught and tired. I wondered if I looked the same to him. I'd been crying most of the day, and my eyes were puffed up and swollen. I hadn't even bothered to put on makeup.

"Hey," I said as his blue eyes clashed with mine from across the room.

He started to move toward me before stopping himself, and that single action, that moment where he stayed away from me instead of coming closer, told me everything.

"How was your last game?" I hadn't looked at the score

or how he had done because I couldn't bring myself to do it.

"I hit like shit. Went oh for four," he said like he couldn't have cared less about the one thing he loved more than anything else on the planet.

"I'm sorry," I said because I was. I knew that I was the reason he hadn't hit well and that Logan was probably throwing a party over what he'd accomplished.

"Can we not talk about my game?" His expression twisted, his eyes pulling together as his body tensed, and I knew that nothing I said was going to relax or calm him. "What happened last night, Christina? You have to tell me. I need to know. I'm going out of my fucking mind." His voice broke, and it took my heart with it.

"I don't—" I started to say as the tears spilled. I promised myself that I'd be strong. That Cole didn't deserve to feel sorry for me, but I couldn't help it. The tears refused to stay put. "I honestly don't know what happened. I don't remember the end of the night."

He looked around before pulling out a chair at the dinner table and sitting down. "Tell me what you do know," he said.

I moved across the room to join him at the table, a box of tissues in my hand. I sat down, put the box in front of me, and proceeded to tell him everything that I remembered. Up until Logan had offered to drive me home. The hours between that moment and when I opened my eyes this morning were still a complete blank. Not a clip of a scene or a blip in my memory bank. It was all a bunch of ... nothingness.

Cole stayed quiet. He looked at me before looking

anywhere else. "God, Christina, I don't want to believe Logan. I really, really don't. But I can't just …" He tugged at his hat, his fingers digging into it, and I could tell how torn up he was inside. "I can't just pretend like it couldn't have happened. Especially if you don't remember. It'll eat me up inside. It already is."

His confession was like an arrow straight to my heart. It punctured, piercing me with its pointed tip.

"I know." I knew that asking Cole to pretend it never happened wasn't realistic and that this was exactly the sort of thing that came back up if you tried to bury it. The ugliness would rear its head in other ways until it left nothing in its wake but what once had been.

"Is it possible?" he asked, his voice sounding so pained. "That you fucked him?"

I visibly winced with his choice of words. I hated them but hated the answer I had to give to him even more. "I guess it's possible. I really don't remember, Cole, but I can't imagine that I would ever let Logan touch me. Drunk or not."

"But he did touch you. He had his arm around you," Cole argued before pulling up the picture on his phone and showing it to me.

I never wanted to see that picture again.

"Maybe I lost my balance? Maybe I didn't know it was him? I don't know." I knew I sounded insane, like a drowning person desperately searching for air to stay alive.

"What were you drinking anyway?" he asked, like the question had just popped into his mind and he needed to get it out before he forgot about it again. "How did you, of all people, get so drunk that you blacked out?"

I still hadn't worked that part out yet in my own head. "I have no idea. I literally did one sake bomb with the band, and then I drank beer the rest of the night. The only thing I can reason out is that I must have had way more than I'd realized. I mean, way more. Because one second I was fine, and then the next, I could barely stand."

"Do you think he drugged you?" Cole's expression turned angry, his jaw tight, eyes narrowed as he held his breath and waited for my response.

"I didn't even know he was there."

Cole looked downright murderous as he worked out whatever was going on inside his head. "Where'd you get your drinks from? The bartender?"

"The server kept bringing them to me. I just assumed they were from the bartender because the guys in the band told him to take care of me earlier."

"Anything could have been in that beer, and you wouldn't know. How did you feel this morning when you woke up?"

Ashamed. Embarrassed. Mortified. "I felt like I had a hangover. My head hurt the most," I said before adding, "until I read my texts."

I wasn't sure what I expected to happen next. Maybe Cole would tell me he had proof that Logan had drugged me and that was why I'd blacked out and that it wasn't my fault and we could fix this and everything would be okay.

"Were you violently ill when you woke up? Like food-poisoning type of sick?" He leaned forward, elbows on the table, and I knew that he wanted my answer to be yes. That if I told him I was sick, then things would somehow make sense.

But I couldn't lie to him. "No." I had thrown up, but it wasn't the kind of violent vomiting he was asking about. I'd thrown up because my actions had made me sick.

He didn't say anything. He leaned away, his jaw unclenched and his fists unfurled, and I knew we were back to being in a situation that wasn't fixable. A situation I had no excuse for.

I sniffed and reached for a tissue. "How did you find out what happened? What did Logan say to you?"

Cole frowned. "He sent me a text. He thanked me for leaving town." He cleared his throat before continuing, "Then, he sent that picture of the two of you and said not to worry, that he kept you warm last night."

All words escaped me. *What can I possibly say to that?*

I had nothing.

No defense.

No case to argue.

No cards to play.

Cole reached for me, his strong hands covering my own as he pleaded, his blue eyes glassy. "God, Christina. I don't want to believe Logan. I really, really don't. Just tell me you didn't do it. Tell me you didn't do it and I'll believe you. Just say it never happened. Please." He looked down, and I watched as his shoulders shook lightly.

Cole Anders was crying.

I looked right at him even though he kept looking

downcast as the tears spilled across my cheeks. The last thing I wanted to do was lose him, but I couldn't do this in order to keep him. And I knew it. My heart ached so badly in my chest that I thought it might crack into pieces and fall out at my feet. A red carpet for him to walk out on.

I couldn't breathe. I couldn't think. All I did was ache.

"I can't say that. I want to, Cole, but I can't." My tears blurred my vision until Cole was barely visible. "I wish I remembered. I wish I could tell you with absolute certainty that Logan was lying and he was only doing this to get between us and mess with your head …"

"But you can't."

"But I can't. And I'm so sorry."

Cole pulled his hands from mine and looked up before wiping at his face, any trace of fallen tears gone. His throat bobbed up and down as he swallowed hard, and he suddenly composed himself in a single breath. "I am too. We can't be together anymore." He pushed up from the table without sparing me another glance.

His steps didn't falter on his way out, and it devastated me even more when he didn't slam the door closed behind him. I wanted to feel his anger, to see if he hated me as much as I hated myself. But Cole had closed it so gently, quietly, and soft, like it might fall off the hinges otherwise.

The door stayed perfectly intact.

I was the only thing falling apart inside this apartment.

Sleeping with the Enemy

Cole

I COULDN'T STAY a second longer. I had to leave. To get out of there and away from her before I lied, told her I forgave her and that everything between us would eventually be okay, when the truth was that nothing would ever be okay again. It'd physically fucking pained me to look at her. I knew how much she was hurting and that she never meant for this to happen, but none of that mattered. Not if she fucked another guy.

And if Logan had done something to her drink, which I wasn't putting past him, would it really change anything? Was I the kind of person who was strong enough to forgive her for sleeping with the enemy? I didn't think that I was. As shitty as that sounded, I knew that forgiveness of that kind came from a place I didn't think I was capable of reaching. It would tear me up from the inside out. Eat away at me until nothing was left.

My imagination was on overdrive, making up scenes and scenarios I couldn't unsee even though they were all in my head. I couldn't stop seeing Logan touching her ... or fucking her. My girl.

My girl.

That was why I had to end things. Why I had to walk away with my head held high even though I felt so damn low that I could barely look up. I had no idea how I'd ever trust her again. And I couldn't live like that—with the constant questioning and wondering. Especially when I was out of town for a game.

The last thing I needed was to be so focused on my girlfriend's whereabouts and actions that I couldn't focus on anything else, like my batting average.

Hopping into my truck, I pounded the steering wheel until my palms went numb. It wasn't enough.

I wanted to hit someone.

Hell, I wanted to hit everyone.

Nothing made any sense. And even though I didn't want to believe what had happened, the fact that Christina couldn't dispute it only made it worse. Part of me was thankful she wasn't blowing up my phone, but the other part of me—the insecure and vulnerable part—hated that she wasn't even trying. *Why isn't she apologizing nonstop and begging for my forgiveness?*

I knew it was irrational and illogical, but I still couldn't help but wonder, *Why am I not worth fighting for? Why does every female in my life walk out of it and never look back?*

I drove on autopilot toward the liquor store, picking up a case of beer before heading back to the baseball house; it was the worst possible place for me to be right now, but unfortunately, it was where I lived, so I couldn't really avoid it.

I was thankful when I didn't see any extra cars parked in the driveway and hoped that I'd be able to get into my room without anyone seeing me. I turned my phone off and decided not to turn it back on until the morning. The idea of what waited for me or how many of my teammates knew about her and Logan was enough to make me never want to turn it back on again.

I was so embarrassed.

Walking into the house, I visibly tensed, but it was unnecessary. No one was in the living room or anywhere near my room. Closing my door behind me, I tossed the twelve-pack on my bed and flung my body on top of my comforter. My plan for the night was to either drink myself into oblivion or fall the fuck asleep ... whichever one came first.

Christina and thoughts of my mom kept mixing together in my head. I didn't have time for that kind of pain. All I wanted to do was bury it, bury them together. I needed to stop thinking, stop feeling, stop ... *fucking ... hurting*, so I popped open my first beer and started drinking.

THANKFULLY, ONE BEER was all I'd gotten down before I passed out, fully dressed. Traveling on a road trip was physically exhausting on its own, but throw in all the emotional chaos from the past twenty-four hours, and I was dead to the world.

I woke up seconds before my alarm went off, thankful that I hadn't slept through it or hit Dismiss instead of Snooze. The last thing I needed was to miss class. I craved all the distractions that I could get right now. Anything that would keep me from thinking about her and missing her and wishing that I were the kind of man who could get past this and just forgive her.

If I had any hopes of forgetting about my situation in my Communications class, I was sorely mistaken. How was I supposed to know that we'd not only be studying word interpretation and how it was used in the press, but that I'd also get assigned the word *cheating* as my paper's focus? *You've got to be fucking kidding me.* Class couldn't end quickly enough.

Pulling my hat down low across my eyes, I made my way through campus without looking at anyone. If Christina was in the vicinity, I wouldn't know, and that was how it had to be. I wasn't sure that I could handle seeing her without getting choked up. And the very last fucking thing I wanted to do on this campus, in front of the whole damn school, was tear up.

Girls grabbed me as I walked by and said lewd shit, but I continued toward the parking lot, doing my best to ignore them as I pried their fingertips from my shirtsleeve without so much as a glance. I had no idea if they knew that I was technically single again, but I didn't care. I was tired of my personal life being public business. It would be fall semester all over again—baseball only, females not welcome.

Once I reached the parking lot, I tossed my shit in the passenger seat and drove over to the sports facilities complex for an early workout before practice. Putting my truck in park, I hopped out before noticing Logan two cars over. He had his keys in his hand and was watching me like a hawk.

"See something you like, LeDouche?" I tried to play it cool, like I wasn't fazed by the knife he'd taken to my relationship as he sliced it apart and then jammed it in my back.

He continued to stare at me like a fucking weirdo. "Not really. Just surprised to see you here, is all."

Did Logan really think it would be that easy to get rid of me? That when he ripped apart my heart, I'd fall with it?

"Why? Because you're so desperate for my spot on the field that you messed with my girl?"

"Wasn't that hard. She was willing enough," he said before smirking, taking three steps toward me.

He wanted me to hit him. He was basically fucking daring me to.

All my previous coolness flew out the proverbial window. What Logan had done was beyond just breaking guy code. There needed to be repercussions for his actions.

"If I find out that you drugged her drink, they'll have to pull me off your corpse."

His expression twisted like I'd already struck him. "Drugged her?" he asked with a sick laugh. "Is that what she told you? I didn't have to drug your girlfriend to get her to fuck me, Cole. All I had to do was ask."

I'd had enough of Logan taunting me, fucking with me, and trying to ruin my damn life in order to get my spot on the team. It was ridiculous, and I was tired of letting him get away with it because I was too worried about getting in trouble with Coach. If Logan wanted to push me past my breaking point, we were quickly heading there at breakneck speed, and I didn't care who saw.

"Bullshit." I dropped my bag to the ground at my feet and closed the space between us even further.

"Come to think of it." He looked toward the sky before looking back at me. "She was pretty drunk. But she still liked it. Told me at least a hundred times while my cock was in her pretty little mouth."

Fuck the consequences. This asshole deserved to get hit.

I pulled my right hand back and let it fly. When my knuckles connected with Logan's jaw, everything moved in slow motion—his head swiveling hard to the right as spit flew from his mouth and my arm fully extended so I couldn't reach him anymore. His eyes rolled back as he stumbled on his feet. I knew that if I gave him even the slightest push, he'd fall to the ground on his ass.

It felt so fucking good to hit him. I'd been holding it inside for so long when he never deserved my self-control.

"Should have done that a long time ago," I said as I braced myself for him to retaliate.

"Don't know what took you so long," Logan said as he spat at my feet.

I stepped back just in time as the blood narrowly missed hitting my shoes.

Logan looked around, and I did the same, realizing for the first time that we had an audience. Our teammates were all pulling up, some of them already out of their cars, watching us, and I noticed Mac and Chance in the distance, sprinting over.

"Hit me back," I growled because I wasn't done. I didn't want this fight to be over until Logan was a bloody fucking heap on the ground, pleading for me to stop. All of my anger and hurt and pain clawed at me from the inside, begging to be let out.

"I can't." He threw his hands in the air, high enough that everyone would see him surrendering. "Don't want to lose my new position since you sure as shit won't be playing it."

As he said the words, I realized that I didn't care that I'd hit him. I didn't care that I'd be getting in trouble and most likely suspended from some games. I only cared that I'd finally given Logan exactly what he always wanted—my spot on the roster and a chance at the draft.

He walked away, dramatically rubbing his jaw as blood spilled over his cut bottom lip, and I watched him go before I looked down at my hand. It throbbed with each beat of my heart, and I realized two things in that moment. The first was that I still had a heart. I hadn't been sure anymore. The second was that I thought I'd broken my knuckles.

"What the hell, man?" Mac said as he ran up to me, followed closely by Chance.

"You just couldn't *not* hit him, huh?" Chance asked.

"You didn't hear the things he said." I shook my hand out, noticing the pretty purple and blue colors it was already turning.

"You need ice," Mac groaned.

"You need an X-ray. Idiot," Chance chastised.

I glared at them both. "No one asked you two to stick around. Per fucking usual," I ground out, but my hand was throbbing.

"Just go." Chance shoved at my back.

I started walking, thankful that neither of them had brought up Christina or the situation. But I knew that they knew. I could tell by the way they looked at me. Did people realize how much they gave away with their eyes?

The two of them, my bodyguard shadows back in action, walked me into the physical trainer's room and dropped me off.

"He fucked up his hand," Chance said to one of the trainers, who was working out a knot in one of our pitcher's shoulders.

"Let me see," he said as he moved toward me.

I shoved my hand in his face.

He squeezed it in a few places, and when I didn't wince because I wasn't a pussy, he said, "It's most likely just bruised. If it was broken, I wouldn't be able to put pressure in those places at all. No matter how tough you think you are. You need to ice it, elevate it, and take ibuprofen. You're lucky."

"Sure," I said because I wasn't feeling so lucky. And that feeling dropped significantly as Coach Jackson screamed my name and told me to get the hell in his office. "I guess I'll take that ice to go," I said, and trainer dude was already filling a bag and reaching for a bandage to secure it in place.

When my hand was firmly wrapped in an ice cocoon, I walked into Coach's office, prepared for whatever hell was about to be unleashed.

"Shut the door," he growled, and I did what I had been told.

"Goddamn it, Anders!" Coach started as he slammed his fist on top of his desk, papers flying in the air as a result. "Sit down." He pointed at the lone chair.

I almost asked if I could stand instead but didn't want to make him any angrier.

"Why did you have to go and hit him?" he asked once I'd finally sat down and rested my iced hand on my lap.

"Does the reason matter, Coach? Will it get me in less trouble?" I wasn't trying to be a smart-ass, but I thought it might have come off that way.

"No. But you could at least tell me why, in your senior year, near the end of the damn season, you'd put everything at risk like this. You could have broken your damn hand!" Coach's face was turning an unnatural shade of red.

"You need some water, Coach?"

"I don't need any dang water. Now, tell me why."

"He messed with my girl," I admitted and waited for Coach to tell me what an idiot I was and how disappointed he was that I'd let a girl come between my dreams of going pro. I waited for the lecture that never came.

"Yeah"—his voice lowered—"I heard about that."

My head fell forward with my surprise. "You heard?"

How the hell did Coach know already? It just happened.

"Repeat this, and I'll deny it. Logan's an arrogant asshole. And he's always been jealous of you. I'm suspending you both for three games. If you aren't playing, neither is he."

I wanted to be pissed. Three games felt like a lifetime, especially at the end of the season when I knew our stands would be filled with scouts. But on the other hand, it was only three games, just one series. I knew I could live through that.

"Why are you suspending Logan? He didn't hit me back," I asked because he hadn't technically done anything that warranted a suspension.

"No, he didn't. He did something worse. You don't purposely mess with someone's girl. I won't tolerate that kind of attitude on my team. It's unbecoming behavior and unsportsmanlike, and I won't have it. Three games. Your hand had better be healed by then. Get out."

I pushed back from the chair, and it scraped against the floor on my way out. "I'm sorry for breaking your rules." I had known that I was going against code when I hit Logan. I would do it all over again, but I didn't want Coach to think I didn't respect him. "But thank you for not kicking me off the team," I added because I'd heard that Coach sometimes took his no-fighting-over-girls policy a little too far. Getting benched was an absolute, but getting kicked off was also a definite possibility.

"That's an urban legend, by the way," he said.

I looked at his face through surprised eyes. This whole time, I'd believed that people actually got kicked off the team because of girl drama.

"No shit?"

"No shit," he said, giving me one of his elusive grins. "Now, get out."

I walked out of his office and toward my locker when Mac and Chance appeared.

"What'd he say?" Mac asked.

"Three games," I informed them both and watched as their faces dropped in defeat. "Logan too," I added with a wicked grin.

"That's fire," Mac said as he made a fist and pounded knuckles with my left hand.

"Oh, Logan's gonna be pissed," Chance added as we all turned around in unison to Coach yelling Logan's name.

Logan had a literal bounce in his step, like he didn't have a care in the world, aside from his busted-up face. He had no idea that he was about to get benched right along with me.

"You going to be okay?" Chance genuinely looked concerned.

"Yeah. You aren't going to spiral into a depression, right? Like, we're not going to have to pick you up from a pile of your own puke or anything?" Mac added with a little too much creative detail.

I tapped the side of his face. "Thanks for the vote of confidence, asshole."

"I'm only asking because, first, you lose your girl, and then you lose three games in your senior year. It's a reasonable question." He sounded flustered, like there was no way on earth that he'd be able to tolerate what I was going through.

I surprised myself at how calm I felt. "I'll be fine. It's only three games. And to be honest, I'm going to need them anyway," I said, holding up my right hand, which was now soaking wet from the melted ice pack.

"No regrets?" Chance asked, and I knew he meant about it all—hitting Logan and the suspension.

"Fuck no."

"Wouldn't it be something if you came back from this suspension even better than when you left?" he asked with a smile that made girls all over campus swoon. Trust me, I'd seen it in action.

"That does sound like something," I said in agreement, suddenly filled with a determination to make this a comeback of epic proportions.

I knew deep down that everyone expected me to come back from this and head straight back down into another hitting slump. They would all assume that I was too rattled to focus because of what Logan had done to my personal life. But I planned to prove them all wrong. Every emotion would get released at the plate. I planned on taking my embarrassment, frustration, and anger out on the ball, and God help any pitcher who tried to get in my way.

The Girl with the Red Hair

Two Weeks Later

Christina

TWO WEEKS HAD passed. It didn't happen in a blur but more of a sluggish haze. It felt like time couldn't even bear to pass itself. That was how slowly it moved, like even it knew that each day simply marked another where we didn't speak. Two agonizing weeks of silence, where I drove myself mad, wondering if Cole missed me or not. Was he hurting the same way I was? I had no idea because not a single text had been sent or received by either one of us. No phone calls or missed calls either.

Did you know that two weeks was more than enough time for the entire campus to hear about what had happened and label me as the villain in this story? Of course you knew that. Anyone with half a brain would know that I'd be called a *whore* or a *slut* whenever I walked by a group of girls.

Fourteen days of not seeing Cole but hearing about him every single time I was on campus was a different kind of pain than it used to be. It felt like all the girls made sure I heard what he had been up to, where he had been, and how happy he seemed without me. Their words were like daggers; they hurt, and I bled. If I didn't have to go to class in order to graduate, I probably wouldn't have left my apartment. At least not until the dust had settled a little more ... or something else had taken my place on the gossip circuit.

Worse than all that though were the questions that random guys hurled at me like they had some sort of right to. They always seemed to do it when they were in packs though, so if I noticed one coming in my direction, I tried to change course. It didn't always work.

"Do you only fuck baseball players? What about the basketball team? You shouldn't discriminate against other athletes," this guy said to me one time as five of his friends looked on and laughed.

"Why don't you guys go fuck each other?" I fired back before walking away and willing myself not to cry.

Even though it looked like I had myself pulled together on the outside, mostly because I had actually started brushing my hair before I left the house, I was completely broken on the inside. And it had nothing to do with all the name-calling and messed up comments.

Heartache was a kind of pain you couldn't see, but it existed with each breath, reminding you that you were slowly bleeding out, slowly dying. The wounds might not be visible, but they ran deep.

I did my best to distract myself with work for The Long Ones and the waffle restaurant as often as I could, but there was only so much research that I could do before my eyes felt like they were going to fall out of my head. Not to mention the fact that anything regarding The Long Ones brought back the night I'd screwed it all up, and anything regarding the waffle restaurant ... well, it made me think about Cole, too, for obvious reasons. He had become so intertwined with every part of me that there was no escaping him.

When the distractions were gone and my thoughts invaded my mind, I crumbled. Every night since Cole had walked out of that apartment door, I'd cradled my phone, wanting to dial his number. But I knew there was nothing I could say that would make things better. Not that he would have even answered the phone in the first place. And that rejection still would have stung even though I deserved and expected it.

I wanted to text him all the time and tell him how much I missed him, just so he knew I was thinking about him, but it felt selfish somehow. Mostly because I knew I would have been holding my breath, waiting for him to tell me he missed me back. That wasn't fair to him, and I refused to do it to make myself feel better.

I sat at the kitchen table one morning, sipping coffee and wondering how long it would take before I forgave myself for what I'd done. *Why is it easier to forgive other people? Is it because we accept their flaws more willingly than we accept our own? Or is it because we hold ourselves to standards so high that there's no margin for error, that we simply aren't allowed to make those kinds of mistakes?*

"Have you called him yet?" Lauren rounded the corner and tapped her finger on the table, breaking me from the trance I had been in.

"And say what? *I still love you, but I still don't remember anything. And I miss you so much that it hurts with every breath I take. And I know you think you hate me for what I did, but you could never hate me more than I hate myself.*"

Her eyes widened. "It's a hell of a start."

"I can't do that."

"Why not?"

"Because nothing's changed. If Cole was willing to forgive me and wanted me back, then he would reach out."

I took a small drink of my coffee, which had now grown lukewarm. Lukewarm coffee was as gross as lukewarm beer. I pushed it away, and Lauren grabbed it as she moved into the kitchen to pour herself a cup.

"He's stubborn. But you also hurt his pride. And his ego. He can't be the one to chase you this time. Not after what happened. It would make him look weak."

"I know. You're right. But I don't know how to fix it. And until I can actually do that, I can't reach out to him."

"Just promise me that you'll think about it. It's been weeks. At least send him a text and tell him you're sorry and that you miss him. Extend that olive branch. After all, he did get suspended for three games because of you." She placed two fresh cups of coffee on the table as she sat down next to me.

"He got suspended for hitting Logan. That was going to happen with or without me in the equation."

"That's not how it happened," she said with a look that told me she knew more than I did on the subject.

"How did it happen? And why are you just telling me now?" I asked, feeling annoyed because the suspension was old news.

"Logan was talking about you, and Cole lost his temper."

Even after everything, Cole still defended me? "Are you sure?"

"I'm very sure. Logan said something awful about you, and Cole punched him in the face for it," Lauren said with a laugh. "Wish I could have seen that. How were we both so wrong about Logan?" she asked, and I knew she was thinking back to when Logan had first pursued me and how she had encouraged me to say yes because he seemed so nice and un-Cole-like.

I blew on my coffee before taking a tentative sip. "I guess he's a really good actor."

"Or a sociopath. He definitely would have sold you into sex trafficking," she said, and I rolled my eyes, assuming I was about to get another lecture. "No. You roll your eyes, but I'm mad I didn't see it. I pride myself on being a good judge of character, and he completely tricked me."

He had tricked us both.

"I don't care about Logan," I said, sounding as exhausted as I felt. "I only care about Cole."

"Yeah? Then, you should tell him." She stuck out her tongue before pushing up from the table.

"I can't mess with his head like that. His season's almost over. And you've seen his batting average."

I gave her an incredulous look because Cole had absolutely been dominating at the plate since he came back from his suspension. He was hitting home runs in almost every game. Not that I'd witnessed any of them in person, but I'd been following him online, quietly cheering on his success from behind my computer screen.

"He is hitting like crazy. But you see how mad he looks? He's only hitting like that because he's picturing Logan's face on the ball. Guarantee it." She gave me a small smile.

"Yeah. Or mine," I argued, and she let out a loud groan as she reached for her coffee.

"I need to get ready for class. But seriously, think about it. Just tell him you heard what he did to Logan. Tell him you love him. Tell him you'll run away to an island and give him a whole baseball team of babies if that's what he wants. Tell him you know he'd never sell you to the black market."

"You're ridiculous."

"But at least I'm cute." She flipped her blonde hair before disappearing into her room and leaving me alone with my thoughts.

I used to love my alone time, craved it even. Being alone never used to bother me. But that was before. Alone time now equaled emotional torture, overthinking, and a brain that wouldn't shut off. Running Lauren's words through my mind, I decided against reaching out to Cole, no matter how badly I wanted to. He needed to focus, and I'd promised myself that I wouldn't screw that up for him.

THAT AFTERNOON, DURING class, the girl next to me kept glancing over at me. I could see her in my peripheral vision, but I didn't turn to make eye contact. I knew I wouldn't be able to keep my composure if I did.

"Aren't you the one who cheated on Cole?" she whispered toward me, and I broke my no-looking rule as I stared but gave her no response. "How could you do that to him? And with Logan of all people. Gross. Are you stupid?" When I continued to stay silent, she ended with, "Yeah. You're obviously stupid. Can't even answer my question."

The girl next to her leaned forward and added, "Who cares why she did it? At least Cole's back on the market. Thanks for fucking up, by the way. I, for one, really appreciate it."

They both started giggling as I packed up my things and walked out, my eyes already misting over, my heart pounding in my chest. Pushing open the glass door, I stepped outside and immediately started following wherever my legs wanted to take me as I wiped at my eyes and sucked in a steadying breath.

"Christina?" a voice I didn't recognize shouted my name.

I knew I couldn't take any more confrontations today. Just that small one had pushed me over the emotional edge I'd been teetering on for weeks.

"Christina! Wait!"

I looked up to see a redhead in the distance, waving at me. I had no idea who she was, but she continued heading my direction, and I stopped walking altogether.

"Hi," she said with a big smile when she reached me like we were long-lost friends.

I tilted my head and knew I had a confused look on my face. "Hi," I said back, sounding unsure, and she laughed.

"Cory." She reached out her hand for me to shake. "We met a few weeks ago."

"We did?" I searched my mind and came up empty.

"Yeah. At The Bar?"

The last time I'd gone to The Bar was the night I tore my relationship apart. "When The Long Ones were playing?" I asked, and she nodded enthusiastically.

"Yeah. I'm actually really glad I ran into you. I just wanted to make sure you were okay after that night. I didn't have your phone number or anything, and I don't fuck with online stuff."

This girl talked a mile a minute, and to be honest, I had no idea what the hell she meant. *Why is she asking if I'm okay?*

"I'm confused," I said, deciding to be perfectly honest.

"I'm not surprised. You were pretty wasted," she said.

I winced. It hadn't been my finest moment, and it had resulted in my biggest regret.

"Yeah. I don't really remember anything past a certain point that night," I admitted, feeling like an idiot.

"Again, not really surprised." Cory smiled. "You could barely tell me how to get to your apartment."

Wait. What? "Come again?"

"Your apartment. When I drove you home," she said the words super slow, assuming that I had remembered at least that part.

But I hadn't. Because I couldn't even remember leaving the bar in the first place. Which was why I'd believed Logan when he said he was the one who had brought me home and insinuated that we'd had sex in his car before I went inside.

All this time, I wasn't sure if I had done it or not. All this time, I'd been hating myself over the possibility.

"You drove me home that night?" I asked as the fog started to clear.

"Yeah."

"Me and Logan, right?" His name was like acid on my tongue, and I wanted to spit it out. I hated how just his name caused a visceral reaction in me.

"Logan? That asshole on the baseball team? Not a chance. I drove you home. Just you. But not for his lack of trying." She sounded annoyed and disgusted but resolute.

"Okay. Wait. I'm really confused." I held up a hand to stop her from saying anything else because I needed to focus. I also needed to know every piece of information that she had for me about that night. "Can I ask you a couple more things? Do you have time to fill in the blanks for me if you can?"

Cory nodded, pulling out her phone and glancing at it before shoving it in a back pocket. "I have class in a bit, but yeah, I have time."

"Okay. Thank you. Sorry, I really don't remember. Um ..." I shook my head, forcing myself to pull it together.

"So, Logan didn't drive me home. But he was there, right?" It was a stupid first question because I'd seen the picture of us together, so of course he had been there.

"Yeah, he was there. He was watching you the whole night. I was ordering a drink at the bar, and I saw him sitting in, like, this dark corner with a weird expression on his face. I wanted to know what he was looking at. And it was you." She fidgeted with her backpack before taking it off and throwing it on the ground. "Shit's heavy."

"He was watching me?"

She nodded and opened her eyes wide. "More like he was stalking your every move, following you with his eyes. He gave me such a bad vibe that I just kind of kept my eye on you the whole time. Which I know sounds super creepy, but we girls have to stick together, right?"

I almost didn't know what to say in response. It was such a surreal situation. "I've just never had someone I didn't know look out for me like that before. Or maybe no one ever has," I said with a laugh, and she smiled.

"Well, I knew who you were," she said like that was the most obvious thing on the planet, which made me feel even worse because I didn't think I'd ever seen her before in my entire four years at this school.

"You did?"

"Yeah. I mean, everyone knows you're Cole's girlfriend. You can't avoid that fact even if you hate baseball and baseball players. Which I do. No offense." She put her hands up.

"None taken."

"It's just that baseball's super boring. I don't know how you stand it." She rolled her eyes and continued, "Anyway, I knew you and I went to school together. I knew you were dating Cole. Which also made the whole Logan looking at you with his beady, little, untrusting eyes even sketchier."

"I can't believe this," I said, shocked by her revelations. "You don't even know what you've done for me. I don't know how to thank you."

"Don't worry about it. It's not a big deal." She played it off like it was nothing, but she couldn't have been more wrong.

We hadn't known each other, yet she'd made sure that I was okay that night. A complete stranger taking care of another for no other reason than she believed it was the right thing to do.

"It is though. It's such an extremely big deal. Anything could have happened to me that night. And this whole time, I thought something had."

"You thought something happened to you?" Her eyes grew big.

I nodded. "I did. Hey, this is random, and I'm sure you don't know, but any idea how I got so drunk in the first place? That's one thing that doesn't make any sense to me. I can usually handle my beer, and I would never get that out of control while I was alone."

"The bartender kept sending you those sake drinks all night. He definitely knew Logan, too, because I saw them talking a lot."

I shook my head, looked up at the sky, and then met her

crystal-green eyes. "Every time I got a beer, there was sake in it?"

"Oh, yeah. You didn't know that?"

"No," I said as things finally started to add up. "I thought I was just drinking beer. I had no idea why I was so drunk."

"I know how strong those sake bombs are. People are always like, *Oh, it's just a rice wine; it's no big deal.* And then you're hammered."

I laughed like we were two old friends because she had just given me the keys to my emotional freedom. She'd cut off the chains I'd bound myself with and set me loose.

"I know you already told me, but I have to ask you again, so I can hear you say it one more time." I let out a crazy-sounding laugh. "Logan did not drive me home?"

She smiled as she reached for her backpack and slung it back over her shoulder. "Logan did not drive you home. I left to go to the restroom, and when I came back, he was dangling his keys in front of you. He got you as far as the parking lot before I took you from him."

"You took me from him?"

She nodded. "He had his arm around you and was telling you something about Cole by the time I got outside. I'm not sure what he said, but I definitely heard Cole's name. And then you got the biggest smile on your face, and he took a picture. The second he lowered his phone, you turned your head, almost like you were realizing he was there for the first time, and you told him to get away from you."

"Wow," I said through my total shock. "That picture looked really bad."

"I bet."

"Then, what happened?" I was enthralled, basically on the edge of my seat, hearing about all the things that had gone on that night that I still had absolutely no memory of.

"I told him that you called me to come get you. He didn't like that very much. Tried to insist that he'd be the one to take you home. He said it was his job to take care of his teammates' girls while they were away, but I think you spit on his shoes. Or at least, you tried."

A loud laugh escaped me. "Go, drunk me." For the first time, I felt almost proud of how I had acted that night.

"You also said that you hated him and that Cole was going to eat him for breakfast when he came home." She started laughing. "He did not like any of that."

"Oh my God." I covered my mouth with my hand. "I can imagine that setting him off."

"He was pretty enraged, but he disappeared as soon as you were in my car and he realized he wasn't going to win."

"I can't believe you drove me home. Did you bring me inside?" I grew nervous that maybe, after that, Logan had still shown up at my place in some sort of fit, and I'd let him in or something.

"I did actually. You weren't the best at walking. I made sure you got inside your apartment, and you told me to be careful of your roommate." She tossed her red hair. "You said she bites."

"I did?" It was so weird, hearing things about myself that I had no memory of. I kept questioning everything—not because I didn't believe her, but because I was learning about it for the first time.

"Yeah. You told me to answer all of her questions and make sure to tell her that I wasn't into sex trafficking and wouldn't get you kidnapped." She laughed, and I laughed too.

There was no way that Cory was lying or making any of this up. She knew way too many things. I was mad that I had been so stupid that night. Honestly, anything could have happened to me, and no one would have known.

"My roommate wasn't there though, right?"

"No. No one was there," Cory said. "I fed you a glass of water and put you in your room."

Suddenly, a vision of me standing in front of the mirror with my shirt on inside out flashed in my head. "Oh! Do we know why my shirt was inside out?"

"Ha!" She started explaining, "Because, apparently, it was too hot in my car, but you didn't want the windows down because it was too cold outside. You took your shoes off, and then you pulled off your shirt and curled into the seat. I told you to put your shirt back on, and you did, but it was inside out. Basically, I was just happy you were dressed."

I covered my face with my hand because my behavior was so embarrassing, but holy shit, it was so much better than what I'd been thinking this entire time. "I'm sorry. I'm honestly mortified right now."

"You were pretty entertaining. Anyway, I'm glad I ran into you, so I could fill in all those missing pieces. I'm also glad you're okay. I was a little worried you might die in your sleep or something, and I am not cut out for prison."

"Not dead. But thank you. You have no idea what you've done. No idea." I leaped forward and wrapped her in a bear hug.

She awkwardly hugged me back before she shifted away. I knew my compliments and affection were making her uncomfortable.

"Can I ask you something?"

"Sure."

"What did you think happened to you that night?"

I let out a cough before launching into it. "Logan said he drove me home and fucked me in the backseat of his car. Then, he texted Cole a picture of us together, and I'm sure you can guess the rest."

"You thought you'd slept with Logan this whole time?" she practically shouted before looking around.

"I couldn't remember anything. Even though I didn't want to believe that I'd do something like that, I had no memory telling me that I didn't."

She shook her head, as if in total disbelief. "What kind of person does that? Who in their right mind lies just to hurt someone else?"

"A competitive person? A vindictive person? A psychopath? I just …" I let out a breath as everything hit me all at once like a wave forcing me underneath it. "I can't believe it was all a lie. That I really didn't do anything with him."

"Except spit on his shoes," she reminded me.

"Except spit on his shoes," I repeated.

She told me she needed to get to class, and I thanked her again. And awkwardly hugged her again. And exchanged phone numbers before she sped away. I stood there, watching her go, her hair looking like a flame against the blue sky, as every piece of information she'd told me started to fully sink in.

Logan had lied. It was all a lie.

Holy shit.

The Truth

Christina

I SAT IN my car, torn between going home to talk with Lauren first or going straight to find Cole and spilling my guts. I glanced at the clock on the dashboard and realized that he would still be at practice. His schedule gave me the answer I needed.

Driving home, I was on edge, antsy, hoping like hell that Lauren would be there. I needed to talk this out with her, tell her what I'd just learned, and figure out the best way to inform Cole. For whatever reason, I felt like I needed an actual plan.

I ran through the parking lot, into the complex, and busted through the door like someone was chasing me.

Lauren screamed, "You scared the heck out of me!"

"I'm so glad you're here!" I shouted, breathing hard. *Damn, I am seriously out of shape.*

"What's going on?"

"I didn't sleep with Logan," I said between labored breaths. "Did you hear me? I. Did. Not. Sleep. With. Logan."

Her eyes grew wide. "How do you know?"

I leaned over, my breathing still erratic as I held up a finger. My heartrate, my mind—everything was firing at a rapid pace. "Let me get some water first."

"Screw your water," she shouted with a laugh. "Get over here and tell me everything."

I poured a glass and quickly downed it before making my way to the couch. She sat there, listening, as I filled her in on Cory, her mouth agape the entire time until I said, "The end."

"I can't believe this. I mean, I can because I never really thought you slept with Logan in the first place, but now, we have actual proof that you didn't."

"I know."

"Does Cole know?"

"Not yet." I shook my head.

"He's going to kill Logan," she said with a stern look, and I realized that I hadn't even really thought about him or what Cole would do to him.

"He deserves it."

"Are you mad? I'm mad! Why aren't you mad?"

I folded my arms into my lap. "I am mad. But mostly, I'm relieved more than anything. I'm happy I know the truth. And that I can stop hating myself every time I look in the mirror."

She placed her hands on the top of my arms. "You need to find Cole."

"He's still at practice."

She cocked her head to the side and studied me. "You could be sitting in the parking lot right now, making sure you see him as soon as he steps off the field. But you're not.

Why?"

I realized that I was nervous. I had wanted this information so badly, but now that I had it, I was terrified that it might not change anything. That maybe it was too late. "I wanted to talk it out first. Do I just tell him everything? We haven't even talked once since he walked out of the apartment that day."

"I know."

"What if he's moved on? Or is totally over me? Or doesn't care anymore that it didn't happen?"

"Let's pretend for a second that any of those options could be real." She rolled her eyes before continuing, "He still deserves to know the truth."

"You're right. You're totally right," I agreed because, of course, Cole deserved to know. "So, what do I do?"

"Honestly? You go find him and talk to him."

"What if he won't listen?" I said, admitting my biggest fear.

"You won't know until you try."

Pushing off the couch, I nodded and walked into my bedroom to pull myself together a little better as Lauren shouted from behind me, "I feel like you should be a little more excited about all this than you are!"

"I am excited!" I lied because I was scared more than anything else even though I wasn't entirely sure why.

I grabbed a hoodie and threw it on over my high-waisted jeans before touching up my makeup to help me look a little less tired and a little more alive. Surprisingly, my hair looked really soft and pretty, so I didn't mess with it. Staring at my reflection for a minute more, I apologized for being so hateful lately. And then I silently promised myself that no matter what happened with Cole, we would get through this and be okay.

I DROVE AROUND town, looking for Cole's truck, desperate to find him so I could repair what I'd thought I'd irrevocably broken. But Cole wasn't at the batting cages, his truck wasn't at the field, and he wasn't at his house. I racked my brain, trying to figure out where he could be, when it hit me.

It was a long shot, but I held out hope as I drove the winding lane all the way to the top. My stomach flipped when I saw his truck in the far corner of the structure, all alone. There wasn't another car up here. Cole's silhouetted frame sat in the bed, and I pulled slowly next to where it was parked and cut the engine, a million emotions running through me.

Unlatching my seat belt, I opened the door and stepped out, placing my elbows on the edge. "Hey," I said.

"How'd you find me?" His voice was cold, and a part of me had expected that, so I tried to tamp down the hurt that followed it.

"I remembered you saying that you liked to come here to think sometimes."

"Yeah? Well, it hasn't been working." He faced straight

ahead, his eyes avoiding mine like the plague.

"It hasn't?"

"I used to come here to clear my head. But no. It doesn't work anymore. Not since that day at your apartment." He turned and looked right through me. "Why are you here, Christina?"

It took effort to swallow. My throat felt closed. I was nervous. *Why am I so nervous to tell him what I considered to be relationship-changing news?* "I came to talk to you."

"Talk then." He waved a hand but turned away from me, his eyes back on the sky as he tossed his baseball hat off.

I wanted to run my fingers through his dark hair. I wanted to touch him again.

"I didn't sleep with Logan. He lied," I blurted out and waited for him to focus his attention back onto me, but he didn't budge. "He lied about everything, Cole."

I watched him slowly nod.

"How do you know?"

"There was this girl. Um, her name is Cory. Anyway, she came up to me today and told me she was glad she ran into me. She was asking if I was okay." I launched into what had happened earlier that afternoon as Cole finally turned to watch me with piqued curiosity. "She was asking me because she drove me home that night from The Bar. Not Logan."

"What else did she say?" He sat up straighter, and I knew I had his full attention.

I filled him in, not sparing a single detail.

When I finished, he asked, "And you believe her?"

"Absolutely."

Cole let out a small laugh, and it practically melted my heart on the spot. "You spit on Logan's shoes?"

"Apparently," I offered with a halfhearted shrug.

"You still don't remember anything?"

"No. I wish hearing the truth had made it all come rushing back, but it didn't."

After talking to Cory, I had hoped to remember something from that part of the night, but it was like it never existed in my head in the first place. It was like trying to grab pieces that weren't there.

"So, Logan lied. About everything," he said in a very matter-of-fact tone that turned downright murderous.

"Yeah."

Cole stayed deathly quiet. He didn't move a muscle. I wasn't sure what I had expected, but a part of me had definitely hoped for a movie-like reaction from him. One where he swept me into his arms and swung me around before kissing me senseless and telling me that we could be together forever now. But none of those things were happening.

Why aren't any of them happening?

"Do you believe me?" I asked, wondering if maybe he didn't think I was telling the truth. I had believed Cory's version of events, but that didn't mean that Cole did.

"I do."

"Then, why aren't you acting like it?"

"I'm sorry." He looked at me, his head shaking. "I do believe you. But it's all so overwhelming, you know?" His eyes pulled together, and he looked so genuinely conflicted.

"All of this information at once, totally contradicting what I'd believed for weeks. Aren't you overwhelmed by it all?"

"Sure. I guess. But, Cole, I still love you. This is nuts. I didn't break us. I didn't do anything." I started getting angry. *Why did I have to convince him to want me back or give me another chance?* "Don't you love me?"

"Of course I still love you," he said in barely a whisper, but I heard it, and the words filled my heart with hope.

"Then, we can fix this, right? Or is it too late?" I asked the question and instantly dreaded his response.

Please don't say it's too late.

The Past Is a Mothereffer

Cole

*W*HAT THE HELL *is wrong with m*e? The only girl I'd ever loved was standing next to my truck, telling me that everything that had broken us up in the first place was all a lie. A fucking made-up story by a guy who was clearly more psychotic than I'd thought. So, why wasn't I taking her into my arms and getting back together with her on the spot?

I knew why. I knew exactly why, but I wasn't sure I wanted to admit it to anyone outside of myself. Honestly, it had been a hell of a realization all on its own when it hit me out of nowhere one night. I felt conflicted after hearing the truth. I'd been through an emotional wringer the past few weeks, and learning that it had all been for nothing ... well, I wasn't flooded with relief like I would have expected. Instead, I was exhausted. A bone-deep tired that came from holding all your emotions inside for way too long. And I was angry. So fucking angry. But not at her.

"Cole?" Her voice sounded sad and deflated.

She must have figured that the truth would instantly fix things between us, and I couldn't blame her for that. Maybe for someone else, it might have. Maybe another guy would have only needed that information to hop right back into the relationship, no questions asked, but I couldn't do it.

I needed to tell her how it had devastated me when she never tried to reach out. Not once had she texted to tell me she missed me or that she was sorry or to beg for my forgiveness. She'd gone completely silent, and that hurt more than anything else ever could have. Her silence had made me feel worthless and forgettable.

"What took you so long?" I asked.

"What do you mean? So long to what?" She was confused.

"You haven't said a word to me in weeks. You let me walk away from you without a fight. You just let me go like it didn't even matter that I was leaving."

She looked completely shocked. She had expected a way different response from me, and I couldn't blame her. If the situation had been reversed, I would have expected one too.

"I," she stuttered, "I … didn't know how to fight for you when nothing had changed."

"But you didn't even try."

"I didn't know you wanted me to."

"Everyone wants to be fought for. Even us guys."

Logically, I understood why she hadn't reached out to me. But emotionally, I hadn't been prepared for it. Her absence had triggered something deep within me that I'd kept buried for the majority of my life.

She hopped into the truck bed, uninvited, and sat next to me. "I'm fighting for you now. I'm fighting for us now. But I can't do it by myself."

"I need some time," the words slipped out before I could catch them, and I watched as her blue eyes crumbled before she quickly pulled herself together.

"You need some time?"

"Yeah. I need to sort through some stuff. You gotta give me at least that."

She bit on her bottom lip, and I could tell that this wasn't at all how she had wanted things to go. But I was currently a fucking mess inside. A tornado of emotions and feelings and past issues I'd never dealt with or even acknowledged until now.

"I really need to go." I stood up, hopped out of my truck, and walked over to the side where she was.

I extended my hand to help her out and then pulled her into my arms and held on tight.

"I'll give you space, Cole," she said against my chest, her breath hot. "But are we okay? Are we not okay?"

Releasing her, I took a step back. "I'll call you," I said, not answering her question because I didn't have any idea what we were, and I didn't want to lie.

She stood still as I got into the driver's seat and started up my truck. As I pulled away, she was still standing in the same spot, her arms wrapped around her middle. I knew that leaving her like that was a little fucked up, but I couldn't ... I couldn't pull my head together with her standing there, looking at me like I was crazy for not making this easier.

Apparently, I had mommy issues, and they couldn't be ignored any longer. They had busted out of the box I'd kept them in and refused to go back inside. I needed to talk to my dad and get his perspective, his advice. I got onto the freeway and headed for home.

When I pulled into the driveway, all of the lights inside the house were on, and my dad's work truck sat outside. I hadn't called him or given him any warning that I was coming over. I knew he wouldn't care, but he wasn't expecting me.

I knocked on the front door a few times before opening it and walking in.

"Cole!" my dad said with a smile.

He looked tired, the bags around his eyes deeper than I remembered them being. He had missed a lot of my games lately because he was working long hours on some new housing development over an hour away.

"Hey, Dad," I said before giving him a bear hug.

"I was just making dinner. You hungry?" He headed back into the kitchen and stirred at something on the stove before opening the oven door and peering inside.

"Sure," I said because whatever it was, it smelled delicious.

"Go set the table," he said with a nod, and just like that, we fell into our old routine.

It used to be like this every night after I'd come home from baseball practice and he'd come home from work. He cooked, and I set the table.

"You're lucky I bought extra at the store; otherwise, we'd have to go out."

"What is it?"

"Salmon." He waggled his eyebrows.

I swore my mouth started watering on the spot. I couldn't remember the last time I'd had seafood, and suddenly, it was all I wanted.

"So, what brings you home?" he asked as he pulled the fish out of the oven to cool, and the smell of spices and seasoning grew even stronger.

"I just wanted to talk," I said, feeling a little uncomfortable because my dad and I didn't usually go around, having heart-to-heart conversations all the time. Or ever.

"Is everything okay?" He glanced at me as he scooped rice out of the pot and into a large bowl and set it on the table before heading back to grab the fish.

"Yeah," I said before contradicting myself. "No."

He laughed, his eyes wrinkling in the corners. "Well, which one is it?" he asked before sitting down and watching me with curious eyes. "Baseball's good, right? I've been following you online. You have the best batting average on the team and the second in the whole league."

I had known about the team part but not about the league. I was too busy actually playing to stalk online stats. Plus, I knew how quickly things could change. All it took was one bad or good game for everything to shift around. "Baseball's great, Dad. But there's this girl."

"There always is."

I gave my dad the CliffsNotes version of Christina's and my relationship as he ate and asked questions every so often. When I got to the parts about Logan and what he'd done and everything we'd been through the past few weeks up until today, he leaned forward, arms on the table like this was the most interesting thing he'd ever heard. When I finished, he stared at me.

Taking a swig of his beer, he asked, "So, what's the problem? You found out it was all a lie, so why are you here with me and not with her? What am I missing? Unless this is about Logan? Do you want to know if I think you should kick his ass again or not?"

He forked more fish into his mouth as he waited for my answer.

"No. I'm not here because of Logan, although I do want to fucking destroy him. Coach might not be so forgiving the second time around."

"Your coach might help you." He shrugged, and I laughed as I tried to imagine Coach Jackson actually fighting a player. "So, if this isn't about Logan, then it's about Christina. I'll ask you again, what's the issue?"

"How do I forgive her, Dad?" I looked at him and felt myself getting worked up. The last thing I wanted to do was lose it in front of my old man, but I was afraid I was about to.

"Forgive her for what exactly? She didn't do anything. There's technically nothing to forgive," he said, and I knew logically that he was right, but my emotions ran deeper than that.

"I don't know how to forgive her for letting me walk away," I said with a wince, feeling like the admission made me weak somehow.

"That's a tough one, son. She was in a position she

couldn't win. Until she knew the truth, what was she supposed to do?"

"She was supposed to do something. Hell, she was supposed to do anything. But she did nothing." I dropped my fork, and it clanged against the plate. "Sorry."

"It's okay," he reassured me before asking, "Why are you so mad?"

"I'm mad because she stayed quiet. And because she stayed away. And because she left me holding a bag of fucked up emotions I couldn't process, just like Mom had done when she left." I hated the things that were coming out of my mouth, but I also felt a sense of relief in saying them. They'd held me hostage for so long, and I hadn't even realized it. All this time, I'd been living with these emotional demons inside of me that had nowhere to go.

"Oh, Cole. This girl is not your mother."

"But it feels the same," I said as a single tear escaped. I quickly wiped it away and cleared my throat.

"But it's not." He reached across the table and covered my hand with his. "You can see that, can't you?" His voice was calmer than I'd ever heard before, and it encouraged me to continue opening up.

"Why am I so easy to walk out on?" the question spilled from my mouth like it had come straight up from my heart, and my dad exhaled like he'd been sucker-punched in the stomach.

"Cole, your mom leaving had nothing to do with you and everything to do with her inability to be an unselfish parent. You were the perfect kid, and I mean that. I couldn't ask for a better son. I could have asked for a better mother for him though, and I'm sorry I failed you on that front."

I cocked my head back and huffed, "You're a great dad. You've never failed me."

"Good. Then, you'll think I'm smart and listen to everything I tell you," he said with a grin, and I let out a small laugh. "Your girl, Christina, did not abandon you. She only walked away because you'd asked her to. And she stayed away because she thought she'd ruined things forever. Imagine how she must have felt, thinking she was the reason you guys broke up. She had to be beating herself up the whole time you were apart. And the second she learned the truth and had the ammunition to win you back, she ran straight to you. And you ran straight here." He frowned before taking a bite of fish.

"I'm an idiot," I said with a sigh.

"You're not an idiot. You're just hurting. But don't punish this poor girl because you never got the chance to punish your mom."

"Shit, Dad. That was brutal." *But is it true? Am I punishing her for what my mom did to me as a kid?* I hated that he might be right.

"Truth hurts." He took a swig of beer as I finished up the rest of my plate. "But you need to go forgive that girl. And apologize for being an ass. You'll regret it if you don't. I can see it in your eyes." He pointed his bottle at me.

I knew he was right. I was already regretting walking away from her earlier without reassuring her that we'd be okay. But I hadn't known it at the time. I'd needed the kind of clarity that could only come after a talk with my old man. I'd needed to come here first.

"I can't believe I'm back in this position," I said as I swallowed my last bite.

"And what position is that?" my dad asked, his tone bordering on smart-ass.

I barked out a laugh. "The one where I'm asking for *her* forgiveness again. She's going to get tired of my apologies."

"Well, you'd better come up with a plan then. Don't just show up at her place half-cocked later, like some late-night booty call. Isn't that what you kids call it these days?"

"Please, don't ever say booty call again," I groaned. "And no, by the way. We don't say that."

I had sort of planned on driving over to Christina's apartment after I left here, but when I looked at the clock on the wall, I realized that my dad might be right. It would be pretty late by the time I got back to Fullton, and I had a game tomorrow.

As much as I wanted to make things right, I needed my rest. The season was almost over, and I couldn't afford to do anything that might mess with my chances to get drafted. My apology would have to wait until tomorrow.

"We'll come up with a foolproof plan after your game tomorrow."

I perked up. "Wait, you're coming?" I loved having him at my games and was honestly bummed out whenever he couldn't make it.

"You bet your ass I am." He slapped his bottle of beer on the table, and it wobbled before falling over. He quickly reached for it and stood it back upright. "We'll go get your girl back right after I slash Logan's tires, pull the spark plugs, unplug the battery, and maybe stick a banana in his tailpipe. She won't be able to resist two of us after she hears about that."

I couldn't stop laughing as I pictured it. And I wasn't sure if he was joking or not. I decided not to ask. I couldn't get in trouble for it happening if I didn't know anything about it, right?

Sounded like the perfect plan to me.

Fight for Him

Christina

COLE LEAVING ME in the parking structure messed with my head more than I wanted to admit. When I got home, Lauren was amped up, expecting me to be practically flying through the door with good news. And when I didn't, she let me walk away and gave me time alone. She knew that when I was ready to talk, I'd find her.

I wasn't ready just yet.

What I was, however, was conflicted and confused. I couldn't stop overthinking and replaying his words in my head. I had no idea how I was supposed to handle things. I'd promised Cole that I'd give him space, and even though I planned on doing exactly that, I started to wonder if that wasn't what he really wanted. In my opinion, what he'd asked for equaled no contact from me, but going no contact with him last time had made him think I didn't care.

Is this a test of some sort?

Is he telling me to do one thing but expecting me to do the opposite?

"Laurennnnn," I shouted from my bedroom, and I

instantly heard her thundering toward me.

"Oh, finally. Please tell me what happened. You know I'm sitting out there, playing it cool, but inside, I'm dying. Fill me in!" She jumped on my bed and landed next to me, sending my pillows flying all over.

I told her what had happened. What Cole had said and how he had interpreted my silence. I'd grown so used to the shocked expression on her face that I swore it was all I saw lately.

"I actually feel really bad for him." She looked so sad.

"I know. Me too." I'd had no idea that Cole would take my being quiet after our breakup as my not caring about him or our relationship. Lauren pursed her lips, and I could tell she was dying to say something. "Say it."

"Your silence. It triggered him. It's practically textbook."

"Okayyyyyy," I said wearily because I knew that I'd upset him, but what did she—

"Oh my God." I clasped my hand over my mouth as it all hit me. "His mom."

Lauren nodded slowly and repeated, "His mom."

I wouldn't have said anything about Cole's mom or even brought her up if Lauren hadn't already known about it. It wasn't my story to tell, but she had found out about it a couple of years back and asked me if it was true. She'd said that it was pretty common knowledge around campus, but I'd never heard anyone talking about it before.

"It makes perfect sense that he would react like that. I should have put it together." She snapped her fingers in the air. "I am a psych major after all." She sounded annoyed with herself for not catching the signs.

"To be fair, you did tell me to reach out to him."

"I know, but if I had told you that your silence might trigger his issues, you might have actually listened to me," she explained before we both started laughing because I still wouldn't have reached out, and we both knew it.

"No, I wouldn't have." I shifted on the bed and tucked my feet underneath my body. "Is it bad that I forgot all about his mom? He never talks about her."

"You couldn't have known. It's easy to put your issues away when you aren't being provoked by them."

I swallowed, feeling the weight of this conversation and topic. I realized that Cole had probably always felt abandoned on some level. And that I had unknowingly contributed to that by staying away from him when he needed me to stay.

"Okay, so now that we've put all that together, what do I do?"

"Obviously, you fight for him," she said like I was an idiot.

"Of course I'm going to fight for him. But I mean, what do I do right now? He told me to give him time, but I'm afraid he doesn't really want it. But he looked like he meant it when he said it. But what if he didn't?"

I felt insane. Trying to read Cole's mind was exhausting, and I kept spinning in circles, overthinking and questioning everything until Lauren put her hand on my shoulder.

"Just send him a text. Tell him that you're giving him space, but you want him to know you're not going anywhere."

"Yeah, that sounds good." I nodded as I reached for my phone, and it vibrated in my hand, surprising me. "Ah," I said as I dropped it.

Lauren bent down to pick it up off the floor, and she couldn't help but glance at the screen. "Speak of the devil," she said before handing it to me. "Read it out loud," she demanded.

I read his text to myself first before doing as she'd asked. "It just says, *Come to my game tomorrow?*"

"What are you going to say?" Lauren was literally bouncing on the bed, and my fingers kept skirting over the keypad as I tried to write him back.

"I told him I was already planning on it," I said with a smile because I had been.

Even if Cole hadn't sent that text, I was still going to go tomorrow night. It was one of the last games of the regular season, and I wouldn't miss Cole's final performance at the plate for anything. Watching these last games online wouldn't have been the same. Because that was what you did when you loved someone. You rooted for their success and cheered them on. I planned on doing both of those things from the stands.

AFTER HIS TEXT, I figured that Cole had most likely left me

and Lauren tickets at Will Call, but I didn't want to be presumptuous and assume. I oscillated back and forth between asking if he had or just using our student IDs and getting a pair of those tickets instead. As we waited in line, the crowd went wild. The game had already started, and we were late.

"If you don't check when we get to the front, I will," Lauren instructed. "I don't want to sit out there." She nudged her head toward the student section. "He always gives us way better seats, and you know it."

"Fine," I said as we inched closer to the ticket booth window.

When it was our turn, I said my name and held my breath. The guy asked me to sign a paper before handing me two tickets.

"I knew it!" Lauren exclaimed, waving her ticket in the air like she'd just won the lottery.

I couldn't help but feel a little relieved with the gesture myself. "It's a good sign," I admitted as we looked for our section before making our way down the aisle toward our seats.

The stadium was packed. Sold out, the announcer had said, and we all knew why. The last games of the year always brought out the crowds. Everyone seemed to stop what they were doing in order to support the baseball team before the playoffs started.

Lowering myself into my stadium chair, I propped my feet up on the built-in cupholder, making sure not to knee the person in front of me in their back.

"I can't believe how many draft people there are," Lauren whispered as she looked around, and I laughed because I actually knew what she meant.

"Scouts. They're called scouts. And I can," I said before taking my own mental notes, grateful that I hadn't missed Cole's first at bat of the game.

You could tell which ones were interested in him by the way they perked up when he stepped into the on-deck circle. They grabbed their notebooks, their pens, their stopwatches, and their cell phones.

"We're sort of surrounded by them," Lauren whispered again, and I realized that there was a group of them sitting directly behind us.

When they announced Cole's name, the crowd exploded. It had always been loud for him, but now that he was hitting like a madman with a bat of fire, things had grown exponentially louder. I added to it, yelling his name as he sauntered toward the plate, a man on a mission that no pitcher could stop.

Before he stepped into the batter's box, Cole turned around and started scanning the stands.

"Oh Lord, not this again," Lauren groaned before smacking her hand over her face.

His eyes found mine, and he locked on for a moment before giving me a head nod. I swore I melted on the spot. A few scouts turned to look at me, and my cheeks burned hot with the attention. Thankfully, it didn't last long before they were refocused on my man at the plate.

I watched as they scribbled furiously in their notepads

while simultaneously trying to film him with their phones. It seemed like every scout in the stands was finally paying attention to the only player I'd been paying attention to for years.

It had always been fun, watching Cole play, but this version of Cole was something else entirely. He dominated the batter's box. His stance looked like a challenge. It was almost like he was daring the pitcher to try to strike him out when we all knew it was never going to happen. *Not today, pitcher.*

The loud clang of the metal bat hitting the ball rang out, and Cole tossed his bat to the ground as he jogged toward first. And when the ball sailed over the center field fence, he started trotting around the bases in confident strides. Pulling his helmet off his head once he stepped on home plate and met his cheering teammates, he looked up at me again and pointed like he had that one time before.

I flashed back to the memory and smiled.

"He just loves to point that hat thing at you, doesn't he?" Lauren shook her head, and I didn't bother correcting her this time.

The scouts behind us were talking loud enough that I could overhear. It took everything in me not to turn around and engage them in conversation, so I did what any good girlfriend—*am I Cole's girlfriend?*—would do; I eavesdropped. They were arguing over who was going to talk to Cole first after the game tonight and which team they thought he'd rather play for. I couldn't help but feel proud. Cole was going to get everything he'd worked so hard for, and no one deserved it more.

When the game ended—we won, by the way—I decided not to wait around. I still wasn't sure what Cole and I were, and I knew that he had scouts literally lining up to talk to him. He needed to focus on his future.

"We should go," I said to Lauren, and she balked at me. "Why the face?"

"I just figured you'd stay, like usual. I go home, and Cole brings you there."

"We aren't back together."

"Technicality."

"Regardless. You heard the guys behind us. And that was just them. Who knows how many other scouts want to talk to him? He needs to handle that first."

"But you'll call him tonight, right?" She stomped her foot and narrowed her eyes.

"I promise." I held out my pinkie, she wrapped hers around it, and we shook.

"Fine. But when Cole asks, I wasn't a fan of this idea." She turned and stalked toward the exit, immediately swallowed up by a sea of people as I followed.

I GLANCED BACK at the field, but Cole wasn't anywhere to be found.

We'd only been home for less than ten minutes when our

front door opened, and Cole flew through it, still wearing his uniform. I was shocked that Lauren hadn't locked it behind us like usual.

"What are you doing here?" I asked at the same time Lauren yelled, "How do you always get in?"

He looked at Lauren first and pointed at her. "I have impeccable timing." Then, he pointed his finger at me. "Why'd you leave?"

"The game was over."

"But I left you tickets. I asked you to come," he said, sounding flustered as he stepped closer to me.

"I know. I was going to call you later," I tried to explain, not understanding what the big deal was. "Wait. Why are you here? I overheard the scouts. They were going to talk to you. Didn't you see them?"

He laughed. "Of course I saw them."

"Well, what'd they say?"

"I don't know." He shrugged.

"You don't know?" I shouted.

"I left."

"What do you mean, you left?" I started freaking out because this was the one thing that Cole had always wanted. I'd known it since the first day I met him.

Cole Anders was baseball. This was his dream, his goal, his whole world.

"Why would you do that? You've been working for this your whole life! Oh my God, go back. Go back there right now."

"Christina," he said my name so sweetly that I knew he

wanted me to calm down, but how could I be calm when he was telling me something like this? "I asked them to wait."

"You asked Major League Baseball scouts to wait?" I repeated the idea like it was the most insane thing I'd ever heard in my whole entire life.

He gave me a smirk and a nod. "I told them to pretend that I was taking a shower. A really long shower. And that I'd be right back."

"Cole!" I shouted again, but he only laughed. "Get out of this house right now and go away." I swatted his back and tried to shove at his large body, but it refused to budge. *Stupid, strong shoulders.*

"No," he said, and I heard Lauren giggling. I'd almost forgotten she was there.

"This is your dream," I started to say, but he closed the space between us and pulled me against him, leaving the rest of the words to die in my throat.

"But you're my dream too," he said.

I wrapped my arms around his shoulders like I couldn't pull him close enough. Our bodies talked in silence, spilling apologies and hope and all the things we needed to say to each other but hadn't yet.

Cole broke the hug, moving barely an inch away before those blue eyes looked right into mine. He tipped my chin up with his hand. "I could have baseball, and I would still be missing something if I didn't have you by my side. I need you both in my life. But I need you more," he said before leaning down to kiss me.

There was no hesitation, no pulling back, and no games. I

wouldn't pretend like this wasn't the outcome I had always wanted. That, when our story ended, I'd be the one by his side. So, when he moved to kiss me, I didn't only allow it; I also threw myself into it, making sure he knew that I was still his. And I always would be.

He pulled away, my face in his hand. "I came over here to apologize to you before it was too late. I'm so sorry for yesterday. I was an idiot. And I know it probably won't be the last time I act like one, but do you think you can forgive me?"

"I thought I just did." I smirked, and he growled.

"Say it out loud. I was just so hurt. I wanted to punish you. It wasn't fair, but it's what I did. Forgive me, and I'll leave and go talk to the scouts like a good boy." He gave me a sexy-as-sin grin that he knew I wouldn't be able to resist. Not that I wanted to. Ever.

"Of course I forgive you." I pressed up on my tiptoes and planted another chaste kiss on his lips. "Do you forgive me?"

"For what?" His eyes pulled together.

"For letting you go without a fight. I won't make that mistake again," I said, my tone resolute.

"There's nothing to forgive." He sounded so reassuring. "Okay, I really do need to go."

"Go!"

He ran out the door but not before telling me he loved me. It slammed shut, and I stood there with a dopey grin on my face as it reopened, and he poked his head back through.

"You have to come with me." He waved, trying to call me over.

"What? No, I'm not coming with you," I started to argue, but he was in the apartment, reaching for my hand and pulling me toward the door as I struggled against him.

"I will pick you up and throw you over my shoulder," he threatened.

"I don't want to go. Why are you making me go with you?" I tried to resist, but it was no use. He was way too strong.

"I want you to meet my dad."

"Oh," I said as I suddenly stopped fighting him, and we practically flew out the door. "Bye, Lauren," I shouted and heard her laughing hysterically as my nerves took over.

He wants me to meet his dad?!

The Draft

Cole

I 'D GOTTEN REALLY nervous when the game ended and I saw that Christina had left. I thought that I'd blown it, totally fucked things up between us forever. That was why I raced over to her place and asked her to forgive me before I did anything else. I apologized to the scouts for asking them to wait around for me. I knew that it was unprofessional, but I'd reassured them that there was something I really needed to do that couldn't wait. If I lost Christina, I wouldn't have ever fully recovered from it.

I had been so desperate to make things right and so fucking relieved when I realized that nothing was wrong. The scouts didn't seem too pissed about my leaving. Coach Jackson, on the other hand, had looked like he wanted to strangle me with both hands.

After showering and getting dressed, I headed out of the locker room to find Christina and my Dad looking like they were scheming. They were basically huddled together and whispering right until the moment I walked up next to them.

"What?" Christina asked all innocently.

"Not sure what you two are up to, but it doesn't look good," I said before wrapping my arm around her and tucking her up against me.

"Don't you worry about what we're up to," my dad said before wrapping his arm around Christina's other side.

I stopped walking. "What the hell?"

"I'm just playing," my dad said, and Christina couldn't stop laughing.

That was how things went with them from that moment on. They sat next to each other at the rest of my games. Lauren too. I convinced myself that my dad was there to actually watch me play ball and not spend quality time with my girlfriend, but I wasn't so sure which one he liked doing more. Not that it mattered. Every time I looked up and saw the two of them together, my heart fucking beat against my chest a little harder.

I met Christina's parents soon after as well. They came to one of my games, and then they came to the rest. They even wore Anders T-shirts that embarrassed Christina but made me feel like a badass. My only regret was that I hadn't met them earlier in the season. I'd never had a big, supportive family unit before, and that was what this felt like. I fucking loved it.

THE DRAFT HAD already started. No one was surprised when

the first round came and went, and my name hadn't been called. I hadn't expected to get picked up that soon anyway.

The living room in the house I had grown up in was currently packed. I looked around and realized that everyone I gave a shit about was in this room with me. My girl, her parents, my dad, Chance, Mac, and even annoying Lauren were all here. A few other guys from the team came by, too, and were currently eating all the snacks Christina had set out, their eyes glued to the television screen or their phones. Even Coach Jackson texted that he might stop by.

Speaking of, Coach had surprised the hell out of all of us by kicking Logan off the team for unsportsmanlike conduct before we headed to the semi-regional playoffs. Rumor had it that he had heard all about what Logan had done and was completely beside himself over it. Apparently, he told Logan that he wasn't getting drafted anyway so to get the hell off his team and out of his locker room. Coach had said he'd never had someone so mentally unstable on his team before, and he wasn't about to start now.

I tried to dig deep inside of myself to feel bad for the guy but couldn't. It was hard to find sympathy for someone who had actively tried to ruin my life and had hurt the girl I loved. More than once. The only reason I hadn't beaten his ass again for it all was because I couldn't find him anywhere.

So, fuck you, Logan. Hope you rot in hell.

"Is everyone ready?" the news anchor asked.

She had introduced herself to us as Alpine Peaks, which was her real name, obviously. They were with a local news crew, and they were about to go live with a draft update.

"What do we need to do to be ready? Just sit here and look handsome?" Mac asked, his tone embarrassingly flirtatious. Of course he'd be the one to speak up. He'd probably be making out with Alpine Peaks before the day was over.

"Just act natural. Pretend we're not even here," she said with a megawatt smile.

I knew I could do that. I'd planned on ignoring them anyway even though them being here made me feel marginally better about my chances in the draft. Why the hell would a news crew be in my home to film my reaction if I wasn't going to be getting the call?

But there was still that small sliver of doubt that lingered in the back of my mind. Nothing was ever guaranteed, and them being here didn't change that fact. I had an advisor who kept telling me that my chances were great, but I still wasn't convinced. I hadn't legally been allowed to sign with him as my agent until today. There were a bunch of collegiate rules you had to abide by in order to remain eligible to play during school. This was one of them.

"Are you nervous?" Christina leaned toward me and asked quietly enough that only I could hear.

I looked at her, wondering how I'd gotten so lucky, and nodded. Hell yes, I was nervous. And she was the only person I'd admit it to.

"We're here with local baseball player Cole Anders. He's expecting a call any second now about the Major League draft. We'll be here with him when it happens, and then we'll share it with all of you. It's so exciting! That's all for now.

I'm Alpine Peaks, reporting live. Back to you in the studio, Ken and Jane."

My stomach twisted, and I had to stop myself from telling Alpine to knock on wood or something. *Doesn't she know how superstitious baseball players are?* She'd just told the entire area that I was getting drafted like it was some guarantee, and it hadn't even happened yet.

Right as I was about to lose it and give her a lesson on the mentality of baseball players, the house phone rang. My dad jumped up to answer it, and I watched as his face broke out into a wide grin.

He held the receiver out toward the living room. "Cole, it's for you."

I pushed to my feet and stepped away, reaching for the phone. "Hello?"

I listened as my agent informed me that I should be the next round pick for Houston. My mind wandered to the fact that they were currently under a lot of scrutiny for cheating. "The scandal doesn't matter, Cole. This is your chance to get paid to play baseball," my agent said through the phone, as if reading my mind.

"I'd be an idiot to say no, right?"

"Very much so. Gotta go," he said before hanging up and leaving me with a mixed bag of emotions. I've wanted to play baseball my whole life, but I was pissed about what Houston had done to the game.

Before I got too deep in my feelings, I reminded myself that nothing was set in stone. Just because he said I'd be their next pick, that wasn't a guarantee. This kind of thing happened more than anyone wanted to admit and it wasn't something that we talked about often, but I'd been with guys whose advisors had told them they were going in the next round of the draft and then they called back and told them that it would be the next round after that. Sometimes, it went on that way all day long until the draft ended, and they still hadn't been picked up. It was extremely frustrating and disappointing to be in that position, and I was terrified that it could happen to me. So, even though I wanted to be off-the-rails excited, I couldn't let myself go there.

I sat back down on the couch next to Christina and refused to answer anyone's questions about what was said on the phone regardless of how hard they harassed me.

Superstitious, remember?

Her parents and my dad were sitting at the kitchen table together like old friends, watching me and Christina instead of the TV. She reached for my hand, and I simultaneously held it and my breath as the next round of draft picks started to commence on live television.

I knew that the cameras were rolling, but I did my best to ignore them. They'd been recording on and off so often that it was easy to pretend they weren't there by this point. The Major League Baseball Commissioner stepped back up to the podium, and even though my advisor had said the next name was going to be mine, I just never knew.

Fuck, I was nervous. I wanted to throw up.

"For their second round draft pick, the Houston Astros pick Cole Anders, a right-handed outfielder from Fullton State, California."

Holy shit, he said my name.

The room exploded in cheers and screams and shouts.

My name.

"Cole!" Christina shouted before kissing my cheek, and I turned to face her, my eyes watering. I kissed her hard before letting her go. "Congratulations! I'm so proud of you!" she said as her own happy tears fell.

I blinked a few times, feeling totally awestruck as my phone started ringing and blinging out text message notifications like never before. If I thought that I would have a problem being drafted for Houston a few minutes ago, all that disappeared the second my dream became a reality.

"How do you feel, Cole?" Alpine shoved a microphone in my face, and I could barely see her through my tears, let alone speak.

"Grateful," was the only word that came to mind, so it was all I said before looking for my dad. Wiping at my face, I tried to stop my emotions from spilling out all over the place, but it was too late. I was a damn blubbering mess, and I couldn't stop.

"You did it," he said with the biggest damn smile I'd ever seen on his face before. "You did it." He grabbed me and pulled me tight.

I felt his body shaking, and I knew he was crying.

"Everyone's going to think we're a couple of pussies," I said as I wiped at my face and sniffed.

"Fuck 'em," he said, and I laughed before swallowing hard. "Think you'll get buzzers in Single-A?" he asked and I started choking on my laughter.

"Buzzers are for big leaguers," I said with a smile before getting emotional again. "Thank you, Dad."

"For what?"

"Thank you, Dad."

"For what?"

"For taking me to every practice and game since I was five years old."

"Well it's not like you could drive yourself," he tried to lighten the mood, but I was too nostalgic and emotional to take the bait.

"Thank you for letting me play travel ball in the summer, and for all the time and money it took to support this dream. I couldn't have gotten here without you."

His eyes shone as he gripped my shoulder, "It was my honor, son."

"You didn't have to, you know? You could have told me that we couldn't afford it, and I would have been sad, but I would have understood. But never once," I sucked in a breath, "Not once, did you tell me that I couldn't play."

"Watching you play ball brought a smile to my face when nothing else did," he said, his voice shaking. "I feel like I should be thanking you."

A breath hitched and I suddenly remembered that we weren't alone as my dad's eyes shifted away from me. I turned to see the camera crew filming us. I hadn't even noticed them approaching.

"I swear to God, lady, if you put any of that on the air, I'll hunt you down," he warned Alpine and I knew it was only because he would never want something that personal to be up for public consumption.

"Dad," I said before reaching for Alpine, noting her shocked expression. "That was kind of personal. It wasn't meant for anyone else to hear," I tried to explain before realizing that I wanted them gone. "I'll give you a brief interview, but then you need to go. I want to be with my family and friends, and you can't be here anymore."

"Okay, sure. I understand. And I won't air that clip," she said before looking at her cameraman and demanding, "Delete that footage."

He looked shocked, his eyes questioning, but then quickly pressed some buttons and did as she'd asked. "Done."

"Great. Let's just go in your backyard," she suggested, and I followed behind, telling her to make it quick.

Once I wrapped things up with Alpine and got the crew out of the house, I looked for Christina, but Chance and Mac stopped me on their way out the door.

"Congratulations. We're so happy for you, man," Mac said, and I gave him a big bear hug.

I had no idea when I'd see either of them again. Life was taking us in different directions.

"Are you going to go grab Alpine's number before she leaves?" I gave Mac a look, and he slapped my shoulder.

"Nah. She scares me," he said, and Chance and I both laughed.

"I didn't know any girl could do that to you," I said.

Chance held out his hand, and I took it, the two of us shaking like business partners who'd just closed a deal.

"Congratulations again. I'm so happy for you. You're going to be great. Just keep picturing Logan's head on all those curveballs," he said, and I laughed because he wasn't that far off.

"Thanks, bud. I'm happy for you too."

Chance had been invited to play in the most exclusive summer ball league program in the country. He was going to show everyone there what real baseball players were made of.

"It's a big deal, you know."

"I know," he said, but it wasn't cocky. Chance was never cocky. "Hey, my dad said to tell you congratulations and that it couldn't have happened to a better guy."

"Wow." I cocked my head back in disbelief. "Tell him thanks so much. Ah hell, I'll text him myself later. Thanks for coming over, you guys. It means a lot."

"Of course. We're Team Cole all the way," Mac said, and I rolled my eyes.

"You literally sound like my teenage sister. You realize that, don't you?" Chance said, pretending to be annoyed.

"Then, your sister must be awesome," Mac sniped back.

"Okay, we're leaving," Chance announced before grabbing Mac and giving him a shove.

"Guess we're leaving. Bye, everyone," Mac shouted into the house before Chance could get him outside.

I watched them walk down the driveway and toward their car before I wandered back in search of my girl. I found her sitting with her parents and Lauren, eating chips and salsa at the kitchen table, and it reminded me of the first time we had eaten Mexican food together in the commissary at school. I remembered asking her if the word *salsa* did anything for her, like an idiot.

"Hi, Mr. and Mrs. Travers. May I borrow your daughter?" I asked, making sure I sounded polite and respectful. I'd never had to impress parents before, and it was important to me that I did—impress hers, that was.

"Just make sure you bring her back in one piece," her dad said, and I gave him a nod.

"Don't try to sell her online!" Lauren shouted before putting two fingers near her eyes and then pointing them at me. "I'm watching you, Anders."

"Where are we going?" Christina asked. Always with the questions, my girl was.

"I want to show you something." I reached for her hand and pulled her down the hall toward my childhood bedroom.

"I've already seen it." She laughed, and I smacked her ass as she walked through the doorway.

"Not that. This." I walked over to my bed and reached for a folder that was sitting on top of it. I handed it to her with a smile I couldn't hold back.

"What is this?" she said as she opened it and started flipping through the pages, her eyes scanning them before she went back to page one and started actually reading.

I'd created a business proposal for her that included all of the pros and cons as to why she should start her own company versus going to work for someone else.

"You made this for me?"

"I did." I watched as her expression morphed from

shocked to excited as she continued to read.

"You really think I could go out on my own already?" She looked up from the papers, her eyes misting over.

I pulled her close and kissed her before reminding her, "You've already been doing it for years."

"I know, but it's not the same," she started to argue, and I knew it was only because she was scared.

"It's exactly the same. Only now, you'd be getting paid for your work. You're amazing at this. Because of you, The Long Ones are actually making money. You did that." I knew she was about to say I was wrong, so I continued with my rebuttal, "You made people take notice of them. You're the reason they started getting views and sponsored ads and publicity. You don't need anyone else telling you how to do this job, Christina."

"Why are you saying all this now? We can talk about me later." She tossed the folder back onto the bed. "Not that I don't appreciate it. But we should be out there, celebrating you right now!"

I wrapped my arms around her waist and kissed her nose. "I'm telling you all this because I want you to come with me."

She tried to lean back and break my hold on her, but I only held on tighter. "You want me to go with you?"

"Yep," I said like it was the most logical and reasonable thing ever. But in my mind, it was. There was no reason for me to go to Iowa, where the team was located, and have her stay here. Not when she could technically work from anywhere.

"But," she said before closing her mouth and exhaling through her nose. She was trying to fight back but knew she had no real argument, and it was adorable.

"But nothing. I plan on being with you for the rest of my God-given life, Miss Travers. I don't see why that can't start now."

"Don't you think it's too soon to move to God knows where and live together?"

My girl was scared.

"Nope."

"What do you mean, nope?"

"I want to be with you. I don't want to live apart if we don't have to, and we don't. Have to, that is. You can work from home, or I'll rent you an office space for you to work out of. Whatever you want, but you can do your job from anywhere, right? I just want that anywhere to be wherever I am."

I hadn't even mentioned the fact that I'd get a pretty hefty signing bonus offer. While the majority of Minor League Baseball players lived on shitty monthly salaries, I wouldn't be one of them. Yes, I'd still get paid that basically unlivable wage to play baseball, but we would also have more than enough money to live comfortably for years to come.

"How can I say no to that?" She smiled before rising up on her toes to give me a kiss.

Thank God she'd said yes; otherwise, I was going to have to pull out the big guns and promise her a puppy—or twenty. This girl made my world complete. She and baseball were the two things on earth I never wanted to live without.

But if I ever had to choose between them, it would always be her. Every time.

Epilogue

One Year Later

Christina

WE'D MOVED TO Iowa less than a week later. I'd skipped walking through graduation with my class, and even though my parents were originally disappointed, they understood. The fact that they adored Cole made their acceptance of me not walking and moving away with him easier. They'd also said they were grateful they didn't have to sit outside and endure a five-hour-long graduation ceremony for a bunch of strangers and two people they actually knew and cared about—myself and Lauren.

Speaking of Lauren, she was back in school, going for her master's in order to open her own practice one day. She and Jason, the drummer, still talked, but between her classes and his tour schedule, it was hard for them to maintain anything other than friendship. I told her that she never knew what the future held.

Oh yeah, did I forget to mention that The Long Ones were touring? <Insert a million screaming fans here.> No, literally. Millions of fans.

Once their social media had started to take off, it never stopped. They hired me to continue handling it all, and the band was making six figures between their online streams and video views before they were ever approached by a record label.

The executive had offered them a four-million-dollar deal, which they'd gladly accepted, and they were currently in the middle of their first nationwide small venue tour. So far, I'd gone to see them play at five different locations, getting plenty of footage to post for months to come, but it would eventually get to be too old. The truth was that they would outgrow me and need to hire someone to travel with them full-time. That wasn't something I wanted to do even though they kept offering me the position each time I brought it up.

Cole and I were apart enough with his insane baseball schedule. Before agreeing to move here with him, I'd had no idea how many games his team played, how little time off he would actually have, and how often he would be on the road. Not that it would have changed my decision if I had known, but I would have been better prepared for it.

I'd tried to travel with him at first, thinking that I could easily balance my work with his schedule, but it was way too disruptive and chaotic. They moved around too often, rarely staying in one place for too long. I'd realized pretty quickly that I needed to be able to sit still for days on end and focus on making my business successful. I struggled doing that whenever I was on the road with him, and too many things fell through the cracks, so I usually stayed home.

I missed him like crazy whenever he wasn't in town, but I loved my job, and that made it all worth it. There were a lot of other girlfriends here who didn't have anything going on for themselves, and even though they genuinely seemed happy with their roles, I knew that I wouldn't be able to live that way. I needed my independence and my own sense of self-worth. Plus, I loved being able to contribute to our lifestyle and make my own money.

Cole had been right to push me to go out on my own instead of working for someone else. Starting my own business had been terrifying at first and taken a huge leap of faith, but everything seemed a little bit easier with Cole Anders by my side. Not to mention the fact that he insisted on being my first paying client, even before The Long Ones started paying me, just like he'd always promised all those years ago. He'd printed up a contract, we'd both signed it, and he'd had it framed. It currently hung on the office wall of our two-bedroom apartment in freaking Iowa.

We could have bought a house here if we wanted with the money Cole had gotten with his signing bonus, but Cole had told me not to get too comfortable. He didn't plan on being in Iowa for long. And if his batting average continued to rise the way it currently was, I knew that he was right. He could get moved up to the next level anytime now. All he needed was a phone call from the higher-ups.

"Are you sure you're cut out for this life? I might get traded or called up. And we'll have to move." Cole nudged

me with his nose, and I looked at him before kissing it. "Like the next day," he warned, and I realized that it didn't matter how many times or how often we had to pack up and go.

"As long as I'm with you, I don't care where we are," I told him before he rolled on top of me and made me forget about everything else in the world, except the way he felt when he was inside of me.

Even though we paid for this apartment in Iowa year-round, we didn't live here during the off-season. As soon as his season had ended last year, we'd headed back home to Southern California, where we bought a small but relatively affordable townhouse in Huntington Beach, not far from the pier. Cole considered it an investment and reassured me that real estate was a good way to save for the future. To be honest, I couldn't complain about having a home near our family and friends. It made being away from them during half of the year easier.

"So we'll always have a place to come back to," Cole said when he gave me the key.

Our apartment door flew open, and Cole walked through it, looking sweaty, gorgeous, and tired. He'd been on a four-day road trip. His T-shirt was tight around his shoulders, his biceps flexing as he dropped his bat bag to the floor.

"Honey, I'm home!" he shouted, and I walked around the corner, so he could see me.

I was wearing an apron and nothing else. It was Cole's favorite outfit of mine. "Hello, dear," I said with a smile.

"How was your day?"

Somewhere in our first year here, we'd fallen into this 1950s role-play routine. It had started as a joke one night, with me pretending to be the perfect stay-at-home wife, but when it'd led to some of the hottest sex we'd ever had before, we'd kept it up. It was sort of our thing now.

"Work was awful, my boss is the worst, and I ran out of gas on the way home." He stalked toward me, hunger in his eyes.

"Did you really run out of gas?" I asked because I wasn't sure if this was part of the role-play or not.

"No," he whispered with a laugh as his eyes ran the length of my body.

I glanced down at his pants, noticing the bulge growing there. It was empowering to know that him seeing me did that to him.

"I missed you," I said, staring straight at his crotch.

He cleared his throat. "My eyes are up here."

"I missed you too," I said into his baby blues before hopping into his arms and wrapping my legs around his middle.

"To the shower," he said before kissing me senseless, his fingers kneading into my bare ass, and I knew it was going to be a good night. Every night spent with Cole was a good night.

I remembered back to when we'd first gotten together, wondering how things could ever get better than they were. But this—living together, making love, and planning a future that included each other—this was definitely better.

And it was easy.

It sounded so cliché, but it was true. Things had fallen into place naturally, without being forced. And it wasn't that there weren't ever any hard times because there definitely were; it was just that they felt almost painless to work through.

Maybe it was the promises we had made to each other when we first got here. How we promised to not take one another for granted, to always be honest and open, and to remember what it'd felt like when we thought we'd lost our chance at forever. Those promises kept us grounded. And they took work to honor, but we still tried.

Cole was still kissing me after the shower, his hands roaming every inch of my body like he couldn't get enough. "I'll never get tired of touching you," he breathed against me, and I knew exactly how he felt because I felt the same way.

"Me either," I said, running my fingertips along the curves of his muscles. His shoulders and arms still did something to me. I knew they always would.

His phone started ringing. I growled before telling it to shut up, and Cole laughed.

"You're so feisty when you've missed your man," he teased before making it stop.

He picked me up and tossed me on top of our bed, and a shriek escaped from my mouth when I landed on it, my body bouncing with the impact. Cole smirked and jumped on top of me, his body covering mine, and my fingers instantly dug into his back, signaling to him what I wanted.

But his phone started ringing again.

I was about to tell him to throw it against the wall, but he looked at me and said, "It might be an emergency. Who calls two times in a row? Don't move." He reached for the electronic cockblocker. "It's Bobby," he said. His team manager.

He answered, stood up, and immediately started pacing. I got nervous and sat up, too, pulling a blanket around me as I watched him.

I started thinking that it might be bad news, but Cole had been playing great all season. Then again, I wasn't up to speed on the actual business side of baseball and how it all worked, so maybe Cole's stats didn't mean what I thought they meant when it came to the front office.

When the call ended, he looked at me and said, "Looks like we're moving to Texas," before giving me that smile that I loved.

"You got moved up to Double-A?" I asked, just to clarify.

"Double-A," he said before kissing me hard. "Now, where were we?"

He tossed the blanket covering me to the floor, and we celebrated.

We celebrated five times.

And we would have made it six, but the neighbors knocked on our wall and begged for us to please stop. They said they needed their sleep.

Freaking Iowa.

Hope our Texas neighbors didn't plan on getting any sleep.

THE END

Thank Yous

You guys! Baseball plus all the romance?! SWOON! I don't know why it took me so long to start writing another baseball series, but here we are, and I couldn't be happier about it. Thank you for always wanting more from me, for never getting enough and being the best damn readers a girl could ask for.

I want to thank Krista and Denise for beta-reading the hell out of this one before I sent it off to my brilliant editor, Jovana Shirley. Jovana, thank you for your time, your skills and your acceptance of me. Michelle Preast, you worked your ass off on all of these baseball covers, and I couldn't be happier! Thank you for your talent and vision and for your patience. I know how much I require it.

Thank you to my Kittens (the best reader group on FB ever)! To all my friends who support me—and not just behind the scenes. To every blogger, reader, author and person who posts about my books on social media and helps me reach new people—I appreciate you so much.

To the man who inspired Jack F'n Carter—can you believe we're back here? It's so much fun doing life with you. Thank you for being by my side for it all.

And to Blake—you're the best kid I've ever had. lol

Other Books by J. Sterling

Bitter Rivals—an Enemies-to-Lovers Romance
Dear Heart, I Hate You
10 Years Later—A Second Chance Romance
In Dreams—a New Adult, College Romance
Chance Encounters—a Coming-of-Age Story

The Game Series:
The Perfect Game—Book One
The Game Changer—Book Two
The Sweetest Game—Book Three
The Other Game (Dean Carter)—Book Four

The Playboy Serial:
Avoiding the Playboy—Episode #1
Resisting the Playboy—Episode #2
Wanting the Playboy—Episode #3

The Celebrity Series:
Seeing Stars—Madison & Walker
Breaking Stars—Paige & Tatum
Losing Stars—Quinn & Ryson

The Fisher Brothers Series:
No Bad Days—a New Adult, Second Chance Romance
Guy Hater—an Emotional Love Story
Adios Pantalones—a Single Mom Romance
Happy Ending

The Boys of Baseball Series:
The Ninth Inning—a New Adult, Sports Romance
Behind the Plate—a New Adult, Sports Romance
Safe at First—a New Adult, Sports Romance

About the Author

Jenn Sterling is a Southern California native who loves writing stories from the heart. Every story she tells has pieces of her truth as well as her life experience. She has her bachelor's degree in radio/TV/film and has worked in the entertainment industry the majority of her life.

Jenn loves hearing from her readers and can be found online at:

Blog & Website:
www.j-sterling.com

Twitter:
twitter.com/AuthorJSterling

Facebook:
facebook.com/AuthorJSterling

Instagram:
instagram.com/AuthorJSterling

If you enjoyed this book, please consider writing a spoiler-free review on the site from which you purchased it. And thank you so much for helping me spread the word about my books and for allowing me to continue telling the stories I love to tell. I appreciate you so much. :)

Thank you for purchasing this book.

Please join my mailing list to get updates on new and upcoming releases, deals, bonus content, personal appearances, and other fun news!

tinyurl.com/pf6al6u

Made in the USA
Monee, IL
07 October 2020